FRON
ON T LAND

THE FICTION OF SINCLAIR ROSS

Maria Roberts
July '95

Fest-Shrift — writings on special occasion
to honour some-one.
Friends invited to read/write in honour.

REAPPRAISALS:
CANADIAN
WRITERS

FROM THE HEART OF THE HEARTLAND

THE FICTION OF SINCLAIR ROSS

Edited by John Moss

University of Ottawa Press

REAPPRAISALS
Canadian Writers

LORRAINE McMULLEN
General Editor

Canadian Cataloguing in Publication Data

Main entry under title:
From the Heart of the Heartland
The Fiction of Sinclair Ross

(Reappraisals, Canadian writers; 17)
Includes bibliographical references.
ISBN 0-7766-0329-9

1. Ross, Sinclair, 1908–   — Criticism and
interpretation. I. Moss, John, 1940–   II. Series.

PS8535.079Z88 1991   C813′.54   C91-090460-X
PR9199.3.R68Z84 1991

UNIVERSITÉ D'OTTAWA
UNIVERSITY OF OTTAWA

© University of Ottawa Press, 1992
   Printed and bound in Canada
   ISBN 0-7766-0329-9

All essays were written for a living audience at 1990 Symposium of editors at University of Ottawa July 1990. Papers have context.

Contents

Introduction

JOHN MOSS

*A*s for *Me and My House* is the quintessential Canadian novel, much the way *The Adventures of Huckleberry Finn* is quintessentially American. Sinclair Ross and Mark Twain have little enough in common, but both of them manage to capture in fictions that could not be taken in any way as mainstream the hearts and perhaps the souls of their respective nations. Twain's novel is the literary equivalent of democratic populism; Ross's achievement is far more enigmatic. *As for Me and My House* seems calm on the surface, almost genteel. The narrative voice suggests self-assurance bordering on the smug. Yet there are, beneath that surface, within that voice, passion and uncertainty, conflict and pain. There are also wit, arrogance, vulnerability, and warmth. Identity is askew; while there is a powerful sense of place, almost overwhelming, there is a disjointed sense of time—of historical time, of duration, of continuity. All this makes it seem very, very Canadian. The fact that it is a fine novel and that it is perhaps somehow more accessible to Canadians than to other readers assures it an important position in the Canadian tradition.

Does this mean that Sinclair Ross is the quintessential Canadian novelist? Probably not. A sensibility so thoroughly rooted in the heartland of the country is not likely to speak for the urban majority, not with the same authority as Mordecai Richler and Margaret Atwood, whose caustic voices are continual reminders that we are merely Canadian, nor with the assurance of Margaret Laurence, who turned Manawaka into Main Street, nor with the urgency of Ernest Buckler, who spoke from a self-defined periphery, nor with the unsettling clarity of Alice Munro, who speaks from memories we share.

Sinclair Ross writes from the heart of the Canadian heartland. Even when his fiction strays to Montreal or elsewhere, it offers a vision of life, a view of the world, from the prairie thirties. His voice is a finely articulated reminder of who we have been as a community, morally and psychologically, a reminder of where we come from. Not only in *As for Me and My House*, and the stories in *The Lamp At Noon*, but in *The Well* and *Whir of Gold* and *Sawbones Memorial*, and in his other stories, he writes with what seems an uncanny authenticity. As with all great artists, his experience of the world becomes our own. He does not circumscribe us, the way Richler does, or even Alice Munro. He expands our limits, our experience of ourselves.

Sinclair Ross is central to Canadian literature. This does not mean his work has been a major influence. Few, if any, Canadian novels have been influential, in terms of shaping our tradition. His work is nevertheless among its major achievements. Tradition is the net we cast upon the past to make our presence in the world seem inevitable, as of course it is, and comprehensible, which it sometimes isn't. Tradition is retrospective: it is the acknowledgement and appreciation of cultural heritage. In this respect, Sinclair Ross is very important to us.

We are as fortunate to have both Ross and, say, Charles Dickens in our past as we are to have grandparents and great statesmen. Without Sir John and Sir Wilfrid, our lives might not have been the same. Without grandparents, we would not have been. Ross is *that* necessary to our being and well-being as Canadians. He is the literary forebear of Margaret Laurence, Robert Kroetsch, Aritha van Herk. Yet it would be foolish to expect that Kroetsch was influenced exclusively by Sinclair Ross who was influenced by, say, Frederick Philip Grove who was influenced by Susanna Moodie, whose principal influence was *Wacousta*. Lines of influence and of descent, in literature as in life, are not equivalent.

The literary achievement of Sinclair Ross might not be fully apparent to those unfamiliar with the Canadian tradition. To someone ignorant of cultural heritage in a Canadian context, the familiar voice and vision in Ross's fiction might seem colonial rather than authentic; his regional authority might seem provincial, his subtlety an evasion, his brilliant fusion of abstract and concrete an affectation. Yet it is the familiar, it is regionalism, ambivalent subtleties, practical metaphysics, that elevate Ross and his fiction to such prominence in our tradition. Recognition does not make him less, on the world's stage; nor does it make him more. But within his own tradition, it places his work among the very best.

Inevitably, in a gathering of Ross specialists, discussion of *As for Me and My House* will dominate. There is nothing demeaning about the selection by critical consensus of one work over the others in a writer's canon. Ross is a great writer not in spite of writing only one great novel, but because he wrote at least one, and in the context of excellence that his other work provides. Half a century after the publication of his most celebrated achievement, it is interesting to see that critical commentary is still generated by his other writing. The short stories especially command attention. This may be in part because several of them are widely anthologized—but that too is a measure of their literary worth. His other novels are less well known, except by specialists. That, however, is *not* a measure of their worth—but rather, of the idiosyncracies of accessibility in the Canadian market.

What must be most satisfying to Sinclair Ross—Jim, as he is known to his friends—is the fact that a symposium such as the one represented by this book can bring established scholars and critics together with some of the newest and brightest, that it can bring together thematic critics and critical theorists, earnest scholars, intellectual entrepreneurs, a radical populist or two, and even a critical anarchist, if there is such a thing. The interest in Jim Ross and his writings is not limited to a particular academic coterie. It is not a matter of cultural history, but of art; not a matter of duty, but of conviction, enthusiasm, and pleasure.

At precisely the same time as the University of Ottawa symposium on Sinclair Ross began in Ottawa, in April 1990, Canadian literary critic Robert Lecker delivered an address to an international congress on Canadian Studies in southern Italy on the virtual canonization of *As for Me and My House*. Lecker's point—that Ross's best and best-known novel is more read about than read—is a provocative reminder that sometimes, in our rush to celebrate what is truly excellent, we obscure the thing itself behind a wall of praise or, worse, of analytic obfuscation. Of even more significance, though, is the ironic fact that—call it synchronicity or critical coincidence—Lecker's presentation on Ross at the exact time of the conference in Ottawa confirmed the classic status of *As for Me and My House*.

The essays in this volume were originally delivered as papers at the 1990 Ross symposium, with the exception of David Latham's bibliographic contribution. Each contributor has used the texts of his or her choice, as indicated in the lists of works cited.

I would like to express my appreciation to my colleagues in the Department of English at the University of Ottawa for their help in preparing the program and, especially, in seeing that the weekend ran smoothly. I would particularly like to thank the indefatigable Frank Tierney for all his efforts in this, as in every other Ottawa symposium. I would also like to thank the participants for attending this edition of what is generally regarded as one of the more pleasant and rewarding functions in the academic year. I would like to thank Julia Moss for her astute editorial assistance and Julie Sévigny-Roy in the Department of English office for her help throughout the project. And finally I would like to thank Sinclair Ross, "Jim," for his inestimable contribution to Canadian life and letters.

Sinclair Ross in Letters and Conversation

DAVID STOUCK

The man whose work we have gathered here to appraise and celebrate has never been awarded a Canada Council grant, has never won a Governor General's Award, has not been made a Companion of the Order of Canada, has never received an honorary university degree or prize. At the same time, no body of short fiction in Canada has been so frequently anthologized, no single Canadian novel has been so often taught, or written about, as *As for Me and My House*. The story of this man and his work, both of which have been ignored and praised, neglected and studied, is the story of a culture that has been slow to develop, that has been ambivalent about its character and worth, and that too often has remained indifferent to what lies outside the boundaries of the popular and successful. It is also the story of a writer from the margins to whom the doors of the literary establishment were never really opened.

There is a scene early in his career as a writer to which Ross returns in memory. Before a trip to New York in 1941 to meet his agent and publisher after the publication of *As for Me and My House*, Ross was advised by his Winnipeg friend Roy Daniells to stop in Toronto and meet E. J. Pratt. When English professor E. K. Brown heard of the young novelist's forthcoming visit, he arranged for a luncheon at Hart House. The late-April stopover in Toronto began badly. Ross went to the office of the wrong Professor Brown, a theologian, but neither was the wiser and the two had lunch together, making polite but desultory conversation. Ross discovered his error before leaving the city and was directed to the office of E. K. Brown, English professor, who proceeded with his arrangements, and Ross found himself in company that included Brown, E. J. Pratt, Earle Birney, Robertson Davies, and Northrop Frye. But for Ross the previous day's error only seemed compounded for he found himself out of his depth surrounded by these literary men, who (or so it seemed to the shy author) not only ignored him but probably looked down on him. This was the Canadian literary establishment—eastern, educated, and exclusively male, whereas Ross was a farm boy from the west, with only grade eleven schooling, and more at ease in mixed company. For the young writer from Saskatchewan this introduction to Canada's foremost authors and educators was largely abortive. He came away, not exhilarated by meeting these men of letters, but disappointed by the certain conviction that he could never be one of their company.

Yet Birney was a westerner and Ross admired his poetry, and so eventually he wrote to him from Winnipeg in January 1942. To date this is the earliest Ross letter that I have been able to locate. It reads:

> Dear Mr. Birney,
> I have read and re-read "David"—and unqualified as I am to pen an opinion on poetry, I would like to let you know how deeply it impressed me. I thought it a moving, sensitively handled piece of work. Some of your lines, particularly "into valleys the moon could be rolled in," and "the last of my youth, in the last of our mountains," made me really envious. I hope you will be publishing more poems like this one—and soon.
> > With kindest regards,
> > Sinclair Ross

Birney replied, warmly thanking Ross for his letter of praise and asking him if he would contribute something to the American magazine *Story*, which was planning an issue on Canadian writing. Ross sent him "One's A Heifer" and Birney thanked him for what he thought was an excellent story.

By the following year both men were enlisted in the army and the *Story* project had been called off, but they continued to write to each other in England. Their letters are concerned largely with arranging a time and place to meet in London and, after the meeting, the acquaintance concluded, because Ross felt intimidated not only by Birney the university professor but also by Birney the commissioned officer, Ross himself being then only a private. Although the correspondence does not really go anywhere, in one of his letters (dated July 26, 1943) Ross speaks of something that would plague him throughout his writing career. He bewails the fact that he cannot turn out the slick magazine fiction that his New York agent wants, "being doomed," he says, "to write what no one wants to read." He would like to write about the army but "cannot 'plot' it to suit *The Saturday Evening Post*."

What is significant here is that Ross was committing himself to meeting American standards and markets for his fiction. His first published (and only prize-winning) piece came out in England's *Nash's Pall Mall* in 1934; subsequently he apprenticed as a short-story writer with *Queen's Quarterly*, publishing eight stories there between 1935 and 1941. But when he came to selling a novel, he turned to an American agent, Max Becker (recommended to him by the Winnipeg writer Kathleen Strange), because if he was going to make his living as a serious novelist he would have to succeed in the United States. For, as William French has observed, in 1941 there was little critical apparatus in Canada to recognize a book's worth; standards and taste in fiction were largely imported.

Ross's correspondence with *Queen's Quarterly* in the 1930s has unfortunately not survived. Ross has said, however, that the letters exchanged with one of the editors, Sir Andrew MacPhail, were cordial but not instructive. MacPhail only once asked for a small editorial change—that the husband's name in "The Painted Door" be changed from Elmer to John. Later, the correspondence at *Queen's Quarterly* was with Dr. G. H. Clarke, whose only editorial concern was to make Ross's vocabulary more literary and refined. He objected, for example, to words like "snotty" and "screwy," and though Ross argued that this usage was "army," he complied and removed such words from his stories.

In contrast, Canadian literature owes a great debt to the discriminating taste and generous offices of the American publisher John Reynal. Independently wealthy, Reynal chose for publication the manuscripts he personally liked without any consideration for their commercial possibilities. When Max Becker sent him the manuscript for *As for Me and My House*, he read it at once and the story was accepted for publication in what must be a record length of time, just two days. Reynal did not have to solicit readers' reports or take his selection to an editorial board. This was extraordinary good luck for Canadian literature. Other publishers might have foreseen the book's failure to sell and Ross would probably have destroyed the manuscript for *As for Me and My House*, as he has done with other works that have been regarded as commercially inviable.

But the book's immediate good fortune ended with its publication. Although there were some fine reviews, *As for Me and My House* failed to sell more than a few hundred copies. A Governor General's award might have helped sales a little in Canada, but the award that year went to Alan Sullivan's *Three Came to Ville Marie*, a book that has since been completely forgotten. So, when Ross came out of the army, he had to return to the Royal Bank to make his living.

One of the good reviews was written by W. A. Deacon for *The Globe and Mail*. He praised Ross's "sincere craftsmanship" and asserted that the novel had social significance and something important to say. During his Toronto visit Ross met briefly with the eminent reviewer and they engaged in a correspondence during the 1940s. It is in a letter to Deacon, dated April 15, 1946, that Ross admits that he is discouraged about his prospects as a writer. He says he is afraid to free-lance because he knows his commercial possibilities amount to very little. He is working on another novel, but he plans to go back to the bank since he must support his mother in Winnipeg, who is 70 years of age, nearly blind, and wholly dependent on him. Deacon writes back with the consoling observation that an artist has advantages in amateur status—he can write what he likes instead of what will sell. Ross accordingly returned to writing stories for *Queen's Quarterly*, which paid $25 each, later $37.

As for Me and My House made a strong impression on a handful of perceptive readers and Ross was not without those who tried to encourage him. In retrospect, however, the advice they gave him was not always helpful. In February 1949 Ross received a letter from Robert Weaver, praising *As for Me and My House* and asking for stories that might be read on the CBC. In the correspondence that ensued Weaver tried to persuade Ross to abandon rural subjects for urban ones. In May 1950 he wrote: "it seem[s] to me that your use of western rural background . . . ha[s] become something of a limiting factor in your work." He wanted to see stories with urban settings, so in 1951 Ross sent him one titled "A World of Good." It concerned a husband and wife awaiting the visit of the husband's friend. The woman receives the guest in housedress and curlers, and only later puts on her evening apparel. The readers at the CBC thought the story unlikely and Weaver rejected it because of the piling up of "sordid realistic details." It was also rejected by *Maclean's*. In a reply to Weaver's rejection, Ross discusses the failure of his story not in terms of material or setting uncongenial to his imagination, but rather in terms of his having taken the story too directly from real life.

But the question of the western rural background being a limiting factor remained with Ross. In a short piece titled "Why My 2nd Book Came 17 Years Later," published on the book page of the *Toronto Star* in September 1958, Ross says he has tried intellectually to get away from prairie farm and small town life in his fiction, but is still emotionally involved with it. He says he tried a novel about the war, and another one about delinquency and crime in the city, because "prairie life was too far removed from the world to matter." He felt he should be writing novels of ideas and of contemporary social significance. But his imagination resisted. Weaver's advice of course reflects popular critical opinion in the post-war period when Canada was rapidly changing from a rural to a largely urban society. By 1970, however, no critic would have urged Margaret Laurence to abandon Manawaka for fiction set in Toronto or Montreal.

One of the true champions of Canadian authors was John Gray, the editor at Macmillan. He encouraged Ethel Wilson in the writing of her best work, and when he returned to Macmillan after the war he sought out the author of *As for Me and My House* with the hope of encouraging him to write another novel. They met for dinner at one of the big hotels in Montreal shortly after Ross had been transferred there by the bank in 1946. Ross remembers Gray as a bluff, genial fellow, who was very good company. Correspondence between Ross and Gray, now in the Macmillan collection at McMaster University Library, does not begin until 1955 when Ross sends Gray his manuscript for *The Well*. What follows, in spite of Gray's good intentions, is a confusing series of failed negotiations, wrong choices, and poor advice.

In *The Well* Ross tried to combine contemporary social problems (in this case delinquency and crime) with the western setting that fired his imagination. As early as September 1955, *Maclean's* said it would consider *The Well* for a $5,000 book award and would want to serialize the novel if it were made shorter. Ross was reluctant to make such drastic cuts and revisions, but Gray wanted both the serialization and the award as a way of promoting the book, so Ross finally sat down to the task. However, the report next April from *Maclean's* was negative, citing among other problems adultery as a taboo subject for a mass audience magazine. In the meantime Ross's New York agent, Willis K. Wing, changed his opinion from enthusiasm to dislike of the manuscript, so Gray took over the task of trying to place the manuscript with a U.S. publisher. Both Gray and the American readers wanted a happy ending for the story. One American reader specifically suggested that Chris be exempt from the murder—that Sylvia should do it while the young man is drunk. Gray got good reports from his Macmillan readers who called it "compelling," "vivid," and "powerful and impressive," but he had no luck finding an American firm for joint publication. Marshall Best of Viking actually gave the manuscript an assessment that probably still stands today; he wrote sympathetically to Ross saying "it is neither a serious psychological novel nor a novel of suspenseful action, but falls somewhere in between."

Ross became discouraged, and on December 10, 1957, he wrote to Gray to say that he was working on another novel but that he hesitated at the prospect of two to three years of hard work, with another long-drawn-out failure as a reward: "as the years go on one's enthusiasms—even one's compulsions—become tempered by common sense. There's not much point in knocking myself out if I haven't got what it takes." Gray wrote back the next week to say they would publish *The Well* in 1958, even if they could not find an American firm to sell it to. Bad reviews followed the book's publication and it sold poorly, but Gray continued to write encouraging words to Ross: "The book at least proves once again, if anyone were in doubt, that you have great talent." But the book continued to draw trouble for Ross. A filmmaker by the name of Julian Roffman of Meridian Films, Toronto (he won the first Oscar for a documentary), wanted to do a film version of *The Well*. Before a deal was struck with the author, he spoke on television with great confidence of this upcoming project. After a contract was signed, Ross saw a script and was dismayed to see that his realistic story was full of stereotyped Indians and Mounties. The film was never made and, although Ross received a small sum for film rights, he felt disappointed that his work should continue to bring failure for everyone in its sphere.

Ross's longest association with a publishing house has been with McClelland and Stewart. It began in 1957 when Malcolm Ross chose *As for Me and My House* as one of the first titles for the New Canadian Library series. Ten years later Robert Weaver, feeling differently now about western fiction, suggested *The Lamp at Noon* collection and an introduction by Margaret Laurence. In the McClelland and Stewart papers at McMaster University there is an interesting letter written by Ross to Jack McClelland describing changes he has made to the stories from their original versions. He did not want the stories simply lifted from *Queen's Quarterly* as was the NCL practice at that time; rather, he insisted on the opportunity to revise for stylistic reasons, making cuts to strengthen an effect, and especially to tone down what he felt was overwriting in "Cornet at Night." Ross reveals himself here to be meticulous about his work and insists on receiving galley proofs to correct himself. The major structural change in the stories, as Lorraine McMullen has pointed out in her book on Sinclair Ross, was to bring two separate stories together under the title "Not By Rain Alone" (53).

With two first-rate and profitable Ross titles in the NCL series (*As for Me and My House* had sold nearly 50,000 copies in its first ten years), McClelland and Stewart were apparently willing to take a chance when Ross, now retired and living on the Mediterranean, offered them a new manuscript. Jack McClelland is quoted by one of his editors as saying, "The day we can't publish Sinclair Ross is the day we shouldn't be in publishing." The new manuscript was *Whir of Gold*, although Ross probably did not think of it as very new because it had a composition history of more than 20 years. "The Outlaw," the story of Sonny and his horse Isabel, is first mentioned in letters in 1949 and was published in *Queen's Quarterly* in 1950. In a letter of March 18, 1952, *Queen's Quarterly* editor Dr. G. H. Clarke thanks Ross for sending a story titled "Sonny and Mad," but says that it does not suit the journal's needs at that time. *Whir of Gold*, in fact, is probably the post-war manuscript about urban crime that Ross refers to in "Why My 2nd Book Came 17 Years Later." No readers' reports appear to have survived for *Whir of Gold* (1970), but when it sold less than 1,000 copies Jack McClelland soured on the venture, said it was not up to Ross's standard, and refused a paperback edition that Ross requested. Had the novel been published when it was first written, it might have fared better. It stands up well beside Morley Callaghan's *The Loved and the Lost* (1951), but with its crew-cut protagonists it seems dated in the company of Atwood's *The Edible Woman* (1969), Kroetsch's *The Studhorse Man* (1969), or Dave Godfrey's *The New Ancestors* (1970).

Nonetheless Ross sent McClelland and Stewart the manuscript for *Sawbones Memorial*. With one exception the readers were very enthusiastic, praising it technically as an important experimental work. Jack McClelland wrote to Ross on January 2, 1974, congratulating him on a major work that charts new territory in terms of form. Anna Porter handled the book and there are three important letters Ross wrote to her about his technique and plans for this novella.

In a letter written November 23, 1973, before it was read or accepted for publication, he describes the dialogue and stream of consciousness form of the manuscript for Porter:

> The material, I'm afraid, is pure prairie corn, but the "way" it is done may have possibilities. You may have to read 10 pages or so before you see what I'm doing . . . . The drawback as I see it now, after this, my first experiment, is that it calls for awfully good dialogue. Working on it I discovered how useful are all those little "He frowned and stubbed his cigarette," "A strange light shone in her eyes, part fear, part passion," how they ease the burden for the writer and help him round the corners.

In the same letter he describes beginning the manuscript as an exercise, to see if it was possible to write a novel in dramatic form. He found it very interesting and continued, completing it in a record eight months. With some confidence in the manuscript he is sending, he sets out terms for the *Sawbones* contract which include a $500 advance, a guarantee of a paperback edition, and a further guarantee that there will be no changes in the writing to bring punctuation, syntax, etc. in line with house standards. In a similarly optimistic vein he discusses plans for future books, which include a sequel to *Sawbones*, two travel books, and three other novels he has been working on. One of these is about an artist who has been shot, is in hospital and is struggling for his sanity. Another concerns the effects of a crime on a small town at the point when the criminal is to be released from jail.

After *Sawbones* was accepted for publication, Ross wrote to Anna Porter on January 15, 1974, about the inspiration for his narrative method in Claude Mauriac's *Dîner en ville*, describing his own efforts as much simpler and less sophisticated than those of the French novelist. Always concerned, however, to be honest, he wants to make his debts known and not be put in the dock for plagiarism. And in a letter of March 4, 1974, accompanying the revised manuscript, he talks in detail about a sequel to be titled "Price Above Rubies," done in the same method, expanding on the lives of the same characters from a point of time 20 years in the future (the late 1960s).

The publication of *Sawbones Memorial* was the one point in his career when Sinclair Ross was in the literary limelight. McClelland and Stewart gave the novel a good promotion, describing it as a major experimental fiction from one of the country's senior writers. In the initial print-run, 5,500 hard-back copies were printed. A handsome book jacket was designed: a prairie wheat field and sky, almost an abstract to fit Philip Bentley's definition of good art. Robert Weaver read a piece from the novel on the CAP, William French flew to Spain to interview Ross for *The Globe and Mail*, and when the book was released there were excellent reviews from influential literary figures including Margaret Atwood, George Woodcock, Margaret Laurence, and William French. Atwood went so far as to claim *Sawbones* to be a better book than *As for Me and My House*.

But Ross, ever plagued by failure, did not enjoy the feeling of success for very long. The Canadian reading public genuinely interested in serious fiction proved still to be very small. *Sawbones* did not sell well—just over 2,000 copies—and McClelland and Stewart held back for four years on their promise of a paperback edition. They had tried eight American publishers, but could not find one that would bring out an American edition. There was talk for a time of a Governor General's Award for Ross for 1974, although it seemed unlikely because Laurence's *The Diviners* came out that year; but when the nominees were announced in the spring of 1975 *Sawbones* was not even on the short list. The real blow to Ross, however, was McClelland and Stewart's rejection of "Price Above Rubies." Ross did not blame the publishing house, but felt discouraged that the manuscript had not convinced the readers. After that, Ross did not talk of his plans for future books, only about his giving up as a writer.

Sinclair Ross's readership for more than 30 years has consisted largely of the students and teachers of his work in colleges and universities. Sales of *As for Me and My House* in the NCL must be close to a quarter of a million copies by now. Feeling sharply the inadequacy of a grade 11 education, Ross has consistently declined invitations to speak or read on school campuses, but a letter of praise for his work has always brought a warm and interested reply from the author. There are numerous letters from Sinclair Ross in personal files across the country (recipients include David Carpenter, Wilfred Cude, Alec Lucas, Lorraine McMullen, John Moss, and many others). I will conclude this paper by describing some of the ones I have received over the years. I was able to locate 17, the first being written in 1971 to decline an invitation to Simon Fraser University, the last a Christmas message for 1986, written through his amanuensis, Irene Harvalias.

What is of present interest in these letters are Ross's discussions of *As for Me and My House*. In a letter of January 10, 1972, he describes the book as beginner's luck—sincere but terribly naive, a book in which he did things much better than he knew or intended: "Keeping Philip off-stage, for instance—it gives him a power, makes him a presence looming in the background more impressive for the reader—I think—than when they see and hear him." Which, he adds, is probably why the novel can't be dramatized, though several have tried. In this same letter he comments on Paul, calling him the ridiculous school teacher who is nonetheless "a useful chorus—a bit of a nut, who could say things for me, quoted by Mrs. Bentley in her diary, which she couldn't say." (In conversation he has said to me that Paul is the character he is closest to, that he identifies with, not Philip or Mrs. Bentley. He is the observer of this marriage, becomes emotionally involved, yet remains an outsider.) In this same letter he writes that one of the themes that really interested him when writing *As for Me and My House* was that of nature's indifference to humanity. He had read so much fiction with an anthropomorphic feeling towards nature which, while understandable to anyone who has experienced a prairie storm, seemed nonetheless entirely false. He concluded on his own, he says, that nature was not hostile to humankind but indifferent, and so he had Mrs. Bentley pen that haunting reflection about her walk along the river: "The stillness and solitude—we think a force or presence into it—even a hostile presence, for we dare not admit an indifferent wilderness, where we may have no meaning at all" (131). And that observation seemed to strike a new note, in Canadian fiction at least. Ross also comments in that same letter on *Whir of Gold*, which he feels is "a shaky novel with some fairly good things in it." He feels the Saskatchewan parts are true and among the best things he has written.

In a letter of August 23, 1973, in response to an article I had written about *As For Me and My House*, he said politely that he was interested in the pattern of relationships I had seen in the novel repeating for three generations. "You understand the [Bentleys] perhaps better than I do, or at least did when I was writing. For when I was writing I was participating and when you participate you often don't understand or see. More was coming I suppose than I knew." In this same vein he has often remarked that critical articles about the novel amaze him—discussions of Chopin and George Sand, of Dante, El Greco, or Michelangelo's *Pietà*, because he had no conscious intention of making them part of the design of his book. Questions about the Canadian landscape and about form and painting were, however, very much on his mind and he feels he was lucky in saying something sensible and of lasting interest on those subjects. In a letter of January 30, 1979, after he had read my introduction to the Bison edition of *As for Me and My House* and had thought about the gender controversy over the Bentleys, Ross wrote: "I am especially pleased that you take a balanced view of Philip and Mrs. Bentley. Myself . . . I have always felt they were both in a trap, both victims."

Although Ross was unable to win a large general readership and make his living as a writer, he has been gratified nonetheless by the steady affirmation of his work by the academy and by the conferring of classic status on his fiction with a western setting. Among other things, he enjoys the irony of a writer with a grade 11 education being taken so seriously at colleges

Gerard

and universities. This conference, he feels, confirms the value of his life's work. It is another one of those encouraging beacons along the way, for he has told me that, several times in his life, just when he had decided to put down his pen for good, there would come some word of encouragement, some invitation to write again, and he would resume what he calls his "scribbling." At age 82, living in Vancouver, he is still scribbling, with the faithful assistance of Irene Harvalias and the steady friendship of the writer Keath Fraser. He suffers from Parkinson's disease and works slowly, but in 1988 he published a "memoir" about his mother, titled "Just Wind and Horses," and is at present completing a novella about two prairie boys leaving Canada for the war and contemplating a cycle of stories about elderly people who are living in a hospital. He will try to give it what he's got and then, as he likes to say, "stand back and laugh, for another Ice Age is coming and what will it matter then."

WORKS CITED

Atwood, Margaret. Rev. of *Sawbones Memorial. Sunday Supplement.* CBC Radio, 15 Dec. 1974.

Deacon, W. A. "The Story of Prairie Parson's Wife." *The Globe and Mail*, 26 April 1941, p. 9.

————. Letters to Sinclair Ross. Thomas Fisher Rare Book Room, University of Toronto.

Gray, John. Letters to Sinclair Ross. Macmillan Collection, McMaster University.

McMullen, Lorraine. *Sinclair Ross.* Boston: Twayne, 1979.

Ross, Sinclair. *As for Me and My House.* Toronto: McClelland and Stewart, 1989.

————. Letters to Earle Birney. Thomas Fisher Rare Book Room, University of Toronto.

————. Letters to Dr. G. H. Clarke. Queen's University Archives, Kingston.

————. Letters to John Gray. Macmillan Collection, McMaster University Library.

————. Letters to Jack McClelland. McClelland and Stewart Collection, McMaster University Library.

————. Letters to Anna Porter. McClelland and Stewart Collection, McMaster University Library.

————. Letters to David Stouck. West Vancouver, B.C.

————. Letters to Robert Weaver. National Archives, Ottawa.

————. "Why My 2nd Book Came 17 Years Later." Toronto *Daily Star*, 13 Sept. 1958, p. 32.

Weaver, Robert. Letters to Sinclair Ross. National Archives, Ottawa.

"Can't See Life for Illusions": The Problematic Realism of Sinclair Ross

ANGELA ESTERHAMMER

Picking up on a dismissive remark made by his mother about his early writings, Sinclair Ross has entitled his recent memoir "Just Wind and Horses." The phrase compels us to consider whether the depiction of prairie life really is the defining element of Ross's work. Most of the existing criticism of Ross has focused on this aspect; while the talk is not just of wind and horses, but also of eyes, mirrors, diaries, marriages, false fronts, and scarlet rompers, Ross's fiction has most often been judged and appreciated as a realistic account of life on homesteads in Saskatchewan during the Depression era. In his recently published *A History of Canadian Literature*, W. H. New places Ross's fiction "among several works which stand out . . . within the confines of conventional realism"; he chronicles the reception of Ross's work among early readers who valued its "representational accuracy" and later ones who looked instead for accurate depictions of the human psyche (175–77). The standard context for reading Ross has been established by critics such as Robert D. Chambers, who paired Ross and Ernest Buckler for their representation of life in rural communities, and Northrop Frye, who, in his "Conclusion" to the *Literary History of Canada*, identified Ross and Buckler as two examples of an "ironic or realistic" world-view (II, 351). Dick Harrison's discussions of Ross in his book *Unnamed Country* fall into chapters subtitled "Prairie Realism" and "The Failure of Imagination." Most recently, Dennis Cooley has praised Ross's stories for being "among the very best in a long line of prairie realist fiction" (140), an observation in keeping with Lorraine McMullen's comment that "in the context of Canadian writing [Ross] follows such early realists as Frederick Philip Grove" ("Introduction" to Ross, *House*). When McMullen qualifies this statement, pointing out that Ross "goes beyond the realism of prairie novelists before him to focus on the psychological impact which environment has on his individuals" (24), she names the two poles around which criticism of Ross has thus far centred: mimesis and psychological realism. Even when they avoid the term "realist," critics implicitly privilege representational accuracy by focusing almost exclusively on the early short stories and on *As for Me and My House*, works that seem to offer mimetic descriptions of struggling farmers and small prairie towns, and by criticizing Ross's stories of war or crime for their lack of verisimilitude.

I would suggest, by contrast, that the real strength of Ross's fiction does not lie in mimesis. His portrayal of everyday reality is most effective when that reality is in conflict with dream or illusion. The short stories of the 1930s and 1940s derive their power from the tension between characters' fantasies of a good harvest, a promising future for their children, or a happy marriage, on the one hand, and the constraints of isolation, poverty, and ruined wheat, on the other. The success of *As for Me and My House* depends on the romantic and artistic dreams of all the main characters, which are in conflict with each other and with actuality, as well as on the possibility that the narrative, coloured by Mrs. Bentley's anxiety and desire, may not correspond to objective truth. Throughout Ross's work, some of the most suggestive passages are dream or nightmare sequences that blend into waking experience and cast doubts on the protagonists' view of their situation. The radical significance of all these fantasy elements comes into focus in *Sawbones Memorial*, a novel about the construction of "reality" through oral and written discourse that has not often enough been recognized as a culmination of the anti-realist tendency in Ross's work. Ross's "realism" is like the cover over a well of dream and delusion, and the resurgence of these elements must eventually make us question whether there is such a thing as objective reality at all.

Imaginative perspectives that conflict with an objective reality are, of course, not uncommon in the realist novels with which Ross's work is most often compared. Much of Frederick Philip Grove's *The Master of the Mill* is recollection in the mind of the main character, while nightmares and daydreams are both essential elements of Buckler's *The Mountain and the Valley*. But Ross's short stories hint more profoundly at the way imagination will eventually undermine realism in his writing. In stories like "Cornet at Night" and "Circus in Town," fantasy has the last word. When the child Jenny, in "Circus in Town," hangs a torn circus poster "furtively . . . over one of the kitchen calendars" (*Lamp* 63), she is blotting out the charted time that represents the daily routine of her parents' farm. Jenny's dream also transcends the predictable schedule by which small-time travelling shows visit isolated prairie towns: Jenny never asks to *go* to the circus, only to be granted the freedom to create one of her own. The narrator leaves no doubt that Jenny's circus, "the splendid, matchless circus of a little girl who had never seen one" (65), constructed by an imagination that transforms Jenny herself and her surroundings, is far superior to the original of the printed poster. Jenny's vision is powerful enough to shape the story itself. The narrative begins and ends with Jenny's circus, with a girl in purple tights on a galloping horse; the picture of farm life is contained within this frame, as if *it* were the dream and the illusion.

For adult protagonists in Ross's fiction there is a more dangerous aspect to imagination, and the attempt to force one's own vision onto the world in spite of reality brings about an instability of perception that we call madness. One of Ross's most characteristic short stories, "The Lamp at Noon," illustrates how close to madness a person's dreams of a better life may be by juxtaposing the delusions harboured by a husband and a wife about their failing homestead. Paul is unable to see past his insistence that "the land's all right" (*Lamp* 11), while Ellen is maddened into believing that she must flee into the storm with her baby. Ironically, it is Ellen—the character we are more likely to think of as insane—who repeatedly calls Paul a fool and accuses him of being blind and uncomprehending (10–11). Both characters waver between insight and delusion, making it hard even for the reader to maintain a sense of objective reality.

"One's A Heifer" also juxtaposes two unstable images of reality: that of the narrator, an impressionable and imaginative 13-year-old, and that of Arthur Vickers, a recluse whose behaviour implies that he is insane. Besides introducing Ross's most compelling portrait of madness, this story illustrates his use of perspectives, dreams, and an unreliable, or at least misleading, narrator. As Dennis Cooley has pointed out in his essay "The Eye in Sinclair Ross's Short Stories," there is a focus on eyes throughout the narrative, and sight is the favoured mode of perception. Yet we cannot necessarily credit what the narrator claims to see, and the accuracy of vision is often called into question. When the boy rides out, his aunt takes leave of him "cautiously . . . through a cloud of steam" (*Lamp* 113) and his home is obscured by "a thin white sheet of cloud spread across the sky" (114). Betrayed by his eagerness, the boy catches sight of his calves "for sure a dozen times" (115), and his claim that he "at last . . . really" sees them is dubious, since dusk has fallen, the boy is exhausted, and visual perception has never yet been entirely reliable.

The night the boy spends with Vickers is, for both of them, a time of dreams, half-dreams, and waking visions. We do not know what Vickers experiences when he suddenly hurls the checkers against the wall; the narrator tells himself that "he'd just been seeing things" (124), an expression that subtly underlines the unreliability of visual perception in Ross's fiction, since it might equally well mean that Vickers has *not* been seeing but has been experiencing delusions. The boy's own plan to stay awake and sneak out to the stable fails when he begins to fall asleep. His account of how the plans he makes while lying awake are repeated as a dream ("I rehearsed it four times altogether, and the fourth time dreamed that I hurried on successfully to the stable," 124) echoes his mistaken identification of the calves a few hours earlier ("I saw them for sure a dozen times . . . . And then at last I really saw them," 115). In both cases, doubts are cast on the distinction between actuality and illusion.

The most significant aspect of the dream, though, is that it seems to reveal more of reality than the boy is conscious of when awake:

> I fumbled with the door a while, then went inside and felt my way through the darkness to the box-stall. There was a bright light suddenly and the owl was sitting over the door with his yellow eyes like a pair of lanterns. The calves, he told me, were in the other stall with the sick colt. I looked and they were there all right, but Tim came up and said it might be better not to start for home till morning. He reminded me that I hadn't paid for his feed or my own supper yet, and that if I slipped off this way it would mean that I was stealing, too. I agreed, realizing now that it wasn't the calves I was looking for after all, and that I still had to see inside the stall that was guarded by the owl. (124)

In the dream, the calves are not in the locked stall (and in fact, as Aunt Ellen reveals at the end, they have already wandered home). The dreamer knows that he really wants to see inside the stall for some other reason than the calves, but his *conscious* realization of this comes at the very end of the story, if at all. In the dream, the natures of characters are transferred to animals, so that the talking owl with yellow lights for eyes represents Vickers, guarding the locked stall with a "wild light in his eyes" (127), and Tim the horse, giving cautionary advice about manners and behaviour, resembles Aunt Ellen. Perhaps this, too, reveals a truth the boy does not fully grasp when awake: that Vickers, like the owl with a broken wing, stays cooped up inside the house because he is, in some way, not quite whole.

The dream, which seems to provide a more reliable guide for behaviour than waking reality, is central to much of Ross's fiction. Sonny's feverish dream of the flicker in *Whir of Gold* appears to contain a key for interpreting both the relationships in Sonny's waking life and the novel itself, since the only direct reference to the "whir of gold" comes up in that dream. The nightmare that Mrs. Bentley has just before she claims to discover Philip and Judith in bed is crucial to the vexed question of whether she is right or not about her husband's infidelity. And dream and reality are just as difficult to separate in "The Painted Door," even by the story's end. The central incident in "The Painted Door," when John appears at the door of the room where his wife Ann is in bed with their neighbour Steven, is first presented as reality, then re-interpreted as a dream, and the surprise ending reveals that it was probably—but not definitely—real after all. An inability to distinguish objects is already suggested by the insistent layering of white on white in the setting of the story: snow, frost on the pane, a "whitish grey" sky, Ann's "blanched" lips and pale face. Ann herself spends the day painting the woodwork in the kitchen white, as if to obliterate distinctions further. Ironically, the crucial mark that should differentiate, finally, between reality and illusion is the white paint showing up against John's frozen white hand. Given the text's move towards obfuscation rather than clear outlines, we may well wonder how reliable such a mark of white on white can be after all.

In the account of Ann's dream, Ross's language misleads us much the way an unreliable narrator might in other stories:

> Then she dozed a while, and the shadow was John. Interminably he advanced. The whips of light still flickered and coiled, but now suddenly they were the swift little snakes that this afternoon she had watched twist and shiver across the snow. And they too were advancing. They writhed and vanished and came again. She lay still, paralysed. He was over her now, so close that she could have touched him. Already it seemed that a deadly tightening hand was on her throat. She tried to scream but her lips were locked. Steven beside her slept on heedlessly. (*Lamp* 109)

"Then she dozed a while, and the shadow was John": the two parts of the sentence sound as if they should both be taken equally seriously because both are simple affirmations, yet the first clause is a literal statement and the second demands some kind of figurative interpretation. Since the shadow seems to be like John when Ann is dozing, we may suspect already that it is a dream. The incident is described in a dream-like manner: perceptions that entered Ann's consciousness a few hours before, like the "swift little snakes" of snow, now resurface, and her sensation of being unable to scream or call out is familiar from dreams. Steven sleeps through it all, and when Ann sits up, startled, John has vanished.

From here on there is a complex and ironic interweaving of reality and illusion. Ann successfully (but wrongly?) convinces herself (and anyone reading the story for the first time) that the vision was only a nightmare, yet it brings her to a realization of the truth she had earlier denied. Though in Steven's calm detachment there seems to be "such sanity, such realism" (111), Ann's love-making with Steven begins to seem almost illusory in the face of her newly realized devotion to John. Ann acknowledges her guilt and her love for John as a result of a dream-image that reveals a more profound reality than the situation in which she actually finds herself; yet, ironically, the "dream" may have been just as real as that situation. Ross's language continues to play with literal and metaphorical meaning as Ann reflects on the face in her dream, "the face that was really John—John more than his features of mere flesh and bone could ever be" (109), and remembers, with double irony, "the shadow that was John" (110). "The Painted Door" shows how a character who is trying to sort out true and misleading

emotions may not be able to differentiate between real and illusory perceptions. Moreover, the language of the story, which deliberately refuses to
demarcate the limits of reality, demonstrates that there is more at stake here
than unreliable perception. This is also a story about the uncertainties of a
written discourse that claims to represent reality—a story that calls the text
into question along with the mark of white paint.

When we consider *As for Me and My House*, what all these instabilities
point to is a more profound mistrust of realism than even the ongoing debate
about Mrs. Bentley's reliability as a narrator would suggest. The novel is, in
fact, fundamentally anti-realistic; it implies that no one can perceive or
describe an objectively existing reality. Given M. H. Abrams's classic association of the mirror with mimetic theories of art, the distortion of objective
reality is aptly suggested by the fact that, in Horizon, there are too many
mirrors for reflection to be true. Mrs. Bentley complains that the whole town
is "too much like a mirror," or "like a whole set of mirrors" in which she
cannot escape distorted reflections of herself (*House* 23). David Stouck, using
the same images as Abrams in his essay "The Mirror and the Lamp in Sinclair
Ross's *As for Me and My House*," presents Mrs. Bentley herself as a mirror
for Philip's psyche, and this may have been part of Ross's intention as he
set out to write the story of Philip as seen through the medium of his wife's
journal (Kostash 34). Yet Mrs. Bentley's typical view of the townspeople is
in the little mirror over the organ, which allows her to see the congregation
only in sections, and Philip's relation to them in reverse. This is the mirror
in which she first observes Philip's reaction to Judith's singing, which may
suggest that her later interpretation of their relationship is in fact distorted.

If reality is misapprehended through the novel's mirrors, dreams
might give access to a more profound reality, as they seem to do in "The
Painted Door" and "One's A Heifer." As in Ross's other stories, though, the
reliability of dream-experience is complicated by the fact that dreams are
always the product of fitful, troubled, feverish, or drug-induced sleep. These
semi-conscious states appear so often in Ross's work that we might even be
reminded of Romantic writers like Keats and De Quincey and their preoc-
cupation with narcosis—remembering that Ross himself implies a Romantic
connection when he has Mrs. Bentley excel at playing the music of that most
intense and subjective of Romantic artists, Franz Liszt.

When Mrs. Bentley, during her illness, dreams and then wakens to
the belief that her husband and Judith are in bed together, her sleep would
seem to be profound because it has been induced by sleeping powders. But
she has not taken enough of them, and while she is already struggling to
awaken out of her stupor she has "a kind of nightmare":

> My hands were tied, and someone was stealing Minnie's hay. I could see El
> Greco sitting on his haunches in the garden, but when I called him he didn't
> hear me. He seemed a long way off, as if I were looking at him through the

wrong end of a telescope. Paul was telling me he was a wolfhound, and wouldn't know how to chase burglars anyway. (123)

The elements of the dream, which have been given a brief but insightful interpretation by David Williams (157), reflect and reverse the circumstances of Mrs. Bentley's waking existence. She feels she is looking at events in the dream "through the wrong end of a telescope": like the mirror over the organ, this symbolizes the distorted perspective by which she distances and diminishes other people. Dreaming that her hands are tied while someone steals Minnie's hay, Mrs. Bentley anticipates the feeling of being helpless to prevent Judith's affair with Philip before it becomes reality. At the same time, the dream may reveal a truth she is not willing to admit about her relationship with Paul Kirby; when Paul, in the dream, tells Mrs. Bentley that El Greco is a wolfhound, he takes the place of her husband by echoing words that were actually spoken by Philip ("He's a wolfhound," 118).

Mrs. Bentley wakes with a start and sits up, recalling Ann's behaviour in "The Painted Door" when she leaves an apparent nightmare for apparent waking reality. As she seizes on the impressions that come back to her about the ensuing events, Mrs. Bentley sounds curiously as if she were still recounting a dream: "I remember how I crouched there . . . ," "I remember the way my mind seized on the thought . . ." (123). Her sensation when she tries to open the door of the lean-to shed that "there seemed to be something forbidding it" is typically dream-like. When she and Philip are both back in their bed, she turns and mutters into her pillow, "as if . . . just about to waken": the idea is to deceive Philip into thinking she has been asleep, but there is at least a chance that she has also deceived herself—or, finally, us. When Ross has his unreliable narrators use language that makes it impossible for the reader to determine where reality ends and dreaming begins, he does not resemble realist writers nearly as much as he does writers of the fantastic, like E. T. A. Hoffmann.

The undercutting of realism in Ross's earlier fiction prepares us for *Sawbones Memorial*, a text that replaces dreams with interior monologues and visions of the future with versions of the past. As characters in this novel, through dialogue or private reminiscence, reconstruct their own histories, it becomes apparent that all the versions are disparate and that it is impossible to locate any objective reality behind them. Sometimes one character exposes the fallacy of another's self-portrait; Doc Hunter summarizes Stan Gillespie's history to show that "the truth is he's just plain no-good," even though the story "breaks your heart the way [Stan] tells it" (32). At other times a character may doubt the accuracy of his own recollections, as when Dunc catches himself fictionalizing his encounters with Nick during the war and concedes, "No, I'm making that up" (55). The most extensive example of a re-imagined past is the history of Ida Robinson, whose experiences as a homesteader's wife are relayed through her grandson Dunc to his bride Caroline. Doc

Hunter, recounting to Caroline his own memories of Ida, informs her that "Ida's experiences never lost anything in the telling" (29). Ironically, Caroline interrupts Doc's reminiscences because she prefers the romanticized version of her husband's family history. The story of Ida Robinson blends back into reality when Ross reveals in his memoir "Just Wind and Horses" that the passage contains a measure of biographical truth—that Ida is, to some extent, a portrait of his mother ("Wind" 92).

The construction of alternative realities becomes a more profound issue when we take into account the novel's emphasis on oral and written discourse. Throughout *Sawbones Memorial*, the local newspaper, the Upward *Chronicle*, is implicitly present as a second narrative about events in Upward that may be juxtaposed with the oral communication going on in the novel. The *Chronicle*'s editors, Nellie Furby and her husband Dan, are the most frequently met characters in *Sawbones Memorial*; present in 21 of its 40 episodes, they are more in evidence than Doc Hunter himself. Nellie and Dan are in the tautological position of listening to the voices of Upward to gather their information, then using this information to write the stories that Upward will be talking about: all of Upward is thus living in a world created by words. While a newspaper, especially one that calls itself a "Chronicle," would seem to constitute an extreme example of realist narrative, Ross leaves little doubt that representational accuracy is a concept foreign to the paper's editorship. The account of Doc Hunter's farewell party, Nellie would have us believe, has essentially been written before the event takes place, which suggests that the paper is not a "chronicle" in the literal sense at all. In fact, it is closer to the fiction that Ross himself is writing in the way it creates a reality independent of all but occasional coincidences with the "real" world.

The climax of our insight into the way the *Chronicle* defies realist narrative comes with Nellie's summing up of the musical fiasco of "Redwing." "An impromptu trio provided a spirited rendering of *Redwing*, with special love-call effects by Mrs. Billy" is her suggested reportage, and her friend Rose reminds her that she must add "supported by Mrs. Jack's rich contralto," to keep the small-town peace (114). The astonished and derisive reactions of the audience during the performance of "Redwing" have told a very different story; and yet, as Nellie claims with both conscious and unconscious irony, "what you read in the *Chronicle* is always right" (17). It becomes clear that at least some of Ross's characters are aware of the degree of illusion, self-deception, and falsification that goes into any observer's verbal account of events—and that they want it so.

Ross's fiction reveals his concern with the many ways we resist objective reality: by imposing our dreams on it, by perceiving only what is significant to us in it, by constructing our own narratives out of it. The façade of realism in his stories and novels, whether they are directed towards a depiction of life on the dust-bowl prairies or in the crime-ridden streets of

Montreal, is undercut by the persistent confusion in his works between waking, dreaming, imagining, recounting, and (re)writing. Rather than representing reality per se, Ross is engaged in analyzing the way in which we all order our particular perceptions and create a reality out of them. Which is to say, if we believe Philip Bentley's claim that art, like religion, is "a rejection of the material, common-sense world for one that's illusory, yet more important" (*House* 112), that Ross effectively highlights that element of artistry we all possess. More radically, the element of undecidability that so often surfaces in Ross's work may testify to the inherent instability in perception and representation that makes realist fiction an impossible dream.

NOTE

I would like to thank John O'Connor and D. M. R. Bentley for reading versions of this paper and offering very helpful advice.

WORKS CITED

Abrams, M. H. *The Mirror and the Lamp: Romantic Theory and the Critical Tradition.* Oxford: Oxford University Press, 1953.

Chambers, Robert D. *Sinclair Ross and Ernest Buckler.* Toronto: Copp Clark, 1975.

Cooley, Dennis. "The Eye in Sinclair Ross's Short Stories." In *The Vernacular Muse: The Eye and the Ear in Contemporary Literature.* Winnipeg: Turnstone Press, 1987.

Harrison, Dick. *Unnamed Country: The Struggle for a Canadian Prairie Fiction.* Edmonton: University of Alberta Press, 1977.

Klinck, Carl F., ed. *Literary History of Canada: Canadian Literature in English.* 2nd ed. Toronto: University of Toronto Press, 1976.

Kostash, Myrna. "Discovering Sinclair Ross: It's Rather Late." *Saturday Night,* July 1972, pp. 33–37.

McMullen, Lorraine. *Sinclair Ross.* Boston: Twayne, 1979.

New, William H. *A History of Canadian Literature.* London: Macmillan, 1989.

Ross, Sinclair. *As for Me and My House.* Toronto: McClelland and Stewart, 1989.

——— . "Just Wind and Horses: A Memoir." In John Metcalf and Leon Rooke, eds., *The Macmillan Anthology I.* Toronto: Macmillan, 1988, pp. 83–97.

——— . *The Lamp at Noon and Other Stories.* Toronto: McClelland and Stewart, 1968.

——— . *Sawbones Memorial.* Toronto: McClelland and Stewart, 1974.

——— . *Whir of Gold.* Toronto: McClelland and Stewart, 1970.

Stouck, David. "The Mirror and the Lamp in Sinclair Ross's *As for Me and My House.*" *Mosaic* 7 (1974), 141–150.

Williams, David. "The 'Scarlet' Rompers: Toward a New Perspective in *As for Me and My House.*" *Canadian Literature* 103 (1984), 156–66.

The Conflicting Signs of
As for Me and My House

FRANK DAVEY

Le récit est une produit d'une application de la force du
pouvoir sur une écriture.

LOUIS MARIN

Recent criticism of *As for Me and My House* has read
much of the selection and interpretation of events in that novel as specific
to the character of Mrs. Bentley, whose diary entries constitute the entirety
of the text (Dooley 1979; McMullen 1979; Cude 1980; Denham 1980;
Godard 1981; Stouck 1984). While this application of Wayne Booth's concept
of the unreliable narrator has often resulted in more complex readings of
her narration, it has also tended to obscure the fact that Mrs. Bentley herself
is a textual construction. She is not a free-standing agent whose "personality"
can explain the emphases and omissions. In reading a fictional first-person
narrative text such as that constituted by Mrs. Bentley's diary entries, we
are in the presence of a double construction—a text which constructs its
narrator by constructing that narrator's construction of events. Although
many of the text's elements that I will examine here—including its peculiar
array of proper names, its lack of information about Mrs. Bentley's childhood, its silence on economic issues—are indeed open to "explanation" in
terms of her personality (she is Eurocentric, self-effacing, humanistic in
cultural perspective), such "explanation" does not remove them or her from
the overall textual operations of the book. Further, a fictionalized first-person
text is not entirely defined by the personality of its narrator. Mrs. Bentley
is not an etymologist, yet both Paul and his reflections on words become

parts of the novel; she has little interest in ranching, yet the male sexuality the text locates in horses and at the Kirby ranch is still signalled by many of the names various horses and bulls in the novel carry. The text's presentation of itself as a diary, its killing of Judith West in childbirth, its construction of Steve as Catholic and "Hungarian or Rumanian," all evade recuperation by appeal to her personality. My interest here, then, is in the text and the kinds of constructions it offers, whether these be through its construction of Mrs. Bentley, through gaps, intrusions or contradictions it allows in her narration, or through other determinations.

*   *   *   *   *

As for Me and My House has become, as Morton Ross observes (1978), a representative Canadian novel and a novel of prairie Canada. Even in 1957, when introducing the New Canadian Library re-issue of a book "unfamiliar to the Canadian public," Roy Daniells emphasized its Canadianness. It belongs to "the Canadian scheme of things," to "the prairie region, of which Saskatchewan forms the central expanse" (v). "Although precise dates, places and historical events are avoided, there is no doubt that these pages present the prairies of the drought and the depression, the long succession of years between the two wars" (ix). "There is even a brief holiday to the Alberta foothills" (ix).

Daniells's assertion of "no doubt" appears to rest more on unstated biographical information about Ross than on marks in the text: "Ross's little town," he suggests, is "a composite of, or rather an abstraction from, little towns he had lived with and endured" (vi). In fact, the absence in the text that Daniells notes of "precise dates, places and historical events" is so pervasive that it is only by geographical inference that a reader identifies the continent on which the novel is set; the text's national setting, and its regional ones such as "Alberta" and "Saskatchewan," are neither specified nor implied. Reverend and Mrs. Bentley have arrived in a "little prairie town" with a "Main Street"; he is a "preacher" for a "Protestant" church referred to throughout the novel as "the Church." He has been educated at a "little university city" in "the Middle West" (32). Here he met his wife, a music student who was "saving hard for another year's study in the East," and wondering if she "might even make it Europe" (16). Her only other suitor had been a violinist who "went to England shortly afterwards, . . . then made a concert tour of South America" (77). The North American place names offered by the text are the mostly small-town names—Partridge Hill, Tillsonborough, Crow Coulee, Kelby, and Horizon—that have referents only inside the novel. The Bentleys at the end of the narrative leave Horizon to operate a bookstore in "the little city" where they used to live, "two hundred miles southeast."

Thus, although the setting is marked as "not-Europe" and "not South America," it is not marked as "not-U.S." Both "Main Street," with its invocation of Sinclair Lewis, and "Middle West" suggest the U.S., while "prairie," "coulee," "Protestant," "the East," "the Church" can mark either Canada or the United States.

The proper names that participate in semiotic systems outside the book tend to gather together under the sign of "not-this-place." These include England, Europe, South America above Buenos Aires—named as the place from which Mrs. Bentley's violinist friend sends a postcard—the names of the composers—Chopin, Liszt, Debussy, Mozart—whose music Mrs. Bentley plays, and those of painters—El Greco, Romney, Gainsborough—that she borrows in trying to characterize her dog. The text constructs a contrast between a non-North America, which possesses "non fictional" names and referents, and an immediate "prairie" context, which not only lacks names with resonant semiotics but from which all reference to specific North American place names and institutions has been excluded. The effect of this contrast is to create a semiotic silence around the Bentleys and Horizon. He has worked in anonymous towns; they met and married in a nameless city to which they are about to return; he has preached for an unnamed church; she orders clothing from an unnamed mail-order catalogue, walks beside an unnamed railroad. Official systems of meaning appear to operate outside this area of silence. One of these is that of art, embodied in the names of three eighteenth-century European artists and outside of which Philip Bentley attempts his near-modernist drawings. Another is music, represented both by eighteenth- and nineteenth-century European composers and by the violinist's concert tour which originates in Europe, centres on South America, and reaches "prairie" North America only by postcard. A third is language, embodied both in the books that Philip Bentley has inherited or collected and in the etymological musings of the Bentleys' friend Paul. Language for all of them is also from somewhere else—from distant places where books are produced and from a distant time when the "original" meanings of words prevailed. The Bentleys' ambiguous connections to these official systems are two institutions in their nameless "little university city"— the university at which they met and the books of Philip's study and of the bookstore he may eventually buy.

*   *   *   *   *

A number of critics have remarked on another silence in the novel, that around Mrs. Bentley's name. Although she is the narrator of *As for Me and My House*, and although most of its male characters carry both first names and surnames, she is identified only as "Mrs. Bentley." The feminist implications of this are inescapable: the woman who tells us she became Philip

Bentley's wife by "yielding" her "identity" and by making her piano take "second place" (16) loses both her given name and surname on marriage. At the very least this loss creates a semiotic inequality between herself and her husband: a reader can construct him as "Philip" or "Philip Bentley" or "Reverend Bentley" and as occupying the various roles those names suggest, but can construct her only as "Mrs. Bentley." One can construct him as young or middle-aged, as a student or as a minister, but construct her only as a married woman. One can *tutoyer* Philip, address him within an intimate discourse but, despite experiencing the narrative through what should be another intimate discourse, a diary, one must continue to consider its fictional writer as "Mrs. Bentley."

An equally profound but less widely noticed silence around "Mrs. Bentley"—and for me it becomes difficult at this point in thinking of the novel to envision her name without quotation marks—concerns her past. Again, this silence creates a marked imbalance between her and her husband. The text offers some detail about Philip Bentley's birth, his childhood identification with his dead father, his defiant interest in art, and his struggles to become a writer and painter by becoming a Protestant minister, but gives no information about Mrs. Bentley's birth or childhood, and only enough about her ambitions as a pianist to establish the negative sign of what she may have given up. This and the silence around her name are particularly ironic in light of the illegitimacy of Philip's birth and the instability—is "Bentley" his mother's or father's surname?—of his name. The one born outside of institutional naming has his name confirmed by the text and his birth story preserved, but the one very likely born within that institution has her story and name effaced.

Mrs. Bentley's relation to naming is shared by most of the women in the novel. There is Mrs. Nicholson, "the station agent's wife" (77), Mrs. Finley, "President of the Ladies Aid," Mrs. Wenderby, Mrs. Ellingson, Mrs. Lawson, "Mrs. Bird, the doctor's wife" (20), Mrs. Pratt, Mrs. Brook. Only one of these is allowed a given name by the text, "Josephine Bird," who foregrounds the male-female issue by complaining early in the book about the "dominating male" and of having to live in "a man's world" (21). The only other married woman who retains her given name is the even more defiant Laura Kirby, whom the text describes as "a thorough ranch woman, with a disdainful shrug for all . . . domestic ties," "a star attraction in rodeos fifteen years before" (93). In this disdain she is a sharp contrast to the women of the town, whose values she implicitly mocks when she mimics Mrs. Bentley "at a Ladies Aid meeting leading in prayer" (95). Interestingly, she is the only married woman whom Mrs. Bentley can manage to call by her given name, and the only one never called "Mrs." by the text.

Laura Kirby's having given up an individual career to become a wife, childbearer and worker on a ranch known in the text by her husband's surname gives her a history very similar to that of Mrs. Bentley. Unlike the latter, however, and unlike any of the other married women in *As for Me and My House*, she was once successful in a career and can still manage to found her identity upon it, since she "breaks broncos and punches cattle a match for any cowboy." She seems to do so in part by inattention to three children whom the text is reluctant even to identify as hers:

> Three half-naked little girls file in and stand watching us eat, and the moment we leave the table make a rush for the sirup jug. The eldest is seven, the youngest two. They look so dirty and neglected I volunteer to wash them . . . . (93)

Laura has also visibly alienated her husband through a brief relationship some summers ago with "a big handsome cowboy." In addition to marking this "thorough ranch woman" as a neglectful mother and a probably unfaithful wife, the text emphatically marks her identity as masculine. She is "a match for any cowboy." She has "a mannish verve." She wears "a man's shirt and trousers, and for riding fine leather chaps studded with silver nails" (93). In this regard Laura resembles all the married women in the novel, who have identities through their relationships to men and usually to men's activities. But, although the text insists that Laura's apparent independence rests both on her participation in male systems of meaning, the cowboy and the rodeo, and on her neglect of the traditional female systems of meaning, mother and wife, it is relatively quiet about the married woman's role as unpaid labour in her husband's employment or profession. It says nothing about the economic basis of Laura's confidence. Only five pages from the end does it have Mrs. Bentley consider a career separate from Philip's, and this because she fears that if she helps him run his new bookstore she'll prove "so much more practical and capable than he is that in a month or two I'd be one of those domineering females that men abominate. Instead I'll try to teach" (160). Embarking on a separate career could be read as the text's recommendation to strong women as a way not of achieving personal fulfilment but of avoiding intimidating one's man.

* * * * *

> His father had lived for a few months in the restaurant, and pushed out of the way in the little room that later they gave to Philip was a trunkful of his books. There were letters and photographs among them. When a lad still, Philip discovered his father's ambition to paint, that he had been as alien to the town and Philip's mother as was Philip now himself. The books were difficult and bewildering, more of them on art and literature than theology; but only half-understood, beyond his reach, they added to the stature of the man who had owned and read them. (30)

Although the connections that the Bentleys retain with officially constituted systems of meaning may be tenuous, one should not underestimate the importance the text places upon them. As the above passage suggests, it is through books, through the printed word, that Philip Bentley is said to have legitimized himself. Lacking a legal father, he has grounded his identity on his biological father's books, on a textual father. When "a preacher who had gone to college with his father" comes to town and suggests that if he enter the ministry "the Church would educate him," one witnesses a convergence of related meaning systems. The "preacher," the speaker of authorized words, offers access to additional books at the university, another authorized keeper of words, through the mediation of the church, the keeper of Word. Although the church and university and university town may be nameless, they nevertheless still guarantee access to word itself, to the Bible from which the novel's title is taken and to the bookstore to which the Bentleys eventually will move. From Philip the illegitimate will emerge both Reverend Bentley and Philip Bentley, Bookseller. Along the way he attempts to write "a book" (64), and later tries "an article for a missionary magazine":

> a sober discussion of a minister's problems in a district that has suffered drought and dust storms for five years—well written, all his sentences and paragraphs rounded out sonorously with the puffy, imageless language that gives dignity to church literature, a few well-placed quotations from scripture, and for peroration unbounded faith in the Lord's watchfulness over flocks and shepherds alike. (110)

The novel here has Mrs. Bentley emphasize the textualized quality of Philip's identity, the dignity constructed through "puffy imageless language" and the faith produced by pastoral metaphor. Behind this and the other musings it allows her on the gap between discursive constructions and the experiences they attempt to represent, the novel repeatedly places the concept of hypocrisy—with its implications of a single and "correct" text.

✳ ✳ ✳ ✳ ✳

It doesn't follow that the sensitive qualities that make an artist are accompanied by the unflinching, stubborn ones that make a man of action and success.

✳ ✳ ✳ ✳ ✳

> Comfort and routine were the last things he needed. Instead he ought to have been out mingling with his own kind. He ought to have whetted himself against them, then gone off to fight it out alone. He ought to have had the opportunity to live, to be reckless, spendthrift, bawdy, anything but what he is, what I've made him. (103)

Although the novel presents Mrs. Bentley as frequently perceptive of the textual constructions of others, it also presents her as unaware of the constructions in which it has her participate herself. The most important one in the novel is that of art and the artist. Her usual notion of an artist is that above—sensitive, "reckless, spendthrift, bawdy," a fighter, implicitly male. This romantic conception is an important part of her belief that Philip's being an artist is incompatible with his being both a minister and a husband, that his being both "[t]he small-town preacher and the artist" is a "compromise" (4), that "as an artist he needed above all things to be free" (33). It is also what moves her to begin gathering money so that he can move to a different career—"For these last twelve years I've kept him in the Church . . . . The least I can do now is help get him out again" (107). This conception sees the artist both as a rebel against institutions like the Church and marriage, and simultaneously as linked to the institution of learning, to the university, to books and the bookstore. This conception belongs as much to the text overall as to its construction of Mrs. Bentley. Philip draws not in a studio, but in his book-filled study; the conflict Mrs. Bentley imagines between the bawdy artist and the dutiful husband is enacted by his withdrawing from the domestic space of the house to his desk and books. When, with Mrs. Bentley's help, he imagines a way to escape the church and small town and move towards acting more as an artist, he imagines himself back in the university town and owner of a bookstore. The bookstore has links back to God's book, to the authority of the word, and thus to "the Church" that Mrs. Bentley perceives as in conflict with the bawdy artist.

This contradiction in the text is replicated by Mrs. Bentley herself, who wishes Philip to be the bawdy artist but is shocked when he sleeps with Judith West, and whose first impulse is to construct this event in institutional terms—"what has happened is adultery . . . he's been unfaithful to me, . . . I have a right now to be free" (124). She later turns to the "bawdy artist" concept, but without much conviction. "[S]he was there, that was all." "The man I see in the pulpit every Sunday isn't Philip. Not the real Philip. However staidly and prosily he lives he's still the artist. He's racked still with the passion of the artist, for seeking, creating, adventuring. That's why it happened" (126). Four times Mrs. Bentley tells herself, in effect, that Judith "just happened to be there" (129), on the last occasion telling us, "I've reasoned it out a hundred times, and the answer every time is the same: she doesn't really mean anything to him: she only happened to be there" (129–30).

* * * * *

One of the best-known readings of *As for Me and My House* is Robert Kroetsch's structuralist interpretation in his essay "Fear of Women in Prairie Fiction." Kroetsch reads the novel as one of several prairie novels that encode a *horse v. house*, prairie versus town dichotomy in which male sexuality is located in the rural—the horse, the cowboy, the coyote—and female sexuality within the walled and institutionalized space of the town. Although the "cowboy" can never feel at ease within the female walls of the town, male and female do come together, Kroetsch suggests, in the "horsehouse" or "whorehouse."

As for Me and My House does locate male sexuality at the Kirby ranch, not only in various male animals, notably the bull Priapus and horses like Paul Kirby's Harlequin, "temperamental" with a "histrionic dash," or the "spirited sorrel" and "rangy bay" that are rejected as suitable horses for Steve, but also in the "mannish" sexuality of Laura. And it offers as the site of Philip's marital transgression a young woman who is linked through her surname "West" to notions of "west" and "wild west," and is from a rural family. But it also locates male sexuality under the sign of the non-British ethnic. Steve Kulanich's father's liaison with another woman is "the only case of open immorality in the town." Steve, said at one point by the text to be "Hungarian, or Rumanian, or Russian," is described in terms similar to the horses: "[s]ensitive and high-strung, hot-blooded" (36). These are also similar to terms used to describe the artist—"sensitive," "reckless" (103)—who is thus linked both to the Kirby ranch at which Philip paints with "strength" and "insight" and to the city in which Philip buys his bookstore. Male sexuality is also located in music, both in the "zest and urgency" (48) of the music of small-town dances and in the serious music of the concert hall. Mrs. Bentley remarks that "one of my teachers used to wonder at what he called my masculine attitude to music. Other girls fluttered about their dresses, what their friends thought about the pieces they played, but I never thought or cared for anything but the music itself" (151).

* * * * *

The complexity and inconsistency of the various codes of As for Me and My House make any dichotomous reading of it in terms of male and female, town and rural, art and church, very difficult. Although Kroetsch's horse/house reading identifies two important meaning systems in the novel, the cowboy/horse and the marriage/house, it is silent about a third, that of music/art/university/concert tour/Europe that is offered as an alternative to both horse and house and which the Bentleys choose at the end of the novel. It is also silent about one of the main sources of power and identity in the novel, the Word—the books in which Philip finds himself, the Bible, the male names that define almost all the women. The novel's conflicting meaning systems also intertwine and overlap; although church and art are conflicting systems within Philip's life, they both participate in the authority of the Word; although the sexuality of music is experienced more by the cowboy than by the small-town churchgoer, it is also experienced in "the East" or in the cosmopolitan centres of Europe or South America.

The small town's view of Judith West is particularly illustrative of the semiotic complexity of the novel. She is introduced to the reader by

Mrs. Bentley in a paragraph that preserves the language of the self-important Mrs. Finley, who is herself "describing" Judith to Mrs. Bentley:

> On the church steps Mrs. Finley told us that she comes from a family of shiftless farmers up in the sandhills north of town. Instead of trying to help them, though, she went out working when she was about seventeen, sometimes as a servant girl, sometimes stooking in the harvest fields like a man. With her savings at last she set off to the city to take a commercial course, only to find when it was finished that little country upstarts aren't the kind they employ in business offices. Now Mr. Wenderby, the town clerk, gives her twenty-five dollars a month and board for typing his letters in the afternoon, and helping Mrs. Wenderby in the morning and evening. They encourage her in the choir because she needs a steadying influence. In summer she's been heard singing off by herself up the railroad track as late as ten o'clock at night. Naturally people talk. (11–12)

Mrs. Finley is president of the church's Ladies Aid. She stands here on the church steps speaking "as if" from the male authority of the church. In fact throughout the novel Mrs. Finley attempts to adopt authoritative, quasi-theological positions—advising the Bentleys against adopting the Roman Catholic Steve, striking Steve during Sunday school when he fights with her twins, informing the Bentleys about decency and respectability when they buy Steve a horse. Her beliefs—that unsuccessful farmers are "shiftless," that children should help their parents, that women should not act like men, that people should not aspire to roles they are not born to, that steadiness is a virtue, that solitary happiness is a sign of instability, that unconventional people are appropriately subject to gossip—are declared as "natural" throughout the paragraph. The notable phrases in the paragraph, "like a man," "country upstarts," "aren't the kind," "steadying influence," are part of a narrowly categorizing discourse that privileges the familiar and resists challenges to role definitions. The story she tells parallels that of both Philip Bentley and Paul Kirby, "the ranch boy with a little schooling . . . [who] fits in nowhere" (20)—a journey by someone born on a farm or in a small town to the city in search of a more satisfying life, followed by a forced return to the town. Judith's ambition to return to the city is the same as that of the Bentleys; her solitary singing connects with Philip's solitary painting or Mrs. Bentley's solitary piano playing. Her having worked "like a man" connects with Mrs. Bentley's feelings that she will bring disapproval upon herself and her husband if she repairs stovepipes or digs her garden, with her "masculine" piano playing, and with the "mannish verve" of Laura. Her employment as secretary and as kitchen help places her in subservient roles unfamiliar to women in western culture and certainly visible in the novel in such concepts as "ladies aid" and "preacher's wife." The various codes of gender, art, farm, small town, and city mix and compete in this passage. Laura is the girl who would transgress gender and class roles, who would refuse conceptions of the normal, the familial, who looks for "something more" (56) than what she has rather than attempting to defend, like Mrs. Finley, an inherited world.

The Kroetsch horse/house reading is also, like the novel itself, silent about the economic implications of the narrative, implications that are more than evident in Mrs. Finley's account of Judith West. The town of Horizon rests on one activity, agriculture. The industrial passes through it, like the railway track beside which Judith walks. The commercial, which presumably includes the market context within which Horizon's agricultural products are priced and sold, is somewhere else, in the unnamed "city." Signs of long-term economic distress appear throughout the text. When Philip was ordained 15 years earlier, he "had counted on a salary of at least fifteen hundred dollars . . . but hard years and poor appointments kept it to a thousand" (33). "Five years in succession" the farmers of the four towns he has served have "been blown out, dried out, hailed out" (19). Together these towns now owe him more than "twenty-eight hundred dollars" (106). The towns are marked by "broken sidewalks and rickety false fronts" (5), "ugly wretched faces" (17), "red chapped necks and sagging bodies" (19). Although the amount and decline of Philip's salary and the five consecutive years of adverse climate suggest the Depression years of the 1930s, no mention appears in the text of other than local economic factors. Economic adversity is displaced in the text to the wind, to which the farmers listen during Philip's sermons, "tense, bolt upright," "their faces pinched and stiffened with anxiety" (37). Repeatedly the wind brings to Mrs. Bentley her own economic plight, "the dust, the farmers and the crops, wondering what another dried-out year will mean for us. We're pinched already" (39). The Lawsons' son dies because he is unable to receive the care of "a city specialist." Judith West dies without hospital care, giving birth at home. The latter pages of the book are dominated by Mrs. Bentley's attempts to recover a thousand dollars from the twenty-eight hundred owed to her husband by the towns he has served; this thousand dollars becomes for her a measure of the value of her future.

The economic structures in the book appear particularly difficult for women, most of whom are presented as sharing the economic lives of their husbands. Mrs. Bentley's relationship to Philip's professional activities, relieving him of unnecessary domestic tasks so that more of his time may be available for his work, is that of all the married women. If these women have ever had their own economic lives, they have given them up, like Mrs. Bentley claims to have given up a musical career, to "be a good companion," to do what "it seemed . . . life was intended for" (16). Unmarried, like Judith West, they have had their ambitions channelled into low-paying male-service occupations—typing and housework.

The horse, house, and university-city alternatives proposed by the text mark not only possible structures of sexuality and ideology but also economic possibilities. All three rest on economic forces. Many of the values of Horizon—its disapproval of ostentation, its fear of the sexual, whether enacted, as by Steve's father, or symbolized, as in Judith's singing—appear founded on such things as shortages of money and the financial dependence of married women on stable marriages. The "horse" cattle-ranching economy in the novel appears oddly prosperous, apparently little affected by problems of either drought or cash-flow. It can evidently accommodate a more extravagant dress code and—although the economic grounds for this aren't particularly clear—a more relaxed sexual code. The city economy, although barely visible, shows vague signs of specialization and scale; here one can take commercial courses and do "good business" in secondhand bookselling.

*   *   *   *   *

From what signs and positions, then, does the novel speak? Mostly it speaks from Mrs. Bentley's position, a position of multiple marginalization that is constructed by both her and the text as for the most part "reasonable" and unchangeable given the time and place she inhabits. She is the woman excluded from economic productivity, the wife excluded from the role of biological mother, the musician excluded from most of the institutions of art and music, the citizen of Horizon who both accepts and refuses the narrow economic and sexual rules through which it manages its fragile family economies. She is the unnamed woman excluded from official discourse, the writer who works in a genre, the diary, of which the first mark is that it is unread. Although the novel sometimes casts irony on what Mrs. Bentley records—particularly on the feelings of superiority she has towards her husband and to most other women—it rarely dissociates itself from the views it gives her: that men and women are essentially different; that there's a "man's way" and a "woman's way" (64); that men dislike visibly strong women (160); that the benchmarks of art and music are exclusively European; that art celebrates the human, celebrates "[f]aith, ideals, reason—all the things that really are humanity" (80). Mrs. Bentley's Eurocentrism, her humanism, her sense that men are stronger and less competitive than women, her rejection of both the small town and the ranch as suitable places for art, are if anything confirmed by the text overall. The text keeps all mention of Canadian or United States places and institutions out of the mouths of other characters. It gives her its last reflection on art, the comment that Philip "hasn't the courage to admit" the humanistic content of his drawings. It makes Judith's baby male, and causes her to die while giving birth to it, thus not only allowing Mrs. Bentley the son she has always wished Philip to have but killing off her competition for both it and Philip. It allows Philip to find and purchase the secondhand bookstore in the little university city that will become the site of the Bentleys' re-insertion into the cosmopolitan.

Canada in *As for Me and My House* is, like Mrs. Bentley, unnamed. In the place of national or regional indicators is a variety of contending meaning systems. There is the ranch/freedom/wilderness system of cowboy, coyote, wolfhound, horse, bull, and the cowgirl Laura. There is the rigid, heavily defended marriage-economy of the small town. There is the Logos, the authority of the word and all the "Eastern" institutions that flow from it: church, university, art, music, Judith's commercial courses, Mrs. Bentley's mail-order catalogue. Within these are further contentions—art as "bawdy" and ranch-like, "raunchy" if you will, contends with the canonical art of El Greco and Gainsborough, and thus implicitly with other constructions like "business" or "family." Paul tells Mrs. Bentley: "there was a French artist who decided one day he couldn't stand his business or family any longer, and just walked off and left them. It's a good sign" (128). The church appears to conflict in Philip's life with art and letters. However, the text itself resolves these latter contentions within the figure "bookstore," under whose sign Philip will be able to paint, shelter his family, and operate a business, as well as re-enter European art and culture. This movement of the text away from the two Horizon choices Robert Kroetsch identifies and towards the "little university city" is not towards the whorehouse but towards Northrop Frye's implicitly Eurocentric "emancipated and humane community of culture" (347).

The text's endorsement of this unnamed university city becomes, by that non-naming, an endorsement of a putative universal over the local. This endorsement leaves the other contending forces of the novel powerless. Although sexuality has been linked in the text to art, and art to the bookstore, signs of the sexual are notably absent in the passages in which Mrs. Bentley foresees their city life. Woman remains through her namelessness a co-opted part of a universal order that is, by its singularity, European, male, and canonical. She carries her husband's name, plays music composed by men, regrets not having borne a male child, acts as mother to an adopted son. Judith West, the woman who attempted both to escape class and gender determinations and to gain sexual pleasure outside a marriage-economy, is obliged by the novel to die giving birth to this son. And behind these determinations still lurks the economic, disguised as wind, drowning "hymns and sermons," silencing Paul's reflections on etymology (38), covering books with dust (73), blowing so thickly one cannot "see beyond the town" (162). Behind marriage, childbirth, death, art, and the word, in some way the text leaves mysterious and unquestioned, lies money. The thousand dollars, earned through labour and wheat and railroads, through some Judith "stooking in the harvest fields like a man," which was the necessary precedent for the coming of Reverend Bentley's Word of God to Kelby and Coulee City, is also the necessary precedent to the Bentleys' return to art, book, and word. Again, ostensibly conflicting signs intertwine. How they intertwine, however, will remain as obscure as the outskirts of Horizon on a stormy day, for in *As for Me and My House*, although one can sometimes find shelter from the wind, the wind itself remains constructed as a "grim primeval tragedy" (59).

WORKS CITED

Cude, Wilfred. "Beyond Mrs. Bentley" and "Getting Philip Straight." In *A Due Sense of Differences: An Evaluative Approach to Canadian Literature*. Washington, D.C.: University Press of America, 1980, pp. 31–49, 50–68.

Daniells, Roy. "Introduction" to Sinclair Ross, *As for Me and My House*. Toronto: McClelland and Stewart, 1957.

Denham, Paul. "Narrative Technique in Sinclair Ross's *As for Me and My House*." *Studies in Canadian Literature* 5 (Spring 1980), 116–26.

Dooley, D. J. "*As for Me and My House*: The Hypocrite and the Parasite." In *Moral Vision in the Canadian Novel*. Toronto: Clarke Irwin, 1979, pp. 38–47.

Frye, Northrop. *Anatomy of Criticism*. Princeton: Princeton University Press, 1957.

Godard, Barbara. "El Greco in Canada: Sinclair Ross's *As for Me and My House*." *Mosaic* 14, 2 (Spring 1981), 54–76.

Kroetsch, Robert. "Fear of Women in Prairie Fiction: An Erotics of Space." *Open Letter*, Fifth Series, No. 4 (Spring 1983), 47–55.

McMullen, Lorraine. *Sinclair Ross*. Boston: Twayne, 1979.

Mitchell, Barbara. "Paul: The Answer to the Riddle of *As for Me and My House*." *Studies in Canadian Literature* 13, 1 (1988), 47–63.

Ross, Morton L. "The Canonization of *As for Me and My House*: A Case Study." In Diane Bessai and David Jackel, eds., *Figures in a Ground*. Saskatoon: Western Producer Prairie Books, 1978, pp. 189–205.

Ross, Sinclair. *As for Me and My House*. Toronto: McClelland and Stewart, NCL edition, 1957.

Stouck, David. *Major Canadian Authors: A Critical Introduction*. Lincoln: University of Nebraska Press, 1984.

Who Are You, Mrs. Bentley?: Feminist Re-vision and Sinclair Ross's *As for Me and My House*

HELEN M. BUSS

> Re-vision—the act of looking back, of seeing with fresh eyes, of entering an old text from a new critical direction—is for women more than a chapter in cultural history: it is an act of survival.
>
> *(Lies, Secrets and Silence* 35)

Adrienne Rich's description of revision as a feminist literary activity has special meaning for feminist readers of Ross's text. Seeking a Mrs. Bentley who accords with female experience is an "act of survival" that demands a revision of the critical reception of *As for Me and My House*, a reception that offers (in the majority of evaluations) viewpoints of the central female character that limit the reading act. But feminist revision also implies attention to the cultural situation of the revisioning critic, as exemplified by Rich's autobiographical stance in *Of Woman Born*, in which she makes her own history a part of the project of re-examining the institution of motherhood. In the same manner I intend to give attention both to the history of critical reception and to my own history as a reader of Ross's text. [1]

A whole series of critical inquiries, mostly written during the seventies, concentrates on Mrs. Bentley in her role as Philip Bentley's wife. As such she becomes a pole of negativity. These critiques are based on the unacknowledged assumption that Mrs. Bentley's primary function in Ross's fiction is as wife in a patriarchal structure. And as wife she does not fulfil the functions of support, service, and submission of self that are to be expected. As wife she is (I quote a collage of various critiques) "manipulative," "hypocritical," "mean," "incorrect" and "less than human," a "barren" woman, with a "sharply voiced" and frightening "power to castrate."[2]

Assessments that concentrate on Ross's craft as writer, rather than the social world created by his text, point out Mrs. Bentley's role as narrator. She may not be the "pure gold" that Roy Daniells thought she was in his introduction to the first paperback edition of the text (1957), but she tends to receive a less negative assessment as narrator than as wife: "[she] is an almost incidental victim of her critics' attack on the real target, her role of narrator; what seems like a calumny is actually designed to expose her as a most untrustworthy narrator" (M. Ross 194). It would seem, by this kind of assessment, that Mrs. Bentley is not "guilty" as a character, but rather the hapless victim of her place in the narrative grammar of the text. But to label her victim is merely to call up the other side of the stereotyping patriarchal coin. If woman acts in the patriarchal world, she is witch, medusa, castrator, i.e., bad woman. If she does not act, she is acted upon, she is vessel, she is victim, i.e., good woman.

It is curious, however, that when critics abandon these two stereo-typical views and Mrs. Bentley begins to be identified as an artist figure, her negative image remains largely intact. The negativity clings to these assessments either because they ignore Mrs. Bentley's actual art, her journal writing, and assess her as pianist, so that "Philip's artistic activities are intrinsically more creative than" hers (Godard 60), or because they see her as a "perverse Pygmalion" who is "turning her spouse into a statue" (Cude 18), or because they view her as "male-devouring" based on "the man in the study or bed-room, drawing failed pictures or pretending to write, white-lipped and crying . . ." (Kroetsch, "Beyond Nationalism" vii).

I think Robert Kroetsch is on the right track when, despite the fear of women implicit in his "failed male" theory of female artistic impulse, he identifies Mrs. Bentley as a "powerful artist-figure . . . busily writing a journal . . . conniving the world into shape and existence . . ." (vii). But I seek a reading of the text that proposes a fuller view of female artistic production in the context of Mrs. Bentley's historical situation. Adrienne Rich makes a good start on such a facilitating position when she describes her own problems as a writer, burdened with the role (as designed by patriar-chy) of wife and mother:

> For a poem to coalesce, for a character or an action to take shape, there has to be an imaginative transformation of reality which is in no way passive. And a certain freedom of the mind is needed—freedom to press on, to enter the currents of your thought like a glider pilot, knowing that your motion can be sustained, that the buoyancy of your attention will not be suddenly snatched away . . . . You have to be free to play around with the notion that day might be night, love might be hate; nothing can be too sacred for the imagination to turn into its opposite or to call experimentally by another name. For writing

is re-naming. Now . . . to be with a man in the old way of marriage, requires a holding-back, a putting-aside of that imaginative activity, and demands instead a kind of conservatism. (*Lies, Secrets and Silence* 60)

In describing her own dilemma as woman artist in the United States in the 1960s, Rich describes the situation Sinclair Ross effectively communicated, writing in Canada in the 1930s. It is interesting that the solutions Rich suggests, both in terms of behaviour and artistic pursuit, are also very similar to the ones found by Ross's female artist figure. Rich realizes that such a woman cannot leave a relationship, fly free like the traditional male artist figure: "There must be ways . . . in which the energy of creation and the energy of relation can be united" (43). Rich finds that relation, not only by privileging the content of female life in patriarchy (home, children, husband, housework), but by abandoning the values of tightly structured composition, taught by her mentors, and by experimenting with a "longer, looser mode" (43) of writing.

Rich could be describing what Mrs. Bentley is doing as *House* opens, as she (at least partially) abandons the structured, practised world of the pianist for the "longer, looser mode" of the diarist. In beginning her diary, Mrs. Bentley leaps immediately into the quotidian activities that Rich feels the female writer must take as her subject matter. She brings together the "energy of creation and the energy of relation" in the intimate privacy of her diary as she explores her husband, the townspeople, her social position as minister's wife, all intertwined with her painful, anxious, resentful, love-hungry and art-hungry negotiation of the implications of such a world.

Towards the end of the first entry, we become aware of the lonely writing space of the diary, the space of a rather terrible "freedom," where she effects what Rich would call her "imaginative transformation that is not passive." The diarist actively embraces the force of the natural world pressing on her imagination to create her text, and eventually to re-create her world. It is in the "wheeling and windy" world of the storm, a subversive place where the church can be re-named the institution that is "black even against the darkness" (5), where she writes alone, despite her terror, a terror that makes her "feel lost, dropped on this little perch of town and abandoned," in a loneliness so intense that she wishes "Philip would waken" (8), so she can once more bury her consciousness in her role as his wife.

My exploration of this recurring phenomenon of the diarist commenting on her writing moment divides into three areas: a consideration of some current theoretical views on diary writing, a close reading of selected portions of the text of *As for Me and My House* with these theoretical considerations in mind, and a concluding section in which I make some speculations on the historical contexts relevant to the constructions of female self made by Ross and by myself as a reader encountering this text, first in the early sixties, then in the early eighties, and again in 1990.

Mrs. Bentley may be understood more fully as diarist/artist by conflating what relevant theories have to say regarding the special characteristics of diary fiction and of women's autobiographical writing. Lorna Martens describes the metamorphosis in journal/letter fiction between the seventeenth and nineteenth centuries, from Richardson's *Pamela*, exemplary of texts that emphasize suspense and action, to Goethe's *Werther* which marks a shift in emphasis to characterization (78). H. Porter Abbott revises Martens's observation to point out that the interest in "character" of the Wertherian fictions is really an interest in "feeling" (32). Martens herself makes an interesting point about the phenomenon of "feeling" in diary literature when she describes what she calls "expressives," statements about the self made by the diarist which "represent a psychic state" more directly than is usual, that is, not as open to slippage between the writing self and its subject, the "I" referent on the page, as in other formats (40–44). If, by such an ability to make "expressive" utterances, diary fiction is particularly suited to exploration of subjectivity, then, as Penelope Franklin points out, the form becomes especially relevant to the lives of women, in which the "act of keeping a diary is often a way for the writer to get in touch with and develop hidden parts of herself—often those aspects for which little support is given by others—and establish emotional stability and independence" (468). Abbott spends a considerable space showing how the exploration of subjectivity, what is called "the special reflexive function of the diary strategy," "not only tell[s] a tale but play[s] a demonstrable role in determining the outcome of that tale" (38), by which "overt acts in the 'external' sequence of the plot can be born in the text. Conversely, acts can fail to occur, and it is in the text that they can be stifled" (42). Thus, the "diarist, through the agency of her writing, can effect an evolution as a human being or, through the same agency, impede or prevent it . . . . She hones a new image of herself" (43) and, by consequence, as she reconstructs herself, she reconstructs the way she relates to others and the world, and to some degree reconstructs the way others and the world relate to her. Abbott sees the reflexive diary as "plotted [so] as to make *the will of the writer in its freedom* [his emphasis] the central mystery and point of focus" (44–45). In fact, Abbott is describing a writing form capable of combining the best of pre- and post-Wertherian styles, a form in which we observe the "feeling" of the diarist reshaping the "action" of her world. By this point in my negotiation of these theoretical positions, which writer is meant, you may well ask, the fictional writer who is a character in the text, or the fiction writer, the name designated as such on the title page? Abbott and Martens are concerned with the actual writer, but advantages exist in the diary-style fiction for the fictional diarist as well, and coincidentally for us as actual readers. Martens outlines several of these advantages. Diary writing itself offers the artist who co-opts that form for fiction writing the advantage of a conflated narrative triangle. The usual triangle of narrator, narrated world, and fictive reader, as illustrated in a spatial relationship, becomes a "folding over of the subject of discourse on himself" (5); that is, the narrator (or diarist) is her own fictive reader, and the world that is narrated is the stuff of her own subjectivity. This intense collapsing of distance is, in diary fiction, contained within another narrative triangle of author, reader, and novel (33), which imposes on one dynamic situation a second dynamic. Martens designates this as the "voice of the author" (34), which can act as a psychoanalytic voice that recovers through his discourse the "repressed material" the subject (diarist) has buried inside the conscious discourse of the diary. Martens proposes that "if we find points where the second narrative triangle intrudes into the first, we can accept these points of intrusion as indications of how to read the text." She adds that these moments are where we can find "traces of the author's hand" (33). By manipulating the relationship "between the first and second narrative triangles" an author "may endorse the narrator and his discourse, or he may choose to undermine him . . . to validate the diarists or to take the opposite attitude of dissent" (37). I would add a third possibility to Martens's two opposites. An author may choose neither to validate nor to dissent, inviting the reader into a third narrative triangle of textual subjectivity, writerly subjectivity, and readerly subjectivity, a triangle indicating an active relationship in which we are never allowed to rest in only one reading of the text. And this is exactly what I feel Ross's text does.

To plot the operation of the three interrelated triangles of textuality, I begin with the assumption that Mrs. Bentley is, as all of us who are women are to one degree or another, a patriarchal woman. Sidonie Smith argues in *A Poetics of Women's Autobiography* that such a woman, attempting to write the self inside the patriarchal symbol system, is a "misbegotten man." Smith's use of Aquinas's label for woman is part of a summary of male symbol systems in which woman is represented as lacking some essential aspect of humanity. From Aristotelian to Lacanian theory "a female of the species results from a deprivation of nature, a generative process not carried to its conclusion" (27). While in Classical-Christian configurations woman is lack because of her lack of full rationality or her lack of spirituality, Modernity (used here in the broad cultural sense that includes postmodernity) changes only the ground of her absence. In the Freudian/Lacanian formulation, woman is still denied full humanity: "she crosses through the mirror of the logos and assumes her position as Other, the object by means of which man defines himself. Independently she cannot assume and presume herself because, according to Lacan, she has no phallus and therefore can expect no access to the patronym. She enters the symbolic order as absence, lack, negativity" (Smith 14–15).

In entering the world of the symbolic, of symbolic language, particularly the discourse of autobiography, she enters a "public arena," as Smith puts it, and attempts a "narrative that will resonate with privileged cultural fictions of male selfhood" (52). But Smith's *Poetics* does not deal with marginal autobiographical forms such as letters, journals, and diaries, writing forms that have always been the sites of female self-engendering, self-empowering, as well as female subversion of the patriarchal order. It is in this space that the "misbegotten man," the patriarchal woman, Mrs. Bentley in this case, begins to shape her own subjectivity. In that first entry (referred to at the beginning of this paper), she begins by describing the church, long the centre of patriarchal order in the western world, as "black even against the darkness, towering ominously up through the night and merging with it" (5). Her diary is the site of the subversion of some aspects of the patriarchal order represented by that church. It is the site of subversion for her as diarist, for Ross as writer, for myself as reader.

I locate many sites of subversion in the text, moments that culminate in a process of awakening for the diarist, that set her towards new self-engendering activities. These moments are, as Martens suggests, expressive in their use of language, sites where the subject of discourse folds over onto herself, in which her words more directly express the condition of her psyche than other language usages. They are, as Abbott would have it, moments where we find the writer closest to his text, directing the diarist to create the conditions of the future self and the future plot, and they are, as I have suggested, sites where the three subjectivities, that of fictional diarist, the text's writer, and the reader, join.

One occurs at the beginning of the diary entry for "Thursday Evening, April 27" and reads as follows:

> It's nearly midnight. Paul's gone, and I've put Philip to bed. There's a high, rocking wind that rattles the windows and creaks the walls. It's strong and steady like a great tide after the winter pouring north again, and I have a queer, helpless sense of being lost miles out in the middle of it, flattened against a little peak of rock. (47)

Mrs. Bentley often represents great changes in herself in figures of the action of the wind. Later she will wait for the "wind to work its will" (57), will note that Judith's voice can "ride up with it, feel it the way a singer feels an orchestra" (51), will record that Paul, the resident philologist of her text, tells her that "fool" in its original sense means "wind bag." Mrs. Bentley often calls herself fool, indeed her husband calls her "little" fool, and as fool she takes on the voice of the wind, in the sense of wind as breath, as articulation, as words. She eventually realizes that it is "better to run off in the wilderness where there's a strong clean wind blowing" (175) than waste her words reprimanding others (on that occasion the women of the church). And at the end of her diary it is the wind she credits with blowing down "most of the false fronts" (212). Thus, in this entry she begins to negotiate her relationship to the "wind," which at first makes her "helpless" and "lost" but eventually will mean the taking-on of linguistic power, of figuratively "stealing" language "to represent herself rather than to remain a mere representation of man" (Smith 41).

Several recorded moments have led to this initial taking-on of the power of language to restructure reality. She has described her psychic dilemma as a woman "impatient with being just [Philip's] wife" (7), of trying to inflict her "mothering" on him too, a mothering left useless in a marriage that has produced no living child. As patriarchal wife who must create herself through identification with husband and child, she is doubly robbed because Philip feels trapped in his profession and resents sharing with her his one escape, his drawings. She has admitted that she hates the house that contains their misery (25) and makes the important series of confessions that allows her to put in words the "hindrance" that locks them both into a life where a "stillborn" child is the only memory of creativity they both share (45). By recognizing that she herself is part of this "hindrance," she begins the working of her solution. The text becomes the site of that working.

Shortly after this April entry, several plot details are contemplated in the diary and shaped to achieve an important first stage of her new version of herself. She has been given a fuchsia plant by Mrs. Ellingson (19), one of the few females she does not dislike, and the plant becomes the one growing thing in the oppressive house, so that while a "haze of dust like smoke" chokes the atmosphere, the bell-like blossoms of the fuchsia promise that she will "need a bigger trellis soon" (57). This is followed in her next entry by a decision to have a garden so that Philip will not "hate the sight of me by fall" (58).

The decision regarding a garden signals the beginning of her "gardening" in a figurative sense, as the people and events of the plot are constructed to facilitate the reality she needs. Very quickly she finds ways to welcome Paul, Judith, and Steve into her world in a way that will preserve her necessary relationship with Philip while instituting the changes that will give new life to their relationship. Paul, who appears to want to be more her friend than Philip's, is encouraged to spend time with Philip in his den, and when Paul hesitates to accept this social order she acts to enforce it: "At the study door he glanced back a second, hesitating; but afraid that he might take sides I turned my back, and pretended to be busy with the dishes" (49).

She initiates a friendship with Judith, who has just been noticed by Philip (52–53), thus creating a situation where she mediates any kind of intercourse between the two. As well, as soon as Steve becomes a factor in Philip's life, she moves quickly to place herself in a mediating position: "I played brilliantly, vindictively, determined to let Philip see how easily I could take the boy away from him" (63). She is, of course, aware of the moral implications of what she is doing, as she writes in the diary that she wishes she "had spared him" (63), understanding Philip's need to assert himself "against a world of matrons and respectability" (64). But she does not stop her shaping, even though, watching the moths drawn into the flame as she writes (65), she would seem to know how dangerous it is to bring together the worlds of creativity and relationship.

But whereas this textual evidence is the same that is used by the critics formerly quoted to judge Mrs. Bentley as manipulative, less than human, castrating, I quote it as evidence that the patriarchal woman, given (and accepting) only the narrow private world in which to exercise her creativity, uses what she has, in the way a male artist might use the larger world at his disposal, as material for the realization of the self. I refuse the double standard implicitly accepted by those who condemn Mrs. Bentley, the standard that deprives women of a sufficient ground of being and then condemns them for attempting to assert any growth potential on that narrow ground. This condition is the result of the sex-gender system operational in our society.[3] In fact, in proposing a feminist revisionary position I necessarily propose a feminist ethic: that the ethical and the aesthetic cannot be separated; that since the personal is the political, the individual prescribed to operate only in the personal world operates in the same way as the individual shaping and being shaped in the public world. Mrs. Bentley must work with what life offers her to construct her subjectivity. What life offers her are individuals whose propensities and needs she observes and integrates into her own reality construct.

This first phase of self/world building culminates in two events, one that happens to her and that she realizes in the diary, another that she makes happen and records as her own decisive act in the diary. She sits beside Steve on his cot in an intimate maternal moment when she understands, through a music metaphor, her own need for a child: "It was as if once, twelve years ago, I had heard the beginning of a piece of music, and then a door had closed. But within me, in my mind and blood, the music had kept on, and when at last they opened the door again I was at the right place, had held the rhythm all the way" (91). Later, she observes that her relationship with Steve is becoming not a companionship but "a conspiracy" (95). Mrs. Bentley takes immediate action on her realization of her maternal needs, and her observation of Philip's need for a son, as two days later, on the first of June, she records that she shows Judith the pictures Philip is drawing of her, and asserts that she knows she is breaking the rules, taking the shaping of affairs into her own hands: "It was a departure from all precedent. I didn't ask his leave, just sailed ahead of him into the study and rummaged through his drawings till I found the ones of Judith" (94). This moment will draw Judith's feelings to the image of Philip. The diarist has created this moment.

But although Mrs. Bentley is an artist shaping the material life presents, she is no god, not even the powerful castrating witch of patriarchal fears. She makes mistakes. For example, when she sees that Philip is about to speak openly to the church hypocrites regarding Steve, she rushes to his rescue, realizing only afterwards that "If I had only kept still we might be starting in to worry now about the future. We might be making plans, shaking the dust off us, finding our way back to life" (96). Having missed the route that silence would have offered her out of Horizon, she must find the route that the words of her diary offer her.

And during the next 50 pages of entries we watch her carrying out her negotiation of events and people. She contemplates the potential of Judith's femaleness. She assents to the horse that will build the relationship between Steve and Philip and that will make Philip feel, as she does, their need for a child. She buys him paints and brushes to inspire his art; puzzles over how he will earn a living. While taking these steps she has not yet faced the full implications of their 12 years in a life that suits neither herself nor Philip. But, by the entry of July 12, when on holiday on the ranch, she is able to face the reality of her existence without sentimentality: "It seems that tonight for the first time in my life I'm really mature . . . . I've contrived to think that at least we had each other . . . . But tonight I'm doubtful. All I see is the futility of it . . . . There doesn't seem to be much meaning to our going on" (136). But this reckoning of the dark side of their marriage does not lead her to give up, but rather increases the pace at which she initiates change in their lives. Three entries later, on their return to Horizon, she begins planning their rescue, the "book and music store" that will give them an alternative living. For the moment she knows she must push Philip to write letters (to churches that owe him money) under false pretences —"for Steve's education, or a trip to Europe" or "an operation coming up" (140)—since he has not realized the extremity of their plight as she has. She is determined now that "This will be our last year. It's got to be" (141).

It is this realization of the need for extreme measures that drives her to the entries of August 9 and 14, in which she uses her diary to construct a version of events that is absolutely necessary to their new life: the shaping of Judith's child. Critics in recent years have questioned the diarist's assumptions regarding the paternity of Judith's child, suggesting that Mr. Finley or Paul could easily claim credit.[4] Such arguments, far from weakening my own regarding the shaping of reality by the diarist, confirm that it is not so much facts that interest Mrs. Bentley, but the way any moment or set of moments can be shaped into a facilitating gestalt for her needs and the needs of the marriage and creativity for which she is fighting. Pausing outside a door, not knowing fully what goes on inside, confirms a suspicion. Interpreting a laugh as a sexual response, rather than the sound of a dreamer, shapes a moment. Characterizing her own reaction to that moment in the diary as the helplessness of a "live fly struggling in a block of ice" (162) gives Mrs. Bentley the belief in Philip's paternity she needs to confirm her own place as rightful patriarchal mother, to rank Judith as surrogate (much as the biblical Sarah claimed Hagar as surrogate, as the "wives" of *The Handmaid's Tale* claim the handmaidens). She really needs so little to make her reality. Note her response when Judith protests leaving because Mrs. Bentley's health is still fragile: "She protested . . . but Philip didn't. And I clung to that, telling myself over and over that he maybe was glad to be finished with her too" (163).

According to my reading of the text, it is no coincidence that another of those "expressive" moments of the diarist writing herself in the present occurs right after the "conception" scene. A phase has been accomplished, put in a favourable perspective by the diarist; new steps are now necessary. At the end of the entry for August 14, Mrs. Bentley mulls over the sexual attitudes of men towards women, the possibility that a woman means much less to Philip than she might suppose, the possibility that Judith had planned the infidelity, the possibility that she herself is "the one who's never grown up, who can't see life for illusions" (164). And then she decides that such a construction of reality has no place in the life she intends to live:

> I must stop this, though. The rain's so sharp and strong it crackles on the windows just like sand. There's a howl in the wind, and as it tugs at the house and rushes past we seem perched up again all alone somewhere on an isolated little peak.
>
> Somehow I must believe in them, both of them. Because I need him still. This isn't the end. I have to go on, try to win him again. He's hurt me as I didn't know I could be hurt, but still I need him. It's like a finger pointing. It steadies me a little. If only it were morning, something to do again. (164)

Once again the "isolated little peak" occurs, the metaphorical space where she takes on the power of language to shape reality. This time there is not only the wind but the rain, the fertilizing but sharp pain of its growth. However, it is not an "I" but a "we" that is perched up on the peak, the "we" she has created that will give her her child. The route she is travelling is full of hurt, and she will realize the fullness of her own hurt later, when she admits in her diary the degree to which her marriage has emptied her, made her a being without "roots" (199), but it is this hurt that allows her a certain creative ruthlessness. In this regard it is interesting that she figures herself as "perched" ready to move, not tied to the peak. The creative ruthlessness allows her to follow the diary's shape which is "like a finger pointing," her own hand writing, shaping the future. She is impatient for the morning, so that, steadied now by her diary, she can begin the action of building the future.

My discussion, thus far, has centred upon the action of the first of the three interrelated narrative triangles of Ross's diary fiction. I have illustrated the first triangle in this detail in order to move more quickly in demonstrating the operation of the other two triangles. Concerning the second triangle, Lorna Martens identifies two important indicators of the "expressive" moment, its context and the use of certain rhetorical devices. A contextualization consistently used by Ross for the moments I have marked is the characterization of the diarist as suddenly switching from reflection on past events to exploration of the present moment. The rhetorical device I identify as constant in these moments is Ross's use of metaphors that imply the active agency of the environment in the shaping of the diarist's subjectivity.

In contrast, Martens sees a repetition of "metaphors of the body to express psychic states" (50) in Goethe's *Werther*. I feel Ross's choice is entirely suitable to his subject, Mrs. Bentley. While the adolescent, romantic, male Werther worries that his "heart is . . . hanging out" and he is "fallen . . . broken," that some precious commodity of self integral to the body is threatened with harm, the middle-aged, childless patriarchally defined female worries that she has "whittled myself hollow that I might enclose and hold him" (99), wonders whether, if she had met another man earlier, Paul that is, "the currents might have taken and fulfilled me" (209). In context it is the currents of the wind that she speaks of, and it is the wind that is figured as the husband who fills her with the fruitfulness that makes words on those occasions when Ross draws our attention to his diarist's writing acts.

But he does not validate or deny the ethical quality of Mrs. Bentley's acts when he draws attention to them (as Martens would have it); rather, he destabilizes certain notions of creativity, relationship, and art. In the stereotypical world of modernity, artists are people like Philip, whom we might characterize as a reluctant Gauguin, who, unable to strip himself of the bothersome habits of making a living and living with a wife, instead tries to create his South Seas escape in the small space of his study. His theory of art matches his actions: "according to Philip it's form that's important in a picture, not the subject or the associations that the subject calls to mind; the pattern you see, not the literary emotion you feel" (105–106). Philip is caught up in the subject/object nature of a visual theory of art. Mrs. Bentley's response is telling as far as Ross's intentions are concerned: "I've heard it all—and still I believe in his little schoolhouse. His little schoolhouse and him . . . there's some twisted, stumbling power locked up within him, so blind and helpless still it can't find outlet, so clenched in urgency it can't release itself" (106). Mrs. Bentley's theory of art is a much livelier one than Philip's. She believes in the content of art, in the importance of the quotidian in creation; she believes in art's function in liberating the self; the artist is always present in the work for her, autobiographically, insistent on the humanness of art. And creativity is always involved with relationship for her. Not for her a running-away to a space where one may make an object, an abstraction, a colonial subject, of the other. For her the form in which one shapes the self while breathing the same air as the other, a moment after one has made love with him, or been humiliated by him, or fought with him. For her the diary.

And in foregrounding this view of artistic production, Ross gives his imprisoned female diarist a theory of art surprisingly close to Adrienne Rich's strategy for artistic survival for feminists in a patriarchal world. This seeming incongruity of historical era and aesthetic position makes a critic such as myself (one concerned with autobiography as a genre, as a method of writing, as a reading strategy) yearn to investigate the personal reasons for some of Ross's choices in *As for Me and My House*. Lorraine McMullen tells us in *Sinclair Ross* that Ross had many things in common with Mrs. Bentley. Being a bank clerk on the prairies in the 1930s would seem to offer at least as much hindrance to undisguised literary pursuit as being a minister's wife, and indeed the anonymous quality of Mrs. Bentley's artistic life is in many ways similar to Ross's own. Like his heroine he lived in a succession of small prairie towns. He had nothing as public as a pulpit from which to speak. His life, like hers, was shaped by his love for, dependence on, and responsibility to another entrapped individual (McMullen 16–19). From Ross's comments concerning his own life, one can see that his intense involvement with his mother was similar to the emotional attachment between Mrs. Bentley and Philip, an education in realizing the self by living through the significant other. The fact that many people who knew Ross did not know he was a writer shows his tendency to hide his creativity like his diarist (21), and I also note that Ross's first art was not painting, the craft he gives Philip, but the piano, the craft he gives his diarist (18).

But beyond these biographical similarities, I find that there is in the diary format a much more compelling reason for choosing it as a means to exercise and re-create the subjectivity of the writer. Lorna Martens points out that recent theories of autobiography "argue that the very project of writing, the act of signification itself, alienates the writing self from the subject" (40). Her extrapolations from Barthes, Lacan, Fredric Jameson, and Philippe Lejeune exhibit a theory of the writing self where representation becomes impossible because the "I" pronoun we use in writing the self is the very one responsible for the formation of the unconscious. The moment I say "I," the subject splits from itself, the speaking subject and the subject of the enunciation drive a third part of the self, the part shy of revelation, into that linguistic darkness hidden from the consciousness of the writer. By this particular theory of postmodernity, autobiographical writing does not yield the self, but acts, as Paul de Man would have it, as a "de-facement" of self. But, you may note, the theorists I name are all men, and their examples are male also. The growing body of feminist theory directly related to women's autobiographical pursuits points to autobiographical writing and reading acts that construct a "nonrepresentative, dispersed, displaced subjectivity" (Brodski and Schenck 6). Certainly Mrs. Bentley's sense of herself is almost completely dispersed in the lives of others, represented only in her intercourse with others, displaced into the acts of others to the point of achieving motherhood through the imaginative literary and actual shaping of another woman's life.

I contend that the diary offers an excellent form to express such a consciousness, not only because of the features of the diary explored earlier in this paper, but because of the special disguises that the particular diary fiction, *As for Me and My House*, offered Sinclair Ross. It offered not only a life situation similar to his own, but a way to avoid, to some extent, the problem of the pronoun "I" driving the real subject underground. Mrs. Bentley gave Ross a doubly safe disguise of his own situation as a struggling Canadian writer on the prairies of the 1930s. She is not doing anything that anybody would identify as respectably artistic, and therefore he can safely uncover aspects of personal creativity inside her diary. His position is especially secure in that Philip provides a nice straw target as "artist," a set-up that fooled his critics for almost four decades. More importantly, Mrs. Bentley is female. Inside her consciousness one may safely speak of all those more tender and more terrifying aspects of human relationship and sexuality that men inside patriarchy must avoid like the plague, if they are to avoid accusations of unmanliness. Like Flaubert creating Madame Bovary, a male writer can create a character who reveals all sorts of intimacies, and construct that second interrelated triangle of relationship of diarist, text, and writer.

Mrs. Bentley offers an excellent disguise—as imprisoned female, suffering as much from her implication as her imbrication in patriarchy—for the Canadian male writer facing a repressive society and the failure of patriarchal commerce and agriculture in the form of the Depression and the dustbowl of the 1930s. I feel that my own experience as a reader of *As for Me and My House* illustrates the richness of Ross's work in its ability to represent, over successive readings, historical and cultural phenomena typical of female subjectivity in the twentieth century. In this regard we need to view Ross's text as an example of what Mikhail Bakhtin calls the "dialogic imagination," in a theory that explains language not simply as a systematic code of signs, but a "discourse which does not maintain a uniform relation with its object; it does not 'reflect' it, but it organizes it, transforms or resolves situations" (Todorov 55).[5] This describes Ross's relationship to his diarist's discourse. Ross began the book with the intention that its primary concern be Philip and found that his narrator became "more central than her creator had anticipated" (McMullen 58). Adapting the diary style, carrying on a creative act of writing through the adoption of a consciousness both displaced yet very close to the self, leads to such a dialogic utterance.

Bakhtin describes three degrees of "presence" regarding the other's discourse: at one end of the spectrum is "full presence, or explicit dialogue. At the other end—the third degree—the other's discourse receives no material corroboration and yet is summoned forth" (Todorov 73) (parody is a typical example of this degree). Between these two there is "hybridization," a form which, though seeming to come from a single speaker, "contains intermingled within it two utterances" (*ibid.*), utterances that direct me to a third utterance as reader. As a reader, I find myself part of the intertextual field that Bakhtin is describing. I do not think that I am Ross's "super-receiver," that reader which Bakhtin claims the author imagines "whose absolutely appropriate responsive understanding is projected either into a metaphysical distance or into a distant historical time" (Todorov 110). My sense of the way in which the third narrative triangle works to create a dynamic relationship between my subjectivity and Ross's subjectivity, as it is embodied in the subjectivity of his diarist, is closer to what Roland Barthes describes as the "desire" I have for the author, not the author as "institution," as "biographical person," but his "figure" in the text: "I need his figure (which is neither his representation nor his projection), as he needs mine . . ." (27). Any text is what Barthes calls a "frigid" text, "until desire, until neurosis forms in it" (5).

I use neurosis in the positive sense that Barthes does, as the impulse that drives the writer to write out of and against his neurosis. The result of this act is the text. Thus the neurosis is necessary for what Barthes calls "the seduction of [its] readers" (5–6). I have been "seduced" into different readings of *As for Me and My House*, depending on the historical era in which I have read Ross's text and the state of my own subjectivity at that historical moment. I find my own reader-response worth characterizing here not only because it spreads over three decades, but because I was born in the year the book was published. Imaginatively speaking, if Mrs. Bentley's/Judith's child had been a real child, had been a girl child, she could have been me.

What kind of subjectivity does such a child bring to her "mother's" diary, and to Ross through the dialogic quality of his text? Mine is the generation of women raised by mothers who led their lives in that twilight world between the first two waves of feminism.[6] Our mothers grew up thinking the battle for equality had been won with the right to vote and the creation of their legal "personhood." But because the deeper social, psychological, political, and cultural issues recently under examination in the second wave of feminism had not yet been raised (except indirectly by writers such as Woolf), such mothers raised their daughters within a context of "double messages." We were the generation who were taught both to have ambitions for the singular self as our brothers did and to subvert that self in the interests of whittling ourselves hollow in order to become suitable patriarchal vessels. We were taught that being female meant we were equal in every way to males. At the same time, we watched our mothers rejoice in our brothers' self-assertion, while ours made them wary or angry. When the first full force of the sixties' brand of feminism hit us and we realized how badly prepared we were for the new demands, we often exhibited our own patriarchal definitions in a stereotypical way: not by questioning patriarchal institutions, but by blaming our mothers for the kind of hybrid women we were.

That is certainly the kind of subjectivity I brought to Ross's text as a young woman in the 1960s. Mrs. Bentley was everything I did not want to be, everything I hated and feared, but unconsciously felt in danger of becoming with marriage and especially with the production of children. No misogynistic readings by literary critics could have matched the vehemence of mine, as I set myself firmly on Philip's side and against the monster he had married. And there are powerful elements in Ross's text that induce such a reading. Female creativity in patriarchy, not completely preoccupied by reproduction, can be a fearful force. Female creativity, not permitted by societal structure and internalized patriarchal views its full expression anywhere else than in motherhood, can seem demonic. I am sure Ross saw this in many women around him in the 1930s, just as I still experienced the possibility of its action in my own life in the 1960s. In such a subjective position, Ross's ending can be experienced as not just ambiguous, but downright wrong. The character whom a girl of my generation identified with was Judith, who struggled to lead her own life and love her man freely without the bonds of patriarchal marriage.

That Mrs. Bentley was Judith with 16 more years of patriarchy under her belt (all puns intended) never occurred to me, was too frightening a possibility to occur to me, but in fact did occur to me when I encountered Ross's text in a graduate-level seminar in my late thirties. But the changed reading was not just a result of my gender or my personal history. It was a change occurring to all of us in the course of the raising of consciousness not just about gender, but also about the nature of artistic creativity, as we began to see it as a production of all libidos, a production capable of many negative and positive expressions, rather than the privileged essence of something called "genius." Witness to the changed critical context in which we read *As for Me and My House* is Robert Kroetsch's change of tone between his remarks on Mrs. Bentley in 1981, when he recognizes her significance as artist but shivers in its "writing obsessed and male-devouring" qualities (vii), and his revision of this view in his afterword to the new edition of the text in 1989 when he sees Mrs. Bentley as writing "the beginning of contemporary Canadian fiction. Her stance as writer prophesies a way in which one might proceed to become or be an artist in the second half of the twentieth century" (217).[7]

Those of us feminists who debated the subjectivity of Mrs. Bentley with Kroetsch as his graduate students are tempted to feel at least partially responsible for his change of heart, but as a woman reading Ross in 1990, I must confess that I view Kroetsch's appropriation of the female figure of

Mrs. Bentley for his use as a metaphor for the Canadian writer figure, and even Ross's use of her to express his own imprisoned condition, with much more ambiguity than I did as a younger feminist ten years ago. At that time I welcomed the purging of the figure of Mrs. Bentley of her negative readings, welcomed her status as artist figure, even as frustrated and male-devouring artist. I could point to her and say, "see, there but for the grace of my wits and my 20-year lead on her, go I, a victim of patriarchy." The more positive aspects of that figure have been this paper's principal concern.

But now that I have been made a maker of fictions myself, made that not by escaping the experiences of wifing and mothering inside patriarchy, but made a writer exactly because of the rigour of that experience, I know the difference between the experience of creativity when it lives in a female body that has experienced the narrow range of female creativity inside patriarchy, and the experience of that creativity in contexts more conducive to its expression. As well, I am aware of the paradox I live with: despite my personal liberation, I live in a body that in its history has borne (all puns intended) both patriarchy's past and its future.

To describe the way in which such a subjectivity now enters the triangle of the reading act with Ross and Mrs. Bentley, I must appropriate the words of Robert Kroetsch to a more feminist purpose than is suggested by the context of his manifesto in *Beyond Nationalism*:

> Our genealogies are the narratives of a discontent with a history that lied to us, violated us, erased us even. We wish to locate our dislocation, and to do so we must confront the impossible sum of our traditions . . . we recognize that we can be freed into our own lives only by terrible and repeated acts of perception. (Prologue vi)

To make a feminist re-vision in the 1990s is to realize that feminists are the revolutionaries who both live with and love their enemies. Those "enemies," for feminist literary critics like myself, are the writers of our tradition, our academic and literary mentors, our fellow artists and fellow critics. They are both Robert Kroetsch and Sinclair Ross. These "fathers" cannot be discarded, ignored, or killed in the Oedipal gesture patriarchy teaches the literary establishment to make regarding literary "fathers": they must be reconceptualized, re-engaged, restructured, revised, re-embraced in "terrible and repeated acts of perception."

However, beloved as the enemy is (and worthy of our continued attention), feminists must be wary of the closures they offer us. Now, as I read *As for Me and My House* in this new decade, I pause at the figure of Judith, as I did when reading as a very young woman. But this time it is not the Judith who has adventured in the city or the Judith imagined in a passionate embrace with Philip that I discover, but Judith weeping while she holds her gift of oranges. She holds the offering sent from a woman who, although in the act of shifting her self-definition, is still imprisoned in the patriarchy and its need for sons. She has sent the oranges to this girl, suffering the worst of patriarchy, to secure the sacrifice of the girl's passionate voicing of self to the crippled woman's need to fill her emptiness. I know that the subjectivity I encounter in Ross's text today is no longer Ross speaking to me through Mrs. Bentley, but the women of that text speaking to me through Ross. They speak to me of the male "Family Romance" that Ross's closure reinforces, in which all subjective possibilities, those represented by Steve, Paul, Philip, and Judith, must be displaced or suppressed in order to realize the Freudian Oedipal family structure of phallic mother and patriarchal son, the son who kills his father by his very birth.[8] "Sometimes you won't know which of us is which," Philip says nervously. "That's right, Philip. I want it so" (216). These words are not her spoken answer to her husband, they are Mrs. Bentley's written ending to her self-constructing diary. They are Ross's chosen closure. The son has achieved the death of the father and the full attention of his mother's creativity. The patriarchy has re-established itself, as it certainly did in the historical world Ross lived in during the Depression and the Second World War, as it does now in the phenomenon of post-feminism.

But desire works in strange ways. As well as that terrible defeat of Ross's closure, I feel in this text a desire that reaches out to mine and speaks of a world denied in all the texts of my tradition, a world that does not demand such scathing binary opposites, such rigid gender-sex stereotypes, a world contained in that gift of oranges and Judith's tears, a world in which mothering does not demand the death of the voice that scales the wind, in which adult womanhood is not a condition of lack, a condition that requires the death of the female voice in the birthing of sons. It makes me imagine a subjectivity in which the voice of the secret diary need not displace the girl's song, indeed where the diary becomes both public and private song, a dialogic utterance birthing mother tongue/daughter tongue.

This new, speculative, deconstructive/constructive possibility for feminist revision of *As for Me and My House* has just begun to occur to me. I can hardly wait to discover how I will read and write to this richly gendered and engendering text through the 1990s.

NOTES

1.   My current stance on "feminist revision" begins with Josephine Donovan's afterword to *Feminist Literary Criticism* in 1975, and involves the evolution of my critical practice, one that is reflected in many of the "emancipatory strategies" summed up by Patricia Jaeger in *Honey-Mad Women* and informed by Ellen Messer-Davidow's "The Philosophical Bases of Feminist Literary Criticism." By this view I foreground gender as my subject while using a plurality of literary theoretical positions to aid my endeavour.

2. See articles by Ricou (85), McMullen (87), Moss (95), McCourt (152), and Stouck (145) for the quoted characteristics.

3. See Messer-Davidow, pp. 80–81, for a description of the sex–gender system and the ways in which feminist literary critics can read the literature in a "self-reflexive feminist" manner.

4. See Evelyn J. Hinz and John J. Tennissen for an argument in Mr. Finley's favour and David Williams for a support of Paul.

5. Tzvetan Todorov's *The Dialogic Principle* is the source used for Bakhtin's theoretical position.

6. In a feminist historical sense it is incorrect to speak of a "twilight" time between two waves of feminism. Both Dale Spender and Gerda Lerner point out that many women continued the feminist project during that time, but their efforts are read out of patriarchal history because they cannot be characterized in the sensationalized and negative terms such history reserves for feminism. However, for actual women and men, reliant on the ordinary cultural signs of the period from the First World War to the 1960s, feminism would not have seemed a major force.

7. Kroetsch's first comments appear in *Mosaic*'s special issue on Canadian literature, *Beyond Nationalism*, and the second remarks introduce his afterword to the 1989 NCL edition of *As for Me and My House*.

8. It was while reading Eli Mandel's *The Family Romance* that I became aware of how differently from Mandel I, and I assume many other feminists, feel inside our Canadian literary tradition. Mandel recognizes this possibility when he destabilizes his own text by prefacing it with his disclaimer that "the theory of literary history proposed here is unequivocally male in its bias" (xi). His denigration of Atwood's poetics, its "dehumanized world" and its "reticences," as compared to his privileging of Kroetsch's "linguistic play" and Dewdney's "breathtaking leap[s]" (123–34), may well be one of the results of the family romance Mandel requires as a patriarchal reader.

WORKS CITED

Abbott, H. Porter. *Diary Fiction: Writing As Action*. Ithaca, N.Y.: Cornell University Press, 1984.

Barthes, Roland. *The Pleasure of the Text*. Trans. Richard Miller. New York: The Noonday Press, Farrar, Straus and Giroux, 1989.

Brodski, Bella, and Celeste Schenck (eds.). *Life/Lines: Theorizing Women's Autobiography*. Ithaca, N.Y.: Cornell University Press, 1988.

Cude, Wilfred. "Beyond Mrs. Bentley: A Study of *As for Me and My House*." *Journal of Canadian Studies* 8 (February 1973), 3–18.

Donovan, Josephine. "Afterword: Critical Re-vision." In Josephine Donovan, ed., *Feminist Literary Criticism: Explorations in Theory*. Lexington: Kentucky University Press, 1975, 74–81.

Franklin, Penelope. "Diaries of Forgotten Women." *Book Forum* 4, 3 (1979), 467–74.

Godard, Barbara. "El Greco in Canada: Sinclair Ross's *As for Me and My House*." *Mosaic* 14, 2 (Spring 1981), 54–75.

Hinz, Evelyn J., and John J. Tennissen. "Who's the Father of Mrs. Bentley's Child?: *As for Me and My House* and the Conventions of Dramatic Monologue." *Canadian Literature* 111 (Winter 1986), 101–13.

Jaeger, Patricia. *Honey-Mad Women: Emancipatory Strategies in Women's Writing*. New York: Columbia University Press, 1988.

Kroetsch, Robert. "Beyond Nationalism: A Prologue." *Mosaic* 14, 2 (Spring 1981), v–xi.

———. "Afterword" to Sinclair Ross, *As for Me and My House*. Toronto: McClelland and Stewart, 1989, 217–21.

Lerner, Gerda. *The Woman in American History*. Menlo Park, CA: Addison Wesley Publishing Company, 1971.

de Man, Paul. "Autobiography as De-Facement." MLN 94, 5 (December 1979), 919–30.

Mandel, Eli. *The Family Romance*. Winnipeg: Turnstone Press, 1986.

Martens, Lorna. *The Diary Novel*. London: Cambridge University Press, 1985.

McCourt, Edward A. *The Canadian West in Fiction*. Toronto: McClelland and Stewart, 1974.

McMullen, Lorraine. *Sinclair Ross*. Boston: Twayne, 1979.

Messer-Davidow, Ellen. "The Philosophical Bases of Feminist Literary Criticism." In Linda Kauffman, ed., *Gender and Theory: Dialogues on Feminist Criticism*. New York: Basil Blackwell, 1989.

Moss, John. *Patterns of Isolation in English Canadian Fiction*. Toronto: McClelland and Stewart, 1974.

Rich, Adrienne. *Of Woman Born: Motherhood as Experience and Institution*. New York: W.W. Norton, 1976.

———. *Lies, Secrets and Silence*. New York: W.W. Norton, 1979.

Ricou, Laurence. *Vertical Man/Horizontal World: Man and Landscape in Canadian Prairie Fiction*. Vancouver: University of British Columbia Press, 1973.

Ross, Morton L. "The Canonization of *As for Me and My House*: A Case Study." In Diane Bessai and David Jackel, eds., *Figures in a Ground*. Saskatoon: Western Producer Prairie Books, 1978.

Ross, Sinclair. *As for Me and My House*. Toronto: McClelland and Stewart, 1941; NCL edition, 1989.

Smith, Sidonie. *A Poetics of Women's Autobiography: Marginality and the Fictions of Self-Representation*. Bloomington: Indiana University Press, 1987.

Spender, Dale. *There's Always Been a Woman's Movement*. London: Pandora Press, 1983.

Stouck, David. "The Mirror and the Lamp in Sinclair Ross's *As for Me and My House*." *Mosaic* 7, 2 (Winter 1974), 141–50.

Todorov, Tzvetan. *Mikhail Bakhtin. The Dialogic Principle*. Trans. Wlad Godzich. *Theory and History of Literature* 14. Minneapolis: Minnesota University Press, 1988.

Williams, David. "The 'Scarlet' Rompers: Toward a New Perspective in *As for Me and My House*." *Canadian Literature* 103 (Spring 1984), 156–66.

The Dark Laughter of
As for Me and My House

WILFRED CUDE

To recycle a sentiment Robertson Davies loves to borrow, the one from the schoolboy summarizing the writings of Matthew Arnold, *As for Me and My House* is undeniably "no place to go for a laugh." Yet Robertson Davies and his analysis of laughter do have a special place in Ross criticism, I would contend, and not merely because our foremost writer of comedy was the first to identify *As for Me and My House* as "a remarkable addition to our small stock of Canadian books of first-rate importance." Davies, in his review of the novel almost half a century ago, correctly observed that "the story is told with great delicacy and sensitivity": and he further insisted that "Mr. Ross is keenly aware of the subtleties of the human mind." No mention here of laughter: on the contrary, Davies went on (with restraint surpassing even his favourite schoolboy source) to remark that the book is "not precisely gay in tone."[1] Between Davies and the schoolboy, there wouldn't appear to be much room to manoeuvre. Nevertheless, we do find an intriguing range of laughter in this most sombre of Canadian works— and Robertson Davies is the right critic to place that phenomenon in its appropriate context.

Not that Davies ever discussed the matter directly. He did, however, underscore the rich possibilities of intertwining comic and tragic elements— and it is that technical wealth we should now explore. Commenting on the more sophisticated productions of those artists passing beyond what he termed the "humorist's climacteric," he itemized in *A Voice from the Attic* features that bring humour "to its fullest ripening." "A sense of tragedy, a sense of the evanescence and dreamlike quality of life, and a sense of the imminence of death," he argued, are things "to be heard" in the finest comic art, "not aggressively, but as a continuing pedal point, supporting the other harmony, whatever it may be" (225). Surely a similar principle applies to the most sophisticated of tragedies, with the dominant and subordinate roles transposed. In a finely worked piece of literature haunted by "a sense of tragedy, a sense of the evanescence and dreamlike quality of life, and a sense of the imminence of death," we will also detect laughter: it will manifest itself "not aggressively, but as a continuing pedal point, supporting the other harmony, whatever it may be." And this, I submit, is precisely what we find in *As for Me and My House*.

There is no human peculiarity so beguiling and mystifying as laughter, nor one (we should confess at the outset) so resistant to the procedures of formal scholarship. Rising out of our recognition of life's incongruities, laughter points up many situations and moods, often in a bewildering perplexity of ways. Ross understands this well, and uses the resulting diversity to attain a variety of emotional tones. Throughout *As for Me and My House*, laughter of one sort or another helps to intensify nuances of feeling. We have the rollicking Chaucerian earthiness of the Ellingsons, their shared mirth no more than rural good humour, as they watch from a distance the new mistress of the manse entering with evident apprehension her tilted and rickety outhouse for the first time. "My neighbor, Mrs. Ellingson, came over this morning to tell me how she and her husband laughed," Mrs. Bentley good-naturedly reports, capturing with candour the lack of malice in the anecdote (13–14). And we have the secretive sensuality of "a frightened, soft, half-smothered little laugh," slipping out during Judith's seduction and paralyzing Mrs. Bentley on the other side of the door. "I just stood there listening a minute," she reports numbly, "a queer, doomed ache inside me, like a live fly struggling in a block of ice" (123). And we have the brittle mockery of Philip's "forced, derisive little laugh," rejecting his wife's claim that her recent piano triumph was for him, rather than Paul. "He's a still-faced, sober man," she reports with horror; "the laughter was unbearable" (145). This is a subtle device, all the more effective because it is employed with understatement and restraint.

Since this device does function as pedal point, though, we should begin our analysis with a brief survey of the dominant harmony. In some of his later correspondence, Ross has repeatedly insisted he was "writing blind" when composing *As for Me and My House*. "I do remember, very distinctly, thinking 'I'm writing blind,' just as a pilot sometimes flies blind, for I was trying to *be* Mrs. B., to enter emotionally into a situation in which I had never been," he explained in a letter to John Moss in 1973.[2] Nonetheless, he immediately added to this standard declaration a qualification of some significance. "However, there are contradictions: I say I let her carry on, but of course I did select, to some extent I did exercise control—I must have, although I don't remember how much—and certainly I knew where I was going." In a postscript to the same letter, he offered this further elaboration: "My basic sympathies are with [Philip]. It was intended to be his story, filtered through her, and of course possessive so-and-so that she is, she took over. But I am not contradicting myself: I still have a great deal of sympathy for her too. She, in a way, is trapped as much as he is." How could we dispute this analysis? The novel depicts two people not only with compassion, but also with considerable insight into their tragic predicament. They are both quite admirable, both very believable, and both bedevilled with personality traits that complicate the situation they are trapped within. The integration of all that into one artistic vision requires the reconciliation of numerous apparent contradictions, and for that task, no tool is better suited than laughter.

But laughter is a tool perhaps best used intuitively, and Ross has constantly asserted that his artistic approach was "not intellectual—nor even analytical."[3] However the thing was done, it was done well, for we do empathize with the Bentleys—despite their often frustrating or infuriating behaviour. In no small measure, this is because Mrs. Bentley is blessed with the gift of laughter, which she shares whenever her constricted circumstances allow. Consider again her account of that first adventure with the manse outhouse, an account that she opens with a brief history of the structure's lugubrious instability. "Last Hallowe'en it was carried off by the hoodlums of the town and left on the steps of the church with a big sign nailed to it *Come Unto Me All Ye That Labor and Are Heavy Laden*" (13). Here, Mrs. Bentley reveals herself as fully in command of the throwaway line, since she doesn't even pause to let us savour the delicious incongruities of the event: these are literate hoodlums with a multiple satiric touch, placing a small building used as a repository of excrement on the steps of a larger building functioning as a repository of hypocrisy, simultaneously mocking both with just the right biblical text. But their rough yet learned irreverence, we know, is endorsed by the Parson's wife; and we accept her implicit rebellion because we are engaged by her attitude, smiling as she carries on to repeat the full details of what brought merriment to the Ellingsons, admiring the frankness of her cheerful relation of a minor jest at her own expense. "'Sven say she look so scared I maybe tank she vaste her time'" (14). Has any character in all English literature ever conveyed with more delicacy the coarse expression "I was scared shitless?" Mordecai Richler should really take notes.

How surprisingly often, in this novel so routinely described as depressing, do we encounter little incidents that encourage us at least to smile. The abrupt invasion of Mrs. Bird, bustling uninvited and unceremoniously into the parlour of the manse, exhorting the Parson's wife to continue with the musical entertainment. "'No—not the rocking chair,'" she deftly declines the hard-seated hospitality; "'it's sure to creak. I don't want to be a distraction'" (21). Steve's ascendancy into artistry and erudition, sketching the outhouse which he christened the Leaning Tower of Pisa, following a geography lecture on "the architecture and monuments of Europe." "A rather good name too," Mrs. Bentley observes dryly, "by virtue of a bad pronunciation" (63). Judith and Mrs. Bentley conjointly elevating the matronly eyebrows of the entire Ladies Aid, perched uncertainly on a handcar coasting right up to Horizon's railway station, the Parson's wife wearing slippers and fighting hair down in wisps around her eyes, the scapegrace Judith lolling about shiftlessly next to her, the one evading her social obligations and the other escaping her housekeeper's chores, both shockingly indecorous with their legs "hanging over the side," two hussy companions of two scruffy gandy dancers who "gallantly helped us off the handcar just as the tea deployed on the platform twelve or thirteen strong." "'You do get around,'" Mrs. Pratt comments acidly. "'We thought you were indisposed. I don't think that even you, Mrs. Bird, could have thought up a cure like that'" (78). The common thread through all this is good fun, plain and simple, and we sympathize with the narrator gracious enough to provide it.

And yet, sadly, these grace notes of laughter cannot and do not prevail. Life-sustaining in themselves, they are still overwhelmed, much like the floral decorations flanking the entrance to the manse. On either side of the "big flat step where callers scrape their feet and introduce themselves" stands "a stunted, bedraggled little caragana." This pathetic pair, dwindling out of existence in the shade of the "small, squat, grayish house," a forlorn structure itself dwarfed in the shade of "the big, glum, grayish church" (13), speak eloquently in their silence about life in this Depression town. The caragana, or pea shrub, is a particularly hardy, resourceful, and tenacious plant that was utilized extensively across the dustbowl prairie for windbreaks and soil retention. But Horizon's godly people, and the church, and the manse, and the relentless and stifling dark, dust, and wind, all these in combination can reduce the pair of caragana to stunted and bedraggled wisps—living shadows, struggling courageously but hopelessly against an increasingly hostile environment, a physical and spiritual murk that chokes off spontaneity and vitality. So it is with the Bentleys. And so, too, with the laughter that might otherwise have flourished with them.

Ultimately, the only laughter that lingers on here is harsh, brittle, and dark. It is life-denying, rather than life-affirming, best represented by Philip's "dead, vacant laugh that he intended to be reckless." This is the town parson's response to the emptiness left by Steve, to the wearying and wearing refrain from his wife that he should abandon the enervating protection of the church, to her almost plaintive reminder that "after all, you're not so old at thirty-six." Philip finds the statement true enough to be funny, in a cruel and twisted sort of way. Pitching small stones across a ravine, displaying an unexpected dexterity at the trivial sport nobody else practises in Horizon except Judith, "he laughed then—a laugh like all his little pebbles clicking quick and hard one after the other on the rock across the ravine" (119). Heed your loving wife's earnest advice at long last, break away from all that damnable smothering security, plunge manfully into the risks and challenges of those Depression storms, take whatever rewards unfettered artistry offers? There comes a time in everybody's life, perhaps, when even the trap is a joke.

For what, finally, is the essence of the trap that so darkens the novel? In the broadest sense, it is the cage of our passions, against the implacable bars of which we beat or flutter in vain. Helpless as the moths in that terrifyingly natural image recurring throughout the work, we thud mindlessly and monotonously about the lamp of our relationships, and some of us veer off singed and smoking into the shadows. But the trap is also, in a more restricted sense, very much of our own making. Before we can abandon ourselves to either love or hate, we must survive; and all too often we tumble into a pit of hypocrisy because we are driven by our need for economic security. The Bentleys are frustrated as artists because they have shackled themselves to what we in the academic community call tenure. The church certainly sustains them economically, during a devastatingly hard era; but it simultaneously drains them spiritually, because they know they have deliberately chosen this life, and their vaunted artistic insight will not ever give them relief from their knowledge. "The money shamed him a little, reminded him how he earned it," Mrs. Bentley assesses Philip's repetitive flinching, "for he's the kind that keeps his hypocrisy beside him the way a guilty monk would keep his scourge" (79). We take what we seek, and loathe ourselves for the taking. And that, in the end, is the darkest joke of all.

Sinclair Ross, who toiled those same long debilitating Depression years as a bank clerk, most assuredly felt how unamusing the entire situation would be. Writing intuitively, writing blind, he wrote passionately and thus touched accurately upon enduring tragic truths—ensnaring with Mrs. Bentley's clear and direct prose the agony of what we can do to ourselves and others as we pander to our lust for security. "There are plenty of others to whom the Church means just bread and butter, who at best assert an easy, untried faith," she says of Philip at the outset, "but that's no solution for him." The problem he faces, ironically, is that he has too much spiritual integrity for his chosen role. "His guilt is that emphatically he does not believe," she marvels. "His disbelief amounts to an achievement" (18). She is writing of a man who has conditioned himself to see without distortions of any kind, and to capture honestly and compellingly on paper or canvas exactly what he has seen. And his daily struggles are chronicled by a woman who shares his artistic values and who hopes to accompany him in an equal artistic quest. What this must mean is driven home by an almost-comic minor interlude, the collegial visit of "the Reverend and Mrs. Albert Downie, to extend a word of brotherly encouragement and cheer."

Mrs. Bentley cannot resist the impulse to initially present the event as funny. The Downies themselves are "a quaint, serene little pair—piety and its rib in a Ford more battle-scarred even than ours—the parson and his wife in caricature." The whole social exchange is restrained, polite, and totally without human contact: a matchless performance in rural hypocrisy. Mrs. Bentley strives heroically to mask what transpired with a brightly irreverent tone. Relating how the Reverend Downie offered "a word of prayer for us, and finished radiant," she mockingly adds this aside: "I glanced at Philip, and for a minute wished that I were the artist, with a pad and pencil at my hand." But of course the comic approach is precisely the wrong emotional gambit. The visit isn't in the least funny, as both the Bentleys painfully understand. "Over the tea and sponge cake I had a few gaunt moments," Mrs. Bentley confesses, "looking down a corridor of years and Horizons, at the end of which was a mirror and my own reflection" (82). The quiet poignancy of this statement is rendered far more agonizing by the desperate tone of failed banter that served as introduction. In a very heart-rending fashion, this is the novel in miniature. Ibsen could do no better, and we Canadians should learn to recognize as much.

I would like to end with a passage I wrote almost two decades ago, since it has become (if anything) far more relevant today. The context is my reappraisal of *As for Me and My House* after 30 years, an evaluative exploration demonstrating the technical excellence of the work, concluding that "the novel is nothing short of brilliant."

This is a Canadian work so finely structured that it invites comparison with fiction in the first rank of English literature. Ross handles personal relationships with all the delicacy of Jane Austen; he handles first-person narration with all the sophistication of Jonathan Swift; and he handles the bluster of a drought-scourged prairie with all the awareness of Emily Bronte. With novels like *As for Me and My House*, English-Canadian fiction reaches full maturity, and can take a rightful place as an integral part of the literature of the English language.[4]

The international community, which is now celebrating Robertson Davies with such delight, will necessarily also go on to celebrate the splendid creativity of Sinclair Ross that Davies himself so generously identified half a century earlier. Hence, we can say with unshaken confidence that the author of *The Lamp at Noon and Other Stories*, *As for Me and My House*, and *Sawbones Memorial* is continuing his steady progression towards his rightful place in our cultural heritage. It is a place among the finest writers, not merely of this country, but of the very language itself.

NOTES

1. This review was initially printed in the *Peterborough Examiner*, April 26, 1941. It is reprinted in Robertson Davies, *The Well-Tempered Critic* (Toronto: McClelland and Stewart, 1981), pp. 142–44.

2. Sinclair Ross to John Moss, May 15, 1973. Quoted with permission.
3. Sinclair Ross to Kathren Mattson, July 12, 1978. Quoted with permission.
4. This passage was initially printed as the conclusion to my essay "Beyond Mrs. Bentley: A Study of *As for Me and My House*," *Journal of Canadian Studies* (February 1973), pp. 3–18. The essay has been reprinted several times, most recently as a chapter in my book *A Due Sense of Differences: An Evaluative Approach to Canadian Literature* (Washington, D.C.: University Press of America, 1980).

WORKS CITED

Cude, Wilfred. "Beyond Mrs. Bentley: A Study of *As for Me and My House*." *Journal of Canadian Studies* 8 (February 1973), 3–18.

Davies, Robertson. *The Well-Tempered Critic*. Toronto: McClelland and Stewart, 1981.

———— . *A Voice from the Attic*. Toronto: McClelland and Stewart, 1972.

Ross, Sinclair. *As for Me and My House*. Toronto: McClelland and Stewart, 1957.

[handwritten annotations:] Tragi-comedy in ending / Do not escape Trap – repeating cycle / but birth of child adds position – leads to future

Horsey Comedy in the
Short Fiction of Sinclair Ross

DAVID CARPENTER

I began reading Sinclair Ross's work around 1970, a bit before the publication of his last story, "The Flowers That Killed Him" (1972). At the time there seemed to be a hunt in progress to find our cultural heroes, who in turn would articulate for us that elusive thing called "The Canadian Identity." The word was out: return to your roots, scour the countryside, haul those skeletons out of the closet. The grimmer the better. As a graduate student in search of a thesis, I canvassed the bookshelves in search of the most unsparing realism I could find. What I sought would have as many broken teeth as Faulkner's stories, as many corpses as Hemingway's. It would vibrate with existential angst and vomit, just like Sartre's *La Nausée*. It would seethe with all the trapped futility of Joyce's *Dubliners*. When I found whatever it was I was looking for, I would feel a shudder in my soul and cry, "The horror! The horror!" And it would be politically relevant too.

I became a card-carrying proselytizer for stark realism, a grim reality snob in the Saskatchewan tradition: grimmer than thou. But was I alone in my glorification of despair, deprivation, and defeat? I think not.

When I came across "The Painted Door" by Sinclair Ross, I knew I had come home. Several other narratives in *The Lamp at Noon and Other Stories* confirmed my discovery: "Not by Rain Alone," "One's a Heifer," and the title story, "The Lamp at Noon." "A Field of Wheat" was powerfully written, but in those days I was like Atwood's surfacer: I was corpse hunting. And as far as I was concerned, "A Field of Wheat" should have ended paragraphs earlier with the dog Nipper lying mutilated on the ground.

I had become a Rosselyte, what critic Morton Ross refers to as the "gladly suffering reader." Looking back at the critics of *As for Me and My*

House in this same era, Morton Ross observes, "It is, I suspect, natural for literary critics to recommend books on the same grounds that castor oil is prescribed; the experience is not pleasant, but it may be good for you" (200).

I felt that to be a true Rosselyte, you had to suffer willingly through these stories; that was part of the aesthetic pleasure. And as I intimated earlier, I was not alone. Here is Laurie Ricou, summing up his impressions of *As for Me and My House* and the grimmest stories in *The Lamp at Noon*: "An empty, unproductive, and oppressive existence in an empty, unproductive and oppressive landscape makes an intense fictional impact. The discovery of meaning in this existence . . . makes Sinclair Ross one of Canada's best novelists" (94). And here is Robert Chambers commenting on the same short stories referred to by Ricou: "Many of the finest moments in Ross' stories combine these few elements: menacing nature, lonely humans, a tightening claustrophobia. The dominant mood is one of attrition, with a terrible harmony between the working of wind upon soil and snow and the slow undermining of human stamina and strength" (13).

Re-reading all 18 of Ross's stories has been a disturbing process for me. So has my reading of the dozen or so critics who have done studies of Ross's short fiction. Virtually every major study seems to emphasize what Margaret Laurence refers to as the "lives of unrelieved drabness" (9) chronicled in these stories. Perhaps she speaks for all the Rosselytes in her groundbreaking preface to *The Lamp at Noon and Other Stories* (1968):

> Throughout Ross's stories, the outer situation always mirrors the inner. The emptiness of the landscape, the bleakness of the land, reflect the inability of these people to touch another with assurance and gentleness . . . . Ross never takes sides, and this is one admirable quality of his writing. Blame is not assigned. Men and women suffer equally. The tragedy is not that they suffer, but that they suffer alone. (11)

Laurence's remark here seems to speak for all the stories in *A Lamp at Noon*, but she has very little to say about Ross's *other* stories in this volume, the comic pieces: "The Runaway," "Circus in Town," "The Outlaw," and "Cornet at Night." Her sombre essay seems to have set the tone for all subsequent treatments of Ross's later volume, *The Race and Other Stories* (1982). Ross's comic work in the short story is either ignored by subsequent Rosselytes or cast in such a dubious light that the stories seem unduly severe in the critical interpretations. Typical of these readers is Paul Comeau, who claims that Ross's short fiction between 1934 and 1952 is written in "the tragic mode." This position forces Comeau to paint Ross's comic stories with a strangely grey brush. After all, these characters in Ross's lighter work "come from the same pioneer stock and cling to variations of the same dream [as the characters in Ross's grim tragedies]. For example, Martha's ambition to have her children properly educated is realized by Tom's mother in

'Cornet at Night,' mainly because she has sufficient time and funds to maintain an orderly household and supervise his music and Bible studies" (178). Stories like "Cornet," which I now claim to be richly comic, are seen by Comeau as merely less severe reflections of Ross's "hostile environment" (176).

Keath Fraser's essay on Ross's stories is much more perceptive than the studies of Comeau, Djwa, Chambers, Mitchell, Friesen, and McCourt. Like Lorraine McMullen, he devotes some serious consideration to these comic stories—as comedy. And even more than McMullen he demonstrates a rich awareness of Ross's comic talents.

My problem with Fraser's essay is one I've seen in the work of most of the Rosselytes: he reads each story within the pervasive context of all the stories in *A Lamp at Noon*. In his treatment of them, the comic stories come across as though they were part of a formally constituted story cycle, such as *Jake and the Kid* or *Go Down, Moses*. According to Forrest Ingram, a short story cycle is "a book of short stories so linked to each other by their author that the reader's successive experience on various levels of the pattern of the whole significantly modifies his experience of each of its component parts" (19). Fraser reads all of Ross's stories in *The Lamp at Noon* "as part of the futility cycle" he claims Ross has established:

> The futile cycle of eking existence from an indifferent world predominates [in] this collection of stories—a kind of rural *Dubliners* in which the same adult impotence replaces a similar childish Araby. Overall, the book spawns variations on the theme of isolation and its haunting melody is unmistakeable . . . . These prairie inhabitants . . . can retreat nowhere that is not whirling vainly in an absurd seasonal cycle . . . . (77)

There is nothing wrong with reading these stories as a unified collection as most critics have done. They are unified by their setting and their time. Indeed, two of these stories were altered by Ross to form a linked sequence. The two-part story we now know as "Not by Rain Alone" was first published as two stories six years apart: "Not by Rain Alone" and "September Snow." In her pioneering study *Sinclair Ross* (1979), Lorraine McMullen notes: "For consistency the original names of the man and wife in 'September Snow,' Mark and Ann, were changed to Will and Eleanor (the names of the man and wife in 'Not by Rain Alone')" (53).

Lorraine McMullen's lengthy treatment of Ross's stories has the advantage of allowing some of them their own separate integrity. Reading them as Comeau or Fraser or Chambers do, as a unified cycle, occasionally forces these critics into a discussion of the comic stories as though they were written to a theme: the impact of the drought on farm economy, or how farm debt affects interpersonal relationships. These stories deserve to be read as individual works that maintain their own comic integrity without the cloudlike encumbrance of an overall scheme or a theme that prefigures their significance.

One story badly neglected and distorted by the readings of the Rosselytes is "The Runaway." Chambers claims it is one of Ross's "best stories" (11), but says nothing about it. Paul Comeau seems to think it has something to do with the price of prosperity exacted by the land, and dismisses it. So does McMullen with the passing thought that "sometimes nature or coincidence works hand in hand with divine retribution . . . . In 'The Runaway' Luke Taylor's own meanness and cheating lead indirectly to his own death and that of all his magnificent horses" (49). By grouping "The Runaway" with Ross's truly tragic stories under the theme of "Nature as Impassive Agent," she obscures the story's comic vitality. McMullen and Fraser are better geared to Ross's comic vision than the other Rosselytes, but even Fraser doesn't know what to say about "The Runaway." His only words on it are: "Sometimes it seems enough that the bad among them are punished (as is Luke Taylor in 'The Runaway' when he dies in his burning barn, and the wife of the man he cheated calls upon her Biblical clichés that justify his death). But when are the good rewarded? Not really ever . . . ." (79).

The only critic bold enough to comment on this story is Ken Mitchell. He gives it a page in his book *Sinclair Ross*. His reflection on the story is only a plot summary, but he does manage to locate it as "a tale of moral justice in the Faulknerian mode" (18). By "Faulknerian mode" I assume Mitchell means the Faulkner of the *Snopes* trilogy. The story's antagonist, Luke Taylor, is a dishonest horse trader who, like Faulkner's Flem Snopes, becomes the richest landowner in the district. And like Flem, he meets his nemesis, dies violently, and not a tear is shed. I like Mitchell's phrase, "a *tale* of moral justice." Perhaps because this story is a tale, it fits less securely into Ross's collection *A Lamp at Noon* than those praised by the Rosselytes for their unsparing portrayal of bleak lives. By "tale" I assume Mitchell means a narrative that is not realistic but has its own kind of brilliance and charm. John Gardner is helpful on this distinction between stories like "The Painted Door" and others like "The Runaway":

 The realistic writer's way of making events convincing is verisimilitude. The tale writer, telling stories of ghosts, or shape-shifters . . . uses a different approach: By the quality of his voice, and by means of various devices that distract the critical intelligence, he gets what Coleridge called . . . "the willing suspension of disbelief for the moment, which constitutes poetic faith." (22)

Nevertheless, the tale writer, like the realist, must document his story from time to time in some way that gives credibility to his narrative voice. We believe the narrative "not just because the tale voice has charmed us but also, and more basically, because the character's gestures, his precisely described expression, and the reaction of others to his oddity all seem to us exactly what they would be in this strange situation" (Gardner 25). The reader of "The Runaway," then, is from time to time given proofs (closely observed details of farm life and human intercourse) that generate a compelling sense of reality—however fantastic or illusory.

Ross uses a nameless boy to tell his tale. This boy obviously loves a good yarn. In the heat of the story's climax, the narrator thinks, "I knew that for months to come the telling of [this tale] would be listened to" (95). He begins in this fashion:

> You would have thought that old Luke Taylor was a regular and welcome visitor, the friendly, unconcerned way he rode over that afternoon, leading two of his best Black Diamond mares.
>
> "Four-year-olds," he said with a neighbourly smile. "None better in my stable. But I'm running short of stall room—six more foals last spring—so I thought if you were interested we might work out a trade in steers."
>
> My father was interested. We were putting a load of early alfalfa in the loft, and he went on pitching a minute, aloof, indifferent, but between forkfuls he glanced down stealthily at the Diamonds, and at each glance I could see his suspicion and resistance ebb. (83)

So far, we have a realistic story grounded in the conventions of verisimilitude. But note how, in the next passage, the narrator's tone and diction modulate when he comes to his description of Luke Taylor's Black Diamonds and their impact on all who behold them:

> For more than twenty years old Luke had owned a stableful of Diamonds. They were his special pride, his passion. He bred them like a man dedicated to an ideal, culling and matching tirelessly. A horse was a credit to the Black Diamond Farm, a justification of the name, or it disappeared. There were broad-rumped, shaggy-footed work horses, slim-legged runners, serviceable in-betweens like the team he had with him now, suitable for saddle or wagon —at a pinch, even for a few days on the plough—but all, whatever their breed, possessed a flawless beauty, a radiance of pride and spirit, that quickened the pulse and brought a spark of wonder to the dullest eye. When they passed, you turned from what you were doing and stood motionless, transfixed. When you met them on the road you instinctively gave them the right of way. And it didn't wear off. The hundredth time was no different from the first. (83)

Note the closely observed details here, the "broad-rumped, shaggy-footed work horses, slim-legged runners," the sort of things one might associate with any group of normal horses. Then note the intangibles, that "flawless beauty, a radiance of pride and spirit, that quickened the pulse," rendering all who saw them "motionless, transfixed." Note, too, the extravagance of the boy's claims—that all people were affected by these magic steeds, even those with "the dullest eye."

Luke Taylor's Black Diamonds turn out to be "balky," which means that at unpredictable times, the very worst times even, they will refuse to move. Once again Luke Taylor has triumphed. The boy narrator's mother, who in this story is always right, had predicted Taylor would manage in some way to swindle them. This was her warning to her husband:

> "But there are things you can't check. All the years we've known [Luke] has he once done what was right or decent? Do you know a man for twenty miles who'd trust him? Didn't he get your own land away from you for half what it was worth?" And she went on, shrill and exasperated, to pour out instance upon instance of his dishonesty and greed, everything from foreclosures on mortgages and bribes at tax and auction sales to the poker games in which, every fall for years, he had been fleecing his harvest-hands right after paying them. (86)

We have in Luke Taylor, of course, the classic villain of romance. Martha Ostenso's Caleb Gare comes to mind as well as Flem Snopes. And Taylor's victims provide an interesting contrast to him in this intensely moral struggle. Here is the boy narrator's description of his father:

> According to his lights my father was a good man, and his bewilderment [over Luke's successful swindle] was in proportion to his integrity. For years he had been weakened and confused by a conflict, on the one hand resentment at what Luke had done and got away with, on the other sincere convictions imposing patience and restraint; but through it all he had been sustained by the belief that scores were being kept, and that he would live to see a Day of Reckoning. Now, though, he wasn't sure. You could see in his glance and frown that he was beginning to wonder which he really was: the upright, God-fearing man that he had always believed himself to be, or a simple, credulous dupe. (88)

The boy's father is in fact in the throes of a spiritual crisis that has been precipitated by envy. His envy is not simply for Luke's handsome greystone house and hip-roofed barn, the "abode of guile" as the narrator calls it, but is a much deeper, more forbidden envy, focused on Luke Taylor's Black Diamonds but eating away at his own soul. So when he trades his four fat steers for the team of Diamonds, he and his wife are suddenly, mysteriously, young again. Our narrator explains it this way: "My father had a team of Diamonds, and my mother had something that his envious passion for them had taken from her twenty years ago" (86).

Seen on its own terms, then, "The Runaway" is a tale told by an ideal teller in the (slightly) hyperbolic tradition about an upright man in danger of losing his soul to a comic embodiment of the devil. Had Ross taken his hyperbole much further, he would have had a yarn in the tradition of "The Devil and Daniel Webster" or "The Black Bonspiel of Wullie MacCrimmon." But like William Faulkner's narrator Ratliff of *The Hamlet,* Ross's narrator reins in his hyperbole so that on the surface, for the most part, this moral conflict remains fairly realistic. I say *fairly* realistic. Note how, even in realistic passages, the innuendoes spread like superstition throughout the narrative. Here is an example. The boy's father loses his hat in a gust of wind. Just as Luke Taylor approaches on horseback, the father reins in his new team of Diamonds so that he can retrieve his hat.

> And after weeks without a single lapse, that had to be the moment for [the Diamonds] to balk again. Was it the arrival of Taylor, I have often wondered, something about his smell or voice, that revived colthood memories? Or was it my father's anger that flared at the sight of him, and ran out through his fingers and along the reins like an electric current, communicating to them his own tensions, his conflicting impulses of hatred and forbearance? No matter—they balked, and as if to enjoy my father's mortification, old Luke too reined in and sat watching. "Quite a man with horses," he laughed across at me. "One of the finest teams for miles and just look at the state he's got them in. Better see what you can do, son, before he ruins them completely." And then, squinting over his shoulder as he rode off, he added, "I'll tell you how to get a balky horse going. It's easy—just build a little fire under him."
>
> "I wouldn't put it past him at that," my father muttered, as he climbed down and started to unhitch. "Being what he is, the idea of fire comes natural."
> (91)

Just as envy of Luke Taylor's Black Diamonds has apparently robbed the narrator's father of his virility, so too have the horses responded, apparently, to his spiritual conflict, "his conflicting impulses of hatred and forbearance," by humiliating him. And we are teased, rather than informed, in wondering at the cause of this humiliation: a man to whom the idea of fire "comes natural."

If we read Sinclair Ross critics and not the story itself, we might at this point be tempted to predict the ending of "The Runaway." Will Christian forbearance and God-fearing piety win out over evil? Will the devil (or his emissary) and his demonic charges be destroyed on a Day of Judgement? Of course not. Ross's blind and uncaring universe, the indifference of his deity that critics often associate with all of his early work, all these resolutely bleak emanations from an absentee or uncaring God will determine the fate of Ross's God-fearing family. Sandra Djwa puts it very well when she says the following: "Because this conflict is intimately connected with the struggle for survival, the tragedy of these stories is that there is often no possible reconciliation of any kind. When an author's horizon is composed of 'the bare essentials of a landscape, sky and earth,' there are no compromises open: if land and weather fail man, the struggle for survival can only end tragically, the extent of the tragedy being largely determined by the strength of the person concerned" (51).

But this is not what happens in "The Runaway." It is not even close. What happens is that Luke Taylor is destroyed, along with his demonic horses, in a fiery inferno. No tears are shed, not even for the horses, and there is only a perfunctory sort of mourning after this apocalyptic incident. In fact, Luke Taylor's death is rather funny. His advice to the narrator and his father is Luke Taylor's undoing. The horses balk again with a load of straw on a cold and windy November afternoon. And this time, exasperated, the father says to his son, ". . . I think I'll take old Luke's advice, and see what a fire will do." The narrator tells it this way:

> I closed my eyes a moment. When I opened them he had straightened and stepped back, and there on the ground between the Diamonds' feet, like something living that he had slipped out of his coat, was a small yellow flame, flickering up nervously against the dusk.
>
> For a second or two, feeling its way slowly round the straw, it remained no larger than a man's outspread hand. Then, with a spurt of sparks and smoke, it shot up right to the Diamonds' bellies.
>
> They gave a frightened snort, lunged ahead a few feet, stopped short again. The fire now, burning briskly, was directly beneath the load of straw, and even as I shouted to warn my father a tongue of flame licked up the front of the rack, and the next instant, sudden as a fan being flicked open, burst into a crackling blaze. (93–94)

The Diamonds bolt, the boy jumps on his entirely ordinary horse Gopher, and the chase is on. "Riding close behind, my head lowered against the smoke and sparks, I didn't realize, till the wagon took the little ditch onto the highway at a sickening lurch, that the Diamonds were going home. Not to their new home, where they belonged now, but to old Luke Taylor's place" (94).

Note how our narrator has personified the fire, with its nervous flickering, "like something living." Note too how the narrator characterizes the Black Diamonds in Luke Taylor's stable. When the flaming wagon is drawn home by the terrified team, it overturns and sets fire to Luke Taylor's barn. His Black Diamonds are inside, and the boy tries to save them from immolation. Instead of fleeing their stalls to safety, they *all* balk. Instead of being portrayed by our narrator as the innocent victims of an uncaring fate, the Black Diamonds are presented to us as monsters. The narrator describes them as follows:

> I ran forward and squeezed in past [the] heels [of the first Diamond I saw], then untied the halter-shank, but when I tried to lead [the horse] out it trembled and crushed its body tight against the side of the stall. I climbed into the manger, struck it hard across the nose; it only stamped and tossed its head. Then I tried the next stall, then the next and the next. Each time I met the same fear-crazed resistance. One of the Diamonds lashed out with

its heels. Another caught me such a blow with a swing of its head that I leaned half-stunned for a minute against the manger. Another, its eyes rolling white and glassy, slashed with its teeth as I turned, and ripped my smock from shoulder to shoulder. (96)

This is the point at which Luke Taylor shows up. He heads straight for his huge burning barn, evading those well-meaning neighbours who try to head him off. He goes through the door. "The same moment that he disappeared, the floor of the loft collapsed. It was as if when running through the door he had sprung a trap, the way the great, billowy masses of burning hay plunged down behind him" (97). It doesn't take long. Luke returns to his element, and the two remaining Diamonds whose fateful trip "home" started the fire mysteriously return to a prosaically horsey identity. The narrator fears that they will balk again. He "mounted Gopher as usual and rode through the gate ahead of them, but at the first click of the reins they trotted off obediently. Obediently and dully, like a team of reliable old ploughhorses. Riding along beside them, listening to the soft creak and jingle of the harness, I had the feeling that we, too, had lost our Diamonds" (97).

The story closes with the mother (who in this story, as I have said, is always right) and the father (whose judgement is usually questionable where horses are concerned) trying to place their own construction upon the events of the day:

> "It's as I've always said [the mother argues] . . . *Though the mills of God grind slowly, yet they grind exceeding small.* His own balky Diamonds, and look what they carried home to him." She hadn't been there to see it—that was why she could say such things. "You sow the wind and you reap the whirlwind. Better for him today if he had debts and half-a-section like the rest of us."
>
> But my father sat staring before him as though he hadn't heard her. There was a troubled, old look in his eyes, and I knew that for him it was not so simple as that to rule off a man's account and show it balanced. Leave Luke out of it now—say that so far as he was concerned the scores were settled—but what about the Diamonds? *What kind of reckoning was it that exacted life and innocence for an old man's petty greed? Why, if it was retribution, had it struck so clumsily?* (97–98)

These last words, which I italicized, are the ones Djwa quotes to arrive at her sombre conclusion about this work. "The good man of 'The Runaway' finds himself troubled by God's justice, especially when the scales are eventually weighed in his favour" (53–54). But "The Runaway" does not end with the man's words; it ends with the narrator's response to the impact of his mother's words. Here are the last lines of the story:

> "All of them," he said at last, "all of them but the team he was driving and my own two no-good balky ones. Prettiest horses a man ever set eyes on. It wasn't coming to them."

"But you'll raise colts," my mother said quickly, pouring him a fresh cup of coffee, "and there'll be nothing wrong with them. Five or six years— why, you'll have a stableful."

He sipped his coffee in silence a moment and then repeated softly, "Prettiest horses a man ever set eyes on. No matter what you say, it wasn't coming to them." But my mother's words had caught. Even as he spoke his face was brightening, and it was plain that he too, now, was thinking of the colts. (98)

Note how the conversation in this closing scene goes in one way, but how the tone moves like an undertow in the opposite direction, away from any possibility of tragedy. And if the father has undergone a spiritual crisis (which might reappear with the birth of Black Diamond colts), so too, perhaps, has Sinclair Ross. To write "The Runaway" he has forfeited that bleak nihilism he has been branded with in all of his early work.

In the above reading, I have characterized "The Runaway" as a tale rich in comic detail. It is much less about the fate of a man and his horses that "wasn't coming to them" than about the damnation of a diabolical schemer and his demonic steeds. Luke Taylor's fire unites the settlement in a common cause. His death restores normality and hope to the characters.

A re-reading of all of Ross's stories has served to focus my attention upon his talents as a comic writer. I hesitate to say what kind of a comic writer, because the very moment I make a formulation of his comedy, I will begin to recall stories in his canon that refuse, like Luke's horses, to conform to a theoretically "normal" category. "Spike" has the structure but not the texture of romantic comedy. "The Race" (an excerpt from Ross's novella *Whir of Gold*) reads like a long joke or a boy's adventure, full of good spirits and friendly contempt for the strictures of the adult world. "A Day with Pegasus," written in what critics would like us to think of as Ross's early black period, is a realistic story about a boy's fantasy lie, and it reads a bit like a Miracle Play. "Barrack Room Fiddle Tune" is Ross's only story written in the first person plural, an anecdote about the impact of a farm boy's terrible fiddle-playing on a group of army recruits. There is really only one character in this story, so again it defies easy classification.

"The Outlaw," "Cornet at Night," and "Circus in Town" have all received fair attention from critics. The only thing I would add to the comments I have read is that these three stories work by means of subversion. The subversive victory in each has something to do with a child's attainment of a vision which is antithetical to that of his or her parents. In each case the child manages to invert the value system that oppresses her or him.

It is interesting to note that the comedy in almost every one of these eight stories is inextricably bound up with horses. For example, in "Cornet at Night" the story proceeds with quiet, almost detached, irony. Our narrator, Tommy Dickson, has tried to remain obedient to the strictures of his parents' parsimony. His orders for his first ever trip to town alone are to hitch Rock (an old, utterly reliable horse) to the wagon, do the shopping, and bring back a hired man to help his father with the stooking.

"Mind you pick somebody big and husky," said my father as he started for the field. "Go to Jenkins' store, and he'll tell you who's in town. Whoever it is, make sure he's stooked before."

"And mind it's somebody who looks like he washes himself," my mother warned, "I'm going to put clean sheets and pillowcases on the bunkhouse bed, but not for any dirty tramp or hobo."

By the time they had both finished with me there were a great many things to mind. Besides repairs for my father's binder, I was to take two crates of eggs each containing twelve dozen eggs to Mr. Jenkins' store and in exchange have a list of groceries filled. And to make it complicated, both quantity and quality of some of the groceries were to be determined by the price of eggs. Thirty cents a dozen, for instance, and I was to ask for coffee at sixty-five cents a pound. Twenty-nine cents a dozen and coffee at fifty cents a pound. Twenty-eight and no oranges. Thirty-one and bigger oranges. It was like decimals with Miss Wiggins, or two notes in the treble against three in the bass. For my father a tin of special blend tobacco, and my mother not to know. For my mother a box of face powder at the drugstore, and my father not to know. Twenty-five cents from my father on the side for ice-cream and licorice. Thirty-five from my mother for my dinner at the Chinese restaurant. And warnings, of course, to take good care of Rock, speak politely to Mr. Jenkins, and see that I didn't get machine oil on my corduroys. (39)

All things considered, Tommy doesn't do too badly. His only major deviation from the rule of the adults is to bring home a trumpet player with slender and smooth white hands to do the stooking. The young musician's name is Philip Coleman. Philip, lover of horses, Paul Kirby might remind us. Tommy cannot keep his eyes off Philip's cornet case, but other than this, he keeps his enthusiasms and old Rock dutifully reined in—until Philip takes his cornet out of the case:

It was a very lovely cornet, shapely and eloquent, gleaming in the August sun like pure and mellow gold. I couldn't restrain myself. I said, "Play it —play it now—just a little bit to let me hear." And in response, smiling at my earnestness, he raised it to his lips.

But there was only one note—only one fragment of a note—and then away went Rock. I'd never have believed he had it in him. With a snort and plunge he was off the road and into the ditch—then out of the ditch again and off at a breakneck gallop across the prairie. There were stones and badger holes, and he spared us none of them. (46)

Note how, when Philip puts the cornet to his lips and Rock explodes, the comedy takes off as well, from a nicely modulated irony in the first 11 pages to a wonderful moment of farce which effectively destroys the parental hold over Tommy's mission. The carefully garnered supplies fly out of the wagon, an egg crate is smashed, items are lost or ruined, and best of all (or worst of all, depending on your politics), Tommy has been seduced into a new vision of soaring possibilities by Philip's cornet.

Ross returns again and again in his comic works to these moments of subversive joy brought about by a young person whose feelings are catalyzed and released by a horse. Even the relatively horseless "Barrack Room Fiddle Tune" does this when the farm boy protagonist jumps a fence to have a conversation with a horse.

Horses in Ross's work are usually associated with freedom, self-sufficiency, release, and sometimes male pride. They are the Pegasus vehicles for a child's dream of freedom and adventure. And in a society in which sexual desire is suppressed so relentlessly, the horse is often the adolescent's substitute for a true object of desire. Isabel, the horse in "The Outlaw" and "The Ride," for example, is a temptress. The horse is the trigger for the body's ecstatic release, so a horse out of control (as in Ovid's story about Phaëthon or Pindar's version of Bellerophon and Pegasus) is a moment of high celebration in the life of a prairie youth. When I re-read my own summary of "Cornet at Night," I can't help but notice how the images I have cast this story in are charged with erotic innuendoes. The story seems to carry this subcurrent.

It is not my purpose here to offer firm value judgements about Ross's comic work. But I have reached the point where I can urge all the Rosselytes to read his eight short comic pieces *as comedy*. Reading these works will remind us most obviously that Ross has unsung talents as a writer of comedy. It does not, as some critics imply, show up only in Ross's later works; it is there right from the beginning.

Also, if we read Ross's short stories without the constrictions imposed by a prearranged scheme—some form of thematic criticism, for example—we can begin to appreciate Ross's subversive sense of the ridiculous, his buoyant affirmations. And best of all, we can rid ourselves of the excesses of the Rosselytes: their insistence upon suffering as a salutory element of aesthetic pleasure.

I have re-read these stories after the rise and fall of postmodernism in North American fiction, after the theatre of the absurd, after Beckett and Pinter, after the quest for the Canadian identity when stark realism was the unchallenged orthodoxy, and I am returning to something Shakespeare must have known a long time ago: that a balanced diet of comic and tragic renderings is healthier than a strict regimen of one without the other. When I think of modern Canadian works that might fit some acceptable definition of tragedy, I can think of very few: *The Stone Angel*, perhaps, or *Under the Volcano*. Both are written by people who had, by my reckoning, a pretty good sense of humour. So did Sinclair Ross.

WORKS CITED

Chambers, Robert D. *Sinclair Ross and Ernest Buckler.* Toronto: Copp Clark, 1975.

Comeau, Paul. "Sinclair Ross's Pioneer Fiction." *Canadian Literature* 103 (Winter 1984).

Djwa, Sandra. "No Other Way: Sinclair Ross's Stories and Novels." *Canadian Literature* 47 (Winter 1971).

Fraser, Keath. "Futility at the Pump: The Short Stories of Sinclair Ross." *Queen's Quarterly* 77 (Spring 1970).

Gardner, John. *The Art of Fiction.* New York: Random House, 1985.

Ingram, Forrest L. *Representative Short Story Cycles of the Twentieth Century: Studies in a Literary Genre.* Paris: Mouton, 1971.

Laurence, Margaret. "Introduction" to Sinclair Ross, *The Lamp at Noon and Other Stories.* Toronto: McClelland and Stewart (NCL), 1968.

McMullen, Lorraine. *Sinclair Ross.* Boston: Twayne, 1979.

Mitchell, Ken. *Sinclair Ross, A Reader's Guide.* Moose Jaw: Coteau Books, 1981.

Ricou, Laurence. *Vertical Man/Horizontal World: Man and Landscape in Canadian Prairie Fiction.* Vancouver: University of British Columbia Press, 1973.

Ross, Morton L. "The Canonization of *As for Me and My House*: A Case Study." In *Figures in a Ground.* Ed. Diane Bessai and David Jackel. Saskatoon: Western Producer Prairie Books, 1978.

Ross, Sinclair. *As for Me and My House.* Toronto: McClelland and Stewart, 1957.

————. *The Lamp at Noon and Other Stories.* Toronto: McClelland and Stewart (NCL), 1968.

————. *The Race and Other Stories.* Ottawa: University of Ottawa Press, 1982.

Other works consulted:

Chapman, Marilyn. "Anjother Case of Ross's Mysterious Barn." *Canadian Literature* 103 (Winter 1984), 184–86.

Friesen, Victor. "The Short Stories of Sinclair Ross." *Canadian Short Story Magazine* II, No. 2 (Fall 1976), 71–73.

Hamilton, Edith. *Mythology: Timeless Tales of Gods and Heroes.* New York: Mentor, 1969, 131–37.

McCourt, Edward A. *The Canadian West in Fiction* (Rev. ed.). Toronto: Ryerson, 1970, 100–105.

Moss, John. *Patterns of Isolation in English Canadian Fiction.* Toronto: McClelland and Stewart, 1974, 115, 149–65.

Whitman, F. H. "The Case of Ross's Mysterious Barn." *Canadian Literature* 94 (Autumn 1982), 168–69.

Telling Secrets: Sinclair Ross's *Sawbones Memorial*

CHARLENE DIEHL-JONES

I'll tell you a secret. When a child friend of mine tells me his stories, he marks the important stuff by hushing his voice. He has already discovered the power that lives in secrets, power enough to generate a whole economy of exchange in fictional small-town Upward, Saskatchewan, where Sinclair Ross sets *Sawbones Memorial*. Telling secrets. Those who know, trading their tellings, trying out new versions, new variations, balancing their accounts. Or sometimes hoarding their knowing. And the secrets, the stories, whispering secrets of their own, secrets about the teller, about the listener, about the reader.

Diana Brydon writes: "Ross's fiction is unusually concerned with the absences, with what is left unsaid and with what cannot be said" (97). *Sawbones* is no exception. As in short stories—and I'm acknowledging here my debt to Dennis Cooley's elegant investigation of secrecy in his essay "The Eye in Sinclair Ross's Short Stories"—Ross's secret fetish roots into all the dark corners of this text, whispers at every juncture. The novel functions through its secrets: the characters all tell or keep their tales, all engage in the subtle and complex network of exchange; the fragmented plot threads unwind themselves, reveal their secrets, the fragmentation prompting one to wonder what remains hidden in the crevices. And because as readers we are pressed to recognize ourselves as eavesdroppers, as secret-gatherers, the text whispers its provocations about the prevalence, even perhaps the necessity, certainly the ethics, of secrets and secrecy in our lives as readers of texts and of the world.

Teasing out the secrets about secrets: hearing the rustling proximity of story, secret's kindred spirit. Story as that elaborate and complex contract that relies on secret-keeping, secret-telling: this is Barthes's "proairetic code,"[1] the plot/action code, the unfolding of narrative; the reader listens to the secrets caught in the creases, guessing past and through her position in the story's events, depending on the text to guard its secrets. Secrecy as a narrative's survival instinct. So: story as secret, unconfessed secret. And secret as story too: Barthes's sense of the enigma, the secret embedded in the narrative that triggers expectation and desire; the secret with its own storyline of disclosure and delay. Narrative as "a game with two players: the snare and the truth" (Barthes, *S/Z* 188), the snare frustrating the disclosure of the secret which is truth. And since truth always finally silences narrative, the (perpetual) seductive dance of the secret's evasion of its own story: secret-telling as strip-tease. Secret-telling also as illumination, bringing into light what has been hidden in shadow; or scrawling/scrolling ornate marginalia, decorations around a periphery. Which brings us to the problem that worries at any investigation of secrets, perhaps to the secret's inaudible, untellable secret: is a secret the story of itself or is a secret the silent space around which a story is told? The story of a secret or the secret of a story? Doc Hunter hoards a secret about his relationship to Nick; Doc Hunter can only ever guess about the nature of that relationship because it is ultimately unverifiable. Is a secret finally unknowable? Or only untellable?

In *Sawbones*, we eavesdrop on Upward; we listen to the secrets that circulate among its citizens. Much of what we hear is chatter, noise, stories that don't pretend to the prestige of secrecy. Ornate marginalia. Perhaps. Frank Kermode, in *The Genesis of Secrecy*, argues that "it is impossible to live in [the world] without repeated, if minimal, acts of interpretation" (49); the chatter we overhear at Doc Hunter's party is largely interpretive chatter.[2] For Caroline, the new(ish) English bride, the outsider, Duncan's stories of his prairie become strategies for making sensible a perpetually secret world, a cultural matrix so much different from her own. And she insists on her stories; when Doc attempts to correct her versions, she launches a vigorous defence: "I'll have you know I married into a family of pioneers and unsung heroes, and that's where I'm going to stay married" (26). The utter necessity of interpretation. Caroline's stories spin themselves around a space that remains secret in its foreignness; other stories in *Sawbones* explain apparently inexplicable (secret) behaviour. A farmer tells of Doc's claiming calves in return for his services, and insists on attributing it to greed; Ernie Harp, faced with Nick's imminent return to the community, reads anger and revenge into the blank space of his motivation. Every story tells its way towards a secret; every secret is covered over with the stuff of story. On a larger scale, the whole novel—a collection of story fragments—whispers of a communal effort to remember and to forget some secret: the magnetic and irresistible power of the enigma eliciting both "the temptation to name and the impotence to name" (Barthes 62). The potential for attaining any truth, any understanding, both fades and becomes more urgent with the increasingly dense interweaving of this community of stories. The citizens of Upward tell their stories, perhaps to save their souls; they are constrained to seek/find narratives that can span the awful silence of (possible) unmeaning and futility. To keep the secret secret. Under the smugness of even the prattling tours of the new hospital lies that nagging insecurity: we speak these stories because there may be nothing else; that is the secret that we fear and that we cannot tell. Only Doc has the courage to prescribe—and practise—"a little humor too in the face of the inscrutable" (*Sawbones* 127).

Every story has its secrets, but a secret and a story are not synonymous. That whisper of difference, the lure of a secret—"our desire to be taken in by a narrative of secrecy" (Cooley 152).[3] I'll tell you a secret. A wildly complex relation of power resides in that pact: the teller, announcing a privilege of knowledge, chooses to confer privilege of initiation on listeners by granting them access to guarded information, privileged by virtue of its restricted availability. All that power in all that privilege. A transgressive narrative —what I shouldn't tell you—that flatters the listener with the broken pact of silence, that hints of trespassing the borders of taboo, the secret also contains its own (secret) contract: secret-telling insists on secret-hearing ("you must listen to me tell my secret") and secret-keeping ("you must not expose my secret, or expose my exposing of my secret"). It also assumes a certain economic weight, a purchasing power. Barthes writes: "narrating is the (economic) theory of narration: one does not narrate to 'amuse,' to 'instruct,' or to satisfy a certain anthropological function of meaning; one narrates in order to obtain by exchanging" (89). The power of dissemination. Sufficient to establish and fuel a whole trading economy.

Which brings us to Doc's party, where "the stories of various lives emerge through the silences, through the taboo areas that are skirted round, hinted at, or deliberately omitted" (Brydon 100). Doc's party and the flash of proven currency. Two old cronies, Doc and Harry, telling and protecting secrets on the opening page:

> "A lot of stories, Doc, that you used to have a pretty good way of fiddling round yourself. Horny old bastard, still shows all over you. I could name two—"
>
> "Just two? I must be slipping. I thought I had a better reputation than that." (*Sawbones* 9)

Nellie and Rose only a few pages later, on Doc's wife and mistress:

> "When you think, though, that she knew, and knew everybody else knew too—always hanging over her, the humiliation—"
>
> "She could forget long enough to buy clothes and rig herself out in them. Remember the new outfits, spring and fall? The beaver coat, and then the Persian lamb? I suppose it was one way to get even."
>
> "For all that, though, she took it hard. I'll never forget the time, years and years ago, when we were all standing on the church steps after service, six or seven of us, and Maisie Bell came along. The way she picked up speed when she saw us and put her head down. After all, we were the Good Women

of the town, the Holier-Than-Thou's, God forgive us, and I suppose she had a pretty good idea of what we were thinking even if we weren't saying it." (17)

Not surprisingly, many of Upward's secrets revolve around sexuality, an explosive and potentially disruptive force in a small and closed community, and a tabooed one too. The stuff of good talk. Doc's sexual exploits have been valid currency for some time clearly, but they also, in pointed ways, frustrate the economy of secrets, and can only with difficulty be accommodated. Doc's indiscretions are not problematic in themselves, but his refusal to keep and trade his secrets presents a challenge to the currency value.[4] His indiscretions are too indiscreet:

> "He probably thought he was doing the right thing—a sort of loyalty—but in fact he made it so hard for her. Stopping to talk to her in the street, having coffee together in Charlie Wong's, sitting close to the window to make sure everybody would see—deliberately giving people something to talk about . . . . Only he never stopped to think that taking a stand made the town take one too—against her, not him. Trust the man to get off scot free—it never fails. I don't suppose many of us really cared if they had a few times together. If they'd just been a little more discreet, kept the blinds down, respectability would have looked the other way." (20–21)

A profoundly conservative force may be secret's child: the town, in the stories it tells about itself, has already cast Maisie in a particular narrative position. Doc's attempts to subvert the script only settle the town against her. Upward tries—and largely succeeds (she is not in attendance at Doc's farewell party)—to make Maisie a secret, to recuperate a different story in order to prevent the devaluation of their currency. Conservatism is often at gossip's core; the exchange of secrets confirms the club of initiates and the hierarchy they establish and perpetuate. Any small town has a finely tuned and entrenched economy of secrets: an elaborate defence against change which might signal dissolution. Nonconformity to a sexual norm obviously poses a powerful threat: Upward's secrets include Doc's promiscuity, Maisie's indiscretions, Eleanor's frigidity, Harry's pimping, Benny's homosexuality, various schoolyard initiations. Racial or ethnic origin poses another. The visible minorities in a town like Upward are swallowed in silence, even as they're acknowledged:

> "These two wheel chairs we've put them out in front just for tonight so people'll be sure to see. Donated, that's right, believe it or not by the Chinamen. Charlie Wong and Wing Ling Ching—or maybe it's the other way round, names like that how can you remember, one's got the restaurant and the other the laundry. Puts the rest of us to shame, now doesn't it?" (32)

An utter lack of regard sounds through the lumpish designation —"the Chinamen"—and the speaker's uncertainty about the names of the

men; these people figure as one of the community's collective secrets. And
the disregard that engulfs them undercuts the sincerity of the final comment:
patronizing superiority whispers around the edges. Upward, in its conservative reading of itself at least, has pretensions to good breeding. Its prej-
udices are strongly WASP, which means that any ethnic variation becomes
suspect, subject to the secret mill. Nick's family, because of his pending
return, are prominent targets. And the rhetoric is startling. Ukrainian, hard-
working, given to unfamiliar food and clothing and customs: the town
responds by generating (not-so-secret) versions of them that label them "hunkies" and even cast them as non-white. A particularly paranoid citizen:

> "They [hunkies] do things a white man wouldn't, that's how [they get through
> college]. Same as the Chinks—live on anything, live like pigs—it doesn't
> bother them . . . . We didn't bring them in to take over and go to college.
> How's your wife going to feel if she gets sick and has to tell him things—
> maybe about her and you? Or take off her clothes for an examination?
> They've got funny minds and don't fool yourself, he's still a hunky. It would
> take a lot more than Medical School . . . . I say somebody ought to step in
> fast. This has always been a white town." (53–54)

"We didn't bring them in to take over and go to college." As if Nick's
education spoke a secret plot. And some of the community even see conspiracy in the fact that Caroline (another stranger) has already met Nick
(48–50). Once, long ago, Doc unsettled the unspoken pecking order, choosing Nick as a favoured apprentice; the town is still responding through its
secrecy campaign. Attempting to assert its reading of itself. As Bok states:
"At the heart of secrecy lies discrimination of some form, since its essence
is sifting, setting apart, drawing lines" (28).

A curious thing about a secret: rustling on the edge of audibility, it
is (oddly enough) never meant to be silent. I'll tell you a secret. Telling built
into the contract, part of the secret storyline. Telling—selective telling—
introduces (or perpetuates) a secret's circulation, allows it to assume a currency value. Several of the Auxiliary women, for instance, want to sell the
piano Doc has donated to the new hospital, and they spread that news; Doc
knows, or at least guesses, but no one will tell him directly. Everyone knows,
then, but the selectivity of the telling maintains the secrecy and ensures a
certain trading value of the secret. Upward survives, perhaps even thrives,
on this elaborate model of secret exchange. Those who know most—Dan,
the newspaper editor, for instance, and his wife Nellie, who traffic in the
half-said and the half-heard—suppose they know everything. Or near
enough to everything. Because they assume that everyone knows and understands and participates in the economy of secrets that underpins the complex
power relations of their town. Indeed, those who don't are often those who
can't because of language or culture barriers: the Chinese launderer and
restaurant owner, for instance, and Little John and Big Anna in their time

too—are covered over with the town's silence, excused (excluded) from the secret-market and thereby from any access to its power.

In this town lives a secret, a secret that remains a secret, a secret that would shatter Upward's power network: Doc's secret, Doc's carefully kept secret. Of all the citizens of Upward, Doc probably knows and understands best its economy of secrets, has played it to protect his investment(s). Not wrapped in silence like the outsiders, he has propagated certain secrets about himself: his reputation with women appears on the first page of the novel, and he's defending it. He has been open about his friendship with Maisie, knowing well it would generate secrets; open too about his friendship with Harry. Dan's reading of Doc—"We've known each other for twenty-seven years and it seems to me his life has always been fairly open" (80)—is typical. And that has been Doc's strategy. Because Doc is not as much a trader in secrets as his fellow citizens; his engagement is superficial, a foil to allow him to protect what must be protected. As Barthes notes, "the more signs there are, the more the truth will be obscured" (*S/Z* 62). Doc cloaks his relationship with Nick in utter and complete secrecy by covering it over with multitudinous signs: he has expressed his concern for Nick's future openly —some of the townspeople even guess that he has helped him through medical school—but always disinterestedly. Doc as keeper of the secret. For those of us with the luxury of perspective on Upward, this begs the question of the actual power in this economy of secrets that generates and guarantees the relative might of its citizens. Doc has the power because he can choose to play the system, or not to enter it at all. The kept secret gestures towards a wholly other power resource, a different economy; it becomes a vacuum that exercises its influence in spite of its invisibility.

So many secrets are told and kept in *Sawbones*, and not only by the characters. Secrets caught in the crevices of the discourse too. Whispers in the cracks of the writing. Text as secret-keeper, secret-teller. If indeed *"the character and the discourse are each other's accomplices"* (Barthes, *S/Z* 178), we would expect the discourse to tell secrets on those constituting (and being constituted by) it. The language that the woman chooses to summon the guests for sandwiches and coffee, for instance, exposes meanness rather than genuine hospitality: "'We don't want anybody going home from Doc's party hungry. Just don't forget about putting your dishes on the floor and then putting your feet on the dishes. We're going to have enough mess to clean up as it is'" (112). Or Sarah: "He looks so tired and lost, that one little tuft God help us standing up pure white—and there used to be so much of it so black and thick—" (57)—an odd and subtle mixture of nostalgia, maternal protectiveness, loss and sadness, even desire. Or the anonymous tour guide, accidently baring her lack of education and sophistication along with her sentiment: "'they say she played just beautiful . . . but what I mean supposing somebody starts playing and doesn't do it very well . . . . Just think if you were real sick say coming out of an operation and could hear somebody hammering away at *Though your sins be as scarlet*" (30–31). Telling secrets. Hearing telling both as verb (narrating secrets) and as adjective, revelatory secrets. Language speaking out of both sides of its mouth.

This text keeps a lot of secrets. It resists the pressure towards the proper noun, the name, for instance, and we only ever locate the speakers by listening for the secrets wound into the text. And many speakers in the novel finally resist our every effort to piece together their identity. The tour guide, the farmers, the paranoid gossipers: many of Upward's citizens remain anonymous to us, remain mysteries; they are among the text's secrets. This textual secret-keeping unnerves us as readers, presses us to become sensitive to our unconscious assumptions about the nature of text and of reading a text. Its refusal to name characters, for instance, draws attention to our desire for names, our anxiety in the presence of the unnamed; it provokes us to investigate the secrets we keep secret from ourselves. In contrast to the short stories which rely heavily on a diegetic narrative position,[5] *Sawbones* abolishes any overt narrative directives. No identification of speakers, of tone, of situation, no narrative bridges. There is no absence of an organizing principle, as the clear chronology of the framing story affirms, but it is entirely inaccessible. Text-maker as secret presence, as absent presence.[6] The diegetic gestures we expect in a novel become conspicuous in their absence. And if we become complacent as we grow accustomed to the structuring, the text reminds us of its gaps: here is a nameless tour guide in dialogue, though only one voice, her voice, is audible:

> "They can read or play cards, listen to the radio—anything they want. And naturally talk. Oh yes, plenty of books, a whole shelf, but just between ourselves they don't look very good. That's right, donated, we went around—ones people borrow and forget who's supposed to get them back . . . ." (30)

What *Sawbones* refuses is what most realist novels offer: a privileged reading position, a position that is oriented and manipulated by the discourse. This novel provides no vantage point from which to view the happenings of the characters, no indication about presumed valuation strategies. It makes difficult any casual surrender to story, instead pointing towards "the knowledge that what we read is not a presentation nor quite even a representation of life, but a making of it, a making that in turn invites us to share its shadings and shapings" (Cooley 150). *Sawbones* foregrounds the reader's participation (responsibility) in the construction of text, of story.

If any role is cast for the reader of this novel, it is the role of eavesdropper. Because this text is so explicitly mimetic—I place the sections of interior monologue (Doc's, Sarah's, Dunc's) in the camp of expressive rather than expository prose; though silent, these patches borrow a speech model—

the emphasis shifts away from the (imagining) eye and settles almost exclusively in the ear. Which brings us the long way back into the world of secrets. The text saying, I'll tell you a secret. Reader not as voyeur,[7] but as auditeur, overhearer (overlistener). And the eavesdropping position offers its challenges, since always one must sift through noise. Like the chatter of the Upward crowd. But noise, Barthes argues, is essential to narrative:

> in contrast to idyllic communication, to pure communication (which would be, for example, that of the formalized sciences), readerly writing stages a certain "noise," it is the writing of noise, of impure communication; but this noise is not confused, massive, unnameable; it is a clear noise made up of connections, not superpositions: it is of a distinct "cacography." (S/Z 132)

Sawbones, I think, takes us towards recognizing this "distinct 'cacography,'" towards recognizing readerly writing: far from the precision of mathematics, precision which exists to release secrets, Ross's novel explores the potential for secret-keeping that accompanies noise. Secrecy, then, as "the carrier of texture and variety" (Bok 24). This text unsettles our naïve tendency to equate secrecy and truth—an assumption that underlies many of our strategies for reading—and points us instead towards a reading position that admits the power of discourse to keep its secrets. Even to consider that the secret of the text may be its refusal of the-secret-of-the-text. I'll tell you a secret. Just in order to tell you. I may not tell you a secret of any value. Or even one that's true. Telling secrets. Just to tell.

Which makes for an unnerving end to an essay. Because we learn to expect or at least to desire the revelation of secrets in our writing about writing. The critical predicament of finding and telling secrets, and knowing the secrets are always finally enveloped in secrecy. But I said at the outset I would tell you a secret. So I'll tell you a (different) secret: at the close of his story "Rebecca," Donald Barthelme writes:

> The story ends. It is written for several reasons. Nine of them are secrets. The tenth is that one should never cease considering human love. Which remains as grisly and golden as ever, no matter what is tattooed upon the warm tympanic page. (144)

The same could be whispered to Ross.

NOTES

1.   I have drawn heavily on the reading strategies in Roland Barthes's fascinating study S/Z: among the five codes he discovers in texts, I would underscore the "proairetic code," which details the forward drive of the plot, and the "hermeneutic code," which establishes and develops a plot's several enigmas (S/Z 18–20).

2.   Bok's study of gossip in *Secrets: On the Ethics of Concealment and Revelation* intersects mine, and helps particularly to focus the moral issues:

> Cheap, superficial, intrusive, unfounded, even vicious: surely gossip can be all that. Yet to define it in these ways is to overlook the whole network of human exchanges of information, the need to inquire and to learn from the experience of others, and the importance of not taking everything at face value. The desire for such knowledge leads people to go beneath the surface of what is said and shown, and to try to unravel conflicting clues and seemingly false leads. In order to do so, information has to be shared with others, obtained from them, stored in memory for future use, tested and evaluated in discussion, and used at times to encourage, to entertain, or to warn. (90)

3.   Claims to referentiality also may distinguish secret from story: a secret at least professes relation to the (however problematic) "real" world. Bok points up this difference: "One could imagine a club dedicated to false gossip, in which members vied with one another for who could tell the most outrageous stories about fellow human beings. . . . Such a club, however, would be likely to have but few members; for gossip loses its interest when it is *known* to be false" (96).

4.   Bataille outlines the power inherent in *expenditure* (non-utilitarian transfer of goods), especially clearly defined in the custom of potlatch. Doc's tendency toward expenditure contrasts sharply with the more retentive/conservative hoarding tendencies of the townspeople.

5.   Cooley shows the inclination towards narrated speech in the short stories, and argues that it "allows the narrator to preside firmly over the discourse, simply because the mode of discourse is what Gérard Genette would call more diegetic than mimetic" (141). The case in *Sawbones* is exactly the reverse: the novel is without narrated speech (excepting speech narrated by another character).

6.   Bowen writes about *Sawbones*: "It is entirely dialogue; hence there is no place for the brooding introspection which marks Ross' other works" (47). Perhaps equally possible: the introspective brooder has effaced itself, has hidden itself in the cracks of the dialogue and the spaces between dialogues.

7.   Compare Ross's strategy in *Sawbones* with Robbe-Grillet's in *Jealousy*: there the language is all filtered, made "objective," and the reader becomes implicated in a voyeuristic project; in Ross, the reader is always listener rather than watcher.

WORKS CITED

Barthelme, Donald. "Rebecca." In *Amateurs*. New York: Farrar, Strauss & Giroux, 1976, 139–44.

Barthes, Roland. *S/Z*. Trans. by Richard Miller. Preface by Richard Howard. New York: Hill & Wang, 1974.

Bataille, Georges. "The Notion of Expenditure" [1933]. In *Contemporary Critical Theory*. Ed. Dan Latimer. San Diego: Harcourt Brace Jovanovich, 1989, 140–56.

Bok, Sissela. *Secrets: On the Ethics of Concealment and Revelation*. New York: Vintage Books, 1989 (1983).

Bowen, Gail. "The Fiction of Sinclair Ross." *Canadian Literature* 80 (1979), 37–48.

Brydon, Diana. "Sinclair Ross." *Profiles in Canadian Literature*, Vol. 3. Ed. Jeffrey M. Heath. Toronto and Charlottetown: Dundurn Press, 1982, 97–103.

Cooley, Dennis. "The Eye in Sinclair Ross's Short Stories." *The Vernacular Muse: The Eye and the Ear in Contemporary Literature*. Winnipeg: Turnstone Press, 1987, 139–65.

Kermode, Frank. *The Genesis of Secrecy: On the Interpretation of Narrative*. The Charles Eliot Norton Lectures, 1977–78. Cambridge, Mass.: Harvard University Press, 1979.

Ross, Sinclair. *Sawbones Memorial*. Toronto: McClelland and Stewart, 1974.

Sinclair Ross's "Foreigners"

MARILYN ROSE

Morton L. Ross has observed in his "case study" of the "canonization" of *As for Me and My House* that the emphasis in recent Ross criticism has been on narrativity (particularly point of view) and self-reflexivity. This has led, he believes, to a distressing valorization of "the vagaries of 'tension,' 'irony,' 'paradox,' and 'ambiguity,'" along with a displacing of "responsibility for contributing meaning" onto the reader, as if the text were without intrinsic meaning (205). What he most laments is the "deregionalization" of the novel, the failure to value the text (as earlier Ross critics had done) as "successfully realistic and regional fiction, as a graphic evocation of life on the Canadian prairies during the depression" (201).

There is a great deal wrong with Ross's argument, of course: he treats "realistic" and "universal" as transparent, disinterested categories and fails to recognize his own interestedness in maintaining, for example, that Canadian literature is valuable when it contributes to the building of "a" Canadian "identity" (201); he glosses over the problematic relationship between regional specificity and universal "truths," terms that would seem to be at philological odds with one another; and, in attacking the idea of the "reader's responsibility" for constructing meaning when reading texts, he impales himself upon such very obvious spears as "authorial intention" and "textual stability."

What is valuable about Ross's argument, however, is his general (however indirectly made) point that Sinclair Ross's fiction is in fact amenable to what might be called "historical" reading—critical approaches that begin with questions of context and deal with the "pastness" of a work and its relation to the present. When Morton Ross speaks of the "graphic evocation of life on the Canadian prairies during the depression," or the novel's success "in conveying what it was to live in a significant section of the country at a significant time in the nation's history," or its "representation of a community and a way of living" (201), he is actually suggesting situating critical discourse within the parameters of "history" rather than of "realism," a term he has used to unfortunate effect.

I wish to suggest an historical approach to two of Sinclair Ross's novels—*As for Me and My House* and *Sawbones Memorial*—but one differing in a number of ways from the kind of historicism that lies silently behind Morton Ross's article. His approach (and that of the critics whom he endorses when they focus on Sinclair Ross's gritty realism—E. K. Brown, Edward McCourt, Roy Daniells, and Hugo McPherson) looks to the centre, the whole, and the universal (the region, the community and its central, symbolic figures). Mine looks to the margins, paying attention to "people and phenomena that once seemed wholly insignificant, indeed outside of history" (Gallagher 43). Where his seeks a single stable version of the culture inscribed in a text ("that common . . . experience which creates a group" [201]), mine assumes that texts embody, directly or indirectly, whatever "breaking, revision, or weakening of the dominant codes" can be seen to prevail at specific times and places in history (White 301). Where Morton Ross echoes Margaret Laurence in simply praising the accuracy of depictions of the "stultifying atmosphere of small and ingrown towns" (201), my approach assumes that texts do not merely describe, but actively interrogate the power structures they portray. In sum, while his approach to *As for Me and My House* reflects organicism, a search for organic unity, mine assumes that literary texts are participants in what Brook Thomas has called "the dynamic field of social conflict in which they were originally produced" (37)—and thus that texts will not be unitary constructions but will be polyphonic, will embody in themselves the competing elements, the conflictual voices, the unresolved strains that characterize any given cultural moment.

I begin with a single word which appears with insistent frequency in *Sawbones Memorial*, the epithet "hunky." When an anonymous woman at Doc Hunter's retirement party dismisses Nick Miller, Doc's Ukrainian-Canadian protégé and soon-to-be successor, with the phrase "'Once a hunky always a hunky'" (33), she expresses a perspective that persists in post-war Upward. "Hunkies" like Nick Miller are unwelcome there, even as Steve Kulanich is someone to be got rid of in Horizon in *As for Me and My House*, for "they" are not "us" (no matter what credentials they may have accumulated): indeed, while "we" may have "brought them in," as one man says, "we" certainly never meant "them" to "take over" (*Sawbones Memorial* 54).

Its status as a term of opprobrium, then, seems clear. Yet "hunky," as Ross uses it, is an interesting, resonant, and surprisingly equivocal word. It has in fact two competing senses, one of which is particularly historically contingent. Ross's characters use the word as North Americans routinely used it from the late nineteenth through the mid-twentieth centuries, as a response to specific immigration patterns and a way of labelling and thereby containing a particular "foreign" element in their midst. The *OED* for example, lists its first recorded use in this sense as a New York *Herald* account in 1896 of the Pennsylvanian use of the term "hunky" (as derived from the word "hun") to refer to "Hungarians, Lithuanians, Slavs, Poles, Magyars, and Tyroleans."[1] (In Canada, "Russians," "Ukrainians" "Ruthvenians," "Galicians," "Slavs," and "Bohemians" would be added to the list.) From the turn of the century, then, through the end of the Second World War, the use of "hunky" and its synonym "bohunk" developed as a derogatory term meant to categorize the uneducated and unskilled Eastern European immigrant to North America as low, rough, and loutish—indeed, to establish his inferiority to the Northern European immigrant class which typically exercised social and civic power in western settlements at this time.[2]

There is, however, a competing definition of "hunky," an older meaning, which derives from the Dutch/Fresian *honk* or *honck* meaning "goal," "home," or "refuge" and comes to mean "being in a good position" and being "all right."[3] Etymologically related usages that persist through our own time include "hunk," indicating "a sexually attractive man," and "hunky," meaning "very satisfactory" or "fine," as in "hunky-dory" (*Collins* 549).

My argument is that, just as "hunky" is antonymical (in that it encompasses opposites within its parameters), so do Ross's narratives interrogate the concept as it was commonly used in the cultural past that his novels depict—not only by questioning its efficacy as a term of definition, or category, but by actually building into these narratives intimations of the word's alternate sense. In other words, while Ross's characters may deal with the figure of foreigner unequivocally, the stories themselves are constructed so as to undermine the stability of that figure as a routinely invoked cultural type in the towns these novels inscribe. Moreover, the two Ross novels to which I turn now (the first published in 1941 and the second in 1974) represent a narrative continuum which records a kind of cultural evolution with respect to the figure of foreigner in the small towns of the Canadian West—without, however, slipping into teleology, into what might be called a myth of "progressive emergence."[4]

While the word "hunky" does not appear in *As for Me and My House*, it is clear that Steve Kulanich belongs to that cultural category in the minds of Horizon's establishment. Son of an alleged drunkard and adulterer, a labouring foreign "section man" who later abandons him, Steve is quickly pigeonholed by Horizon as inferior and as irremediable. His very type is immoral, says Mrs. Wenderby, reminding Mrs. Bentley of Steve's father and his woman and maintaining that "'we women should have run them out long ago'" (49). His lineage is tainted, a townswoman says: he has "bad blood," and "blood will out" (61). His religion is both false and entrenched, so that, as Miss Twill says, "'At his age you'll never change him over. Catholics are like that, you know'" (55). A church board member echoes her in insisting that Horizon needs "no popery"—which is what accepting Steve would amount to (72).

Mrs. Bentley herself classifies Steve as foreign and records her wariness, her misgivings about him, from the start. At first glance she sees him as "an ominously good-looking boy" (41)—and a rather inscrutable one with his "Oriental"-looking eyes which are like "a blind drawn over a window that could be seen through only from inside" (40). There is something "dubious" about him and something "a little impetuous" in his foreign-inflected speech, his "quick and insistent" voice (40–41). His taste and social manner are deficient: the pictures he hangs in his room (religious lithography and dogs carrying gory ducks [52]), his musical sensibility (she has to play in "the style of very bad Liszt" to please him [69]), and his uncivilized table manners (50) betray his lack of breeding. Worst of all, there is a kind of latent opportunism, she thinks, in Steve Kulanich—he is "scheming" (76), "astute and calculating" (112), all in all a "shrewd little realist" (94) who needs to be watched.

The established families of Horizon, then, subject the foreigner to a kind of cultural "gaze" which fixes him as the "barbaric other"—a practice that reflects Canadian historical experience as it survives in other accounts of the period.[5] Then, having assigned this kind of immigrant to that category, it demands of itself a response to this "stranger within the gates."[6] One possibility is that the establishment attempt to assimilate the foreigner. When Mrs. Bentley declares that she is taking Steve in "just to teach him table manners" (50), approves his wearing Philip's tie (52), or takes him to Sunday school, she is echoing a well-publicized official policy of assimilation in Canada in the thirties—one whose aim was (to paraphrase the words of Gerus and Rea) to render the immigrant as British and as Protestant as possible as quickly as possible (10).[7] And when she fails in her efforts to civilize him, Mrs. Bentley falls back on the alternate response (which much of Horizon had favoured all along), rigorous gatekeeping: Steve Kulanich is summarily banished from Horizon, sent to live with his "own" elsewhere, and a troublesome presence is neatly dispensed with so far as the town is concerned.

Through the figure of Steve, then, Ross ascribes to Horizon a conscious attitude towards the foreign, the "other," which is exclusionary and unequivocal: that presence must be altered or erased. At the same time, however, the novel inscribes fissures in that position. To begin with, the category itself is slippery: Steve is "Hungarian, or Rumanian, or Russian [or Ukrainian?]" (50); no one knows, and indeed there is talk that he may not even be Kulanich's real son (49)—and if he is not, then how can he be defined and managed? It is impossible to police that which one cannot demarcate; while Horizon may have easily dispatched this one foreign boy, an unstable category is precarious as a position from which to attempt to exercise entrenched power in any broad sense.

Equally destabilizing, as far as the construction of a social reality based upon marginalization of the foreign is concerned, is Ross's insistence in this novel on a kind of unacknowledged erotic response to the foreigner on the part of those "matrons" who seek to impose "respectability" upon him (48). It seems significant that Mrs. Bentley perceives Steve as pubescent: she notes his "broadening shoulders" in contrast to his otherwise "slender, undeveloped body" (41). She consistently links him in her diary with the horse, Harlequin, who is impudent and ungovernable, who "slavers" on her dress and yet hears himself praised by her as "handsome and astonishing" (40). She enjoys a covert rivalry with Philip for Steve's affections ("when Steve wants companionship or affection it's always to me he comes" [94]), and repeatedly attempts to seduce the boy to her side through her music. Nor does she stop with Steve: when she and Judith West ride on the handcar, in Mrs. Bentley's most rebellious act while in Horizon, the two are jubilant in their daring as they are literally pressed into the company of the foreign-looking men who operate it, the "grizzled, dirty-looking men, one dark and oily-skinned, the other broad-nosed and stolid like a Slav" (78) whose pumping propels the car. What Ross is suggesting here is a contradictory attitude towards its immigrant class on the part of mainstream Horizon: while the foreigner is seen as reprehensible in the main, and viewed as in need of regulation, his volatility is also perversely experienced as attractive—which exerts further pressure on an already compromised social category.

A temporal relationship between *Sawbones Memorial*, Ross's second small-town Saskatchewan novel, and its predecessor, *As for Me and My House*, is carefully established in that novel's opening pages. Thirty-three-year-old Nick Miller, a Ukrainian-Canadian physician, is poised to return in 1948 to Upward, the town he had left at 14 (in 1933) after his mother's death. Nick's experience thus overlaps (and indeed comes close to coinciding) with that of Steve Kulanich, who left Horizon at "twelve or thirteen" some years into the Depression of the 1930s. And the parallels between them (which extend through their being taken in by their "own" after leaving their xenophobic hometowns) suggest that the novels and their towns can be seen as representing an historical continuum, one that is particularly defined by an evolving relationship between the town and its foreign, its "others."

In Upward it might seem that the campaign against the "other" is far more entrenched, far more overt, and far more virulent than was Horizon's. Not only is Nick Miller's outright abuse as an immigrant child in Upward's past—where he was labelled "hunky," laughed at, spit upon, mocked even by his schoolteacher—set out in wrenching detail (as was not the case with Steve Kulanich), but the category of foreigner itself has been recast along racist lines. Having divided its inhabitants into "us," the "white," and "them,"

the "not-white," Upward routinely indulges itself in broad-brush defama-
tion: the "Hunkies" and the "Chinks" can be lumped together and made to
conform to the same stereotypical model, that of people who "do things a
white man wouldn't" (53), who "stick together, cousins, friends, half a dozen
to a room, three to a bed" (53), who "live like pigs" (53), and who smell of
cabbage but eat cats (36)—allegations that are generic on the whole, and
can be conveniently ascribed (by those who feel themselves above them) to
almost any first-generation immigrant group.[8]

In fact, however, Upward is less fixed, less univocal, less monolithic
in its antipathy to foreigners than Horizon and less able to effect "govern-
ment by category," despite the vehemence of some of its citizens. For the
stranger has now effectively breached the gates: the "Chinamen" are prosperous enough to donate wheelchairs to the new hospital and must be invited
to the reception (although it is still too much to expect the Ladies' Auxiliary
to know their names [32]); and Nick Miller is poised to return to Horizon
within the week—as its centrepiece, its physician, its healer and keeper of
intimate secrets. And while the old guard, like the Harps, may continue to
rail against Nick as "hunky," as "not white," as not "real white," not "one of
our own" (54), in fact Nick is now the one who will govern their fates and
Upward will just "have to get used to" it (21). Moreover, he has come not
only with the blessing of Doc Hunter, but at the request of the most powerful
social figures in Upward, the Gillespies, and particularly Dunc who is President of the Board and "beat down all the rest of the Board" in order to
bring Nick back (41–42)—a Nick he now thinks of as "*our* Nick" (56) who
ought to come "back where he belongs" (42). The civic solidarity which had
served Horizon in managing the foreigner has ruptured and a new hegemony, wherein the margins are shifting towards the centre, appears to have
begun to take shape.

What has happened to Upward is a matter of history. Within the
history that is Doc's story, as it unfolds on the eve of his retirement, is the
history of Upward, a small prairie town. Where Horizon was all isolation,
with infinitely outreaching rail lines signifying its distance from other towns
and "the city," the Upward of *Sawbones Memorial* is consistently seen as linked
to a wider community. From the neighbouring town, Comet, Upward's rival,
to Regina where difficult surgical cases have had to be sent, or Saskatoon
where Doc will live in his retirement, or Winnipeg where Nick had gone to
live with a "Ukrainian" family, Upward is impinged upon by the larger West
as Horizon was not. The Second World War, moreover, has radically chal-
lenged Upward's previously constructed social categories: when Nick and
Dunc meet in England, Nick is both a medical doctor and a Captain in the
Canadian army, and now literally outranks Duncan. And Dunc's gesture in
using his acquaintance with Nick to impress Caroline when they are courting
in England ("I wanted her to know that in Upward they weren't all horses

big and dumb like me" [52]) prefigures the shift in power which Dunc will effect in post-war Upward in bringing Nick to town in 1948.[9]

Given the temporal relationship between *As for Me and My House* and *Sawbones Memorial*, so that the latter can be seen as succeeding the former in historical time, and given the fact that the cultural hegemony that militated against the foreigner in the first novel has clearly collapsed by the time of the second, ought one to see Ross as having constructed a single combined narrative of "progressive emergence" attesting to the triumph of the "foreigner" in the Canadian West?

It seems not, for just as Ross has undercut the sense of cultural solidarity inherent in *Horizon's* story of its foreigner, he undercuts in *Sawbones Memorial* the myth of ethnic triumph that Nick Miller's story might seem to represent. In the first place, Upward's categories ("white" and "nonwhite") have permitted Nick to slip through, for he is "white" and cannot, by whatever verbal sleight of tongue Upward attempts, be confined to the category of "non-white." But that category holds firm, still proves efficacious, when it comes to the Chinese immigrants: while invited, Charlie Wong and Wing Ling Ching do not show up at Doc Hunter's reception (32); ever "polite," they still acquiesce, it seems, to Upward's expectation that because they are "not white" they must "try harder," and "[keep] out of things" (55).

Even more problematic is Nick's own transformation from "hunky" to "Dr. Miller." That Nick's victory is to some extent Pyrrhic is suggested by the way in which he has had to erase his personal identity in order to ensure public success. In re-naming himself—dropping "a few Ukrainian z's and s's" so as to become a "Miller" (21), and acquiring the title *Dr.* Miller, a way of getting around the Ukrainian name "Nick"—he has clearly turned his back on his personal past, and particularly on his mother, "Big Anna." Whether Anna arranged for Doc Hunter to father Nick or simply arranged for Doc Hunter to think that he fathered him, it is she who has in fact engineered Nick's escape from the underclass to which he had been consigned by Upward. That the indomitable Doc Hunter takes Nick up, sees himself as Nick's "Daddy" (138), seemingly educates him, then stage-manages his triumphant re-entry into Upward in 1948, is all owing to a single calculated act ("'You vant?'") on Anna's part on a Wednesday afternoon in January 1915 (135). That Nick is now "hunky-dory" (and indeed a certified blond-haired, blue-eyed "hunk," appropriate game for the glamorous and predatory Miss Carmichael) is Anna's doing. In "bleaching himself" (55), in eradicating all traces of his parents, his history, and his ethnicity, it seems evident that Nick Miller has not so much beaten Upward as joined it on its own terms in an act of erasure, of silent complicity with the very categories he appears at first glance to have successfully resisted.

My interest in Ross's foreigners, and in a tandem reading of *As for Me and My House* and *Sawbones Memorial* which focuses on his "hunkies," is not particularly thematic. The plight of the immigrant might be emphasized in reading these texts, it is true, given Ross's rendering of both Steve Kulanich and Nick Miller as voiceless—as silent or nearly so.[10] If silence is "the condition of visible ethnicity" and if "articulating the silence" is the central task of writers who deal with immigrant experience, as Gary Willis suggests (243), then Ross might be read as a writer of immigrant experience.[11] Similarly, it is possible to see parallels between Ross's foreigners and other kinds of marginalized figures in his fiction. The figure of the "other woman" (like Judith West in *As for Me and My House* or Maisie Bell in *Sawbones Memorial*) is one such similarly silenced constituency. Another is the homosexual presence in Ross's small towns. Benny Fox in *Sawbones Memorial* is repeatedly linked as cultural outsider with Nick Miller, with whom he "had a lot in common" (98). And some might make a related case with respect to Philip in *As for Me and My House*—whom Frances Kaye, at least, has convincingly seen as latently homosexual. His foreigners, then, could be seen as representing, or even standing in for, marginalized groups whom, for one reason or another, Ross has chosen not to foreground in these novels.

My own concern, however, is less with a drive towards any particular "meaning" with respect to Ross's "foreigners" than it is with seeing Ross as a kind of cultural historian whose stories participate in what Jane Tompkins calls the "cultural work"[12] of recovering voices and figures from the past. In attending to those who are marginalized in, or indeed absent from, other accounts of a particular historical moment, and in documenting significant shifts in social power that are evident over time with respect to these "others," Ross raises questions about hegemonic power and its abuse—in social practice, to be sure, but more significantly in the *documenting* of social practice, which is known as "history."

Indeed, it is in this last regard—that of the writing of "history"—that Ross excels, it seems to me. Through what Clifford Geertz has called "local knowledge" and "thick description,"[13] Ross manages to register competing social forces, contradictory strains, and persistent cultural instability as characterizing the experience of Horizon and Upward. That is, rather than offering a monolithic, static view of a particular cultural moment, Ross constantly undercuts the unitary, the univocal, and produces instead a dynamic field of unresolved social conflict wherein one can "affirm" nothing without qualification. In his refusal to be reductive (or readily reducible), then, Sinclair Ross is at his contentious best in novels like *As for Me and My House* and *Sawbones Memorial*, novels that clearly develop out of his own experience in the small towns of the Canadian West in the first half of the twentieth century.

NOTES

1. *Oxford English Dictionary*, 2nd ed. (London: Oxford University Press, 1989), 7: 496.

2.   For a survey of the usage of "hunky" and "bohunk," see the *Oxford English Dictionary*, 496, and *A Dictionary of Americanisms on Historical Principles*, 850. According to these sources, these terms make their literary appearance as contemporary slang in early twentieth-century realist fiction such as that of Sinclair Lewis (*The Man Who Knew Coolidge*, 1928), John Dos Passos (*42nd Parallel*, 1930), and John O'Hara (*Appointment in Samara*, 1934). Canadian literary use of the terms tends to occur later and in works that fictionalize the recent past, such as Hugh Garner's "Hunky" (1963) and Robert Kroetsch's *But We are Exiles* (1965), as well as Ross's own *Sawbones Memorial* (1974).

3.   *The Compact Edition of the Oxford English Dictionary*, 2 vols. (London: Oxford University Press, 1971), 1: 1349.

4.   My use of this phrase owes something to Brook Thomas's attempt to distinguish between the emphasis on progress that characterizes traditional historicism and the attempt by new historicism (shaped as it is by post-structuralism and deconstruction) to avoid teleology in writing of the past. Thomas says, for example, that ". . . de Man's work is not an escape from history but an effort to make us rethink what we mean by 'history.' Most importantly it challenges the notion that history is a chronological development through linear time, a notion of history assumed by narratives of progressive emergence." Brook Thomas, *The New Historicism and Other Old-Fashioned Topics* (Princeton, New Jersey: Princeton University Press, 1991), 35.

5.   Other historical accounts of the period also record the "cultural gaze" which habitually fixed, categorized, and judged the unskilled Eastern European immigrant as a type: "the Galicians are all mighty noise makers and fighters, crazy guys," writes a Dutch immigrant, Willem de Gelder, in *A Dutch Homesteader on the Prairies*, trans. Herman Ganzevoort (Toronto: University of Toronto Press, 1973), 16. The Galicians are "one of Western Canada's knottiest problems—there are so many of them," writes Elizabeth B. Mitchell in 1915, in *In Western Canada Before the War: Impressions of Early Twentieth Century Prairie Communities*, intro. Susan Jackel (Saskatoon: Western Producer Prairie Books, 1981), 11–12. "That's what we called them, Bohunks. Today it's an insult, they don't like it, but then it was the same as calling a Scotsman Scotty," declares one of Barry Broadfoot's pioneers, oblivious to the difference between hegemonic and non-hegemonic epithets, in *The Pioneer Years 1895–1914: Memories of Settlers Who Opened the West* (Toronto: Doubleday Canada, 1976), 161.

6.   The phrase echoes J. S. Woodsworth's assimilationist tract, *Strangers Within Our Gates*, intro. Marilyn Barber (1909; rpt. Toronto: University of Toronto Press, 1972).

7.   Organizations such as the YMCA, Frontier College, and the Protestant churches were instruments of this public policy, offering programs designed to assimilate Western Canadian immigrants. O. W. Gerus and J. E. Rea, *The Ukrainians in Canada* (Ottawa: Canadian Historical Association, 1985), 10.

8.   Whether Upward's recorded expressions of such feelings really do represent an escalation in anti-foreigner sentiment in comparison to Horizon, though, is a moot point, given the way the novels are "told." *As for Me and My House*, after all, is narrated by a single person, a minister's wife, around whom epithets like "hunky" might tend to be suppressed—or whose delicacy might militate against reproducing them if in fact she heard them. The structure of *Sawbones Memorial*

(with its montage of spoken and unspoken voices unmediated by a single narrative perspective), as well as the kind of social experience it depicts (a party where the included can derogate the excluded with impunity), more readily admits expression of the raw, the crude, and the xenophobic in characterizing the way towns like Upward *and* Horizon spoke of their foreigners.

9.   Gerus and Rea observe that the Second World War generally "impelled" Ukrainian-Canadians (and presumably other Slavic-Canadians) "closer to the mainstream of national life." That so many of them enlisted, and served so heroically (as in the case of the Winnipeg Grenadiers, with its high proportion of Ukrainian Canadians), "helped to make [them] more acceptable in the eyes of the host society" (15).

10.   Nick is not only absent from the narrative, but also virtually unquoted in *Saw-bones Memorial*. And by my count Steve makes only four statements in *As for Me and My House*: "I'd like to be on [Harlequin] when he jumps like that"; "And I wouldn't fall off either"; "I do go riding—and I don't fall off" (41); and, about his new suit, "I was wondering if you knew that altogether I've got ten pockets" (68).

11.   Gary Willis, "Speaking the Silence: Joy Kogawa's *Obasan*," *Studies in Canadian Literature* 12 (1987): 239–50; related articles include Robert Kroetsch, "The Grammar of Silence: Narrative Pattern in Ethnic Writing," *Canadian Literature* 106 (1985): 65–74 and Terrence L. Craig, "F. P. Grove and the 'Alien' Immigrant in the West," *Journal of Canadian Studies* 20 (1985): 92–100.

12.   Jane Tompkins, *Sensational Designs: The Cultural Work of American Fiction* (New York: Oxford, 1985).

13.   Clifford Geertz, *Local Knowledge* (New York: Basic Books, 1983).

WORKS CITED

Broadfoot, Barry, *The Pioneer Years 1895–1914: Memories of Settlers Who Opened the West*. Toronto: Doubleday Canada, 1976.

Collins Concise Dictionary of the English Language. 2nd ed. (London and Glasgow: William Collins Sons & Co., 1988.

Compact Edition of the Oxford English Dictionary. 2 vols. London: Oxford University Press, 1971.

Craig, Terrence L. "F. P. Grove and the 'Alien' Immigrant in the West." *Journal of Canadian Studies* 20 (1985), 92–100.

de Gelder, Willem. *A Dutch Homesteader on the Prairies: The Letters of Willem de Gelder 1910–13*. Intro. and trans. Herman Ganzevoort. Toronto: University of Toronto Press, 1973.

Gallagher, Catherine. "Marxism and the New Historicism." In *The New Historicism*. Ed. H. Aram Veeser. New York and London: Routledge, 1989, 37–48.

Geertz, Clifford. *Local Knowledge*. New York: Basic Books, 1983.

Gerus, O. W., and J. E. Rea. *The Ukrainians in Canada*. Ottawa: Canadian Historical Association, 1985 (Canadian Ethnic Group Series, No. 10).

Kaye, Frances W. "Sinclair Ross's Use of George Sand and Frederic Chopin as Models for the Bentleys." *Essays on Canadian Writing* 33 (1986), 100–11.

Kroetsch, Robert. "The Grammar of Silence: Narrative Pattern in Ethnic Writing. *Canadian Literature* 106 (1985), 65–74.

Mathews, Mitford M., ed. *A Dictionary of Americanisms on Historical Principles.* Chicago: University of Chicago Press, 1951.

Mitchell, Elizabeth B. *In Western Canada Before the War: Impressions of Early Twentieth Century Prairie Communities.* Intro. Susan Jackel. Saskatoon: Western Producer Prairie Books, 1981.

Oxford English Dictionary. 2nd ed. London: Oxford University Press, 1989.

Ross, Morton L. "The Canonization of *As for Me and My House*: A Case Study." In *Figures in a Ground: Canadian Essays on Modern Literature Collected in Honor of Sheila Watson.* Ed. Diane Bessai and David Jackel. Saskatoon: Western Producer Prairie Books, 1978, 189–205.

Ross, Sinclair. *As for Me and My House.* 1941. Toronto: McClelland and Stewart, 1957. New Canadian Library edition.

———. *Sawbones Memorial.* Toronto: McClelland and Stewart, 1974.

Thomas, Brook. *The New Historicism and Other Old-Fashioned Topics.* Princeton, New Jersey: Princeton University Press, 1991.

Tompkins, Jane. *Sensational Designs: The Cultural Work of American Fiction.* New York: Oxford, 1985.

White, Hayden. "New Historicism: A Comment." In *The New Historicism.* Ed. H. Aram Veeser. New York and London: Routledge, 1989, 293–302.

Willis, Gary. "Speaking the Silence: Joy Kogawa's *Obasan.*" *Studies in Canadian Literature* 12 (1987), 239–50.

Woodsworth, J. S. *Strangers within Our Gates.* Intro. Marilyn Barber. Toronto: University of Toronto Press, 1972.

Name people when we want to accost them "Nick the Hunky" (104)
severe and judgemental attitudes in Mrs B's naming of this storefront
art.

Cultural Codes — nouns.
Lexical Domains — Sunday Afternoon / Preacher's Wife.
(Presbyterianisms — Strict Communions — observance of Sabbath —
eat only cold food.
whole day spent in Silence / No Movement)
These attitudes come down to Ross thru' mother.
Extreme Asceticism.
Words & power they have thru' all associations in different cultural
positions / aspects.

Mrs B intends her naming to be beyond equivocation, but
interpreted by reader differently.
Verbs omitted. Action (verb) evident in the naming.
"The minister's wife and Sunday afternoon" (HOUSE 28)

"It" is closed / grounded within confines

"Lexical domains" / "semantic domains"

An Awful Stumbling Towards Names: Ross and the (Un)Common Noun

DENNIS COOLEY

Our readings of contemporary texts are replete with awareness of gender and of how gender constitutes texts. We are growing accustomed, too, to tracing the female figure as she is named, unnamed, misnamed, renamed. We measure that naming, knowing how crucial it is to definitions of the self and to ideologies that constrain those definitions.

We find ourselves in Sinclair Ross turning to Mrs. Bentley, that intriguing figure who, even as she presides over her own text in *As for Me and My House*, represents herself only within the double removal of her name: no maiden name, no personal name. Just Mrs. Bentley, that bent name. So engendered, she is inserted into a lexical set which in a sense obliterates her and which perhaps denies her a self sufficient to become the artist she has always wanted to be. New name, changed name. She struggles under something like a pseudonym, false name, name which misrepresents. The pseudonym masks the real self, misleads the reader. I am Mrs. Bentley, our narrator tells us, but we know she is not, not really, or not just. That is obvious enough.

She is only one such figure in Ross. They are everywhere, these characters who wrestle with nouns, names—synonyms, antonyms, homonyms, anonyms, pseudonyms, patronyms; assumed names, partial names, place names, initialled names, shared names, nicknames, shortened names, aliases, symbolic names, secret names, repressed names, Biblical names.[1] There are proper names and common names, misnomers, unavailable nouns, circumlocutions, family names, unspeakable nouns, pro-nouns.

We "name" people when we mean to censure them. We call them names. There is "popery" and "bad blood." What is more, "bad blood was bad blood and always would be," we learn from the town bigots in Horizon

(72). These are the names of exclusion, all those named into the margins: "Nick the Hunky" (37) and the "Scarlet Woman" (23), for example (these in *Sawbones Memorial*). "We called Benny names too," one of the characters in *Sawbones Memorial* confesses (41). Consider the name the locals have chosen for Nick Miller—"Nick the Hunky." It goes a long way to explaining his change in name to Miller, "just short of a few Ukrainian z's and s's," as one character describes it (25). The appositive, "Hunky," reconstitutes the actual name, "Nick," and constricts it. The construction consigns the name to some realm of fixed and inescapable limits that will not allow Nick even his own new naming. In return, in retaliation, Nick "must have had names in Ukrainian for me too," Dunc says (41).

We call names, then, name names, call people by their names, hold positions in name only, blacken names, take names in vain, make names for ourselves. The list goes on. Mrs. Bentley—she who years earlier gave birth to a baby who never rose into the presence of an actual name—is perhaps only the best known and most obvious example of characters who labour towards a naming whose occasion is for them by no means certain or desirable.

*   *   *   *   *

To name. The varieties of name. The antonym for one. She's good at that, Mrs. B.—the contra-diction, she brooks no other naming. There shall be no other names before her. There is her first description of Philip's painting. "And as usual he's been drawing again." How do we read that "as usual"? Approving (that's my boy)? Snide (wouldn't you know it, the fool)? How do we hear Mrs. B. when she says "sure enough," there was a painting? She describes this painting in some detail, insists on how its Main Street scene is "like all the rest" (7), consigns the subjects to a category which perhaps blinds her to those people she so easily judges, so quick is she to name unflatteringly. Philip wrote a book once, she says, but "it was a failure, of course" (45). Of course. How sure she is in her own naming:

> False fronts *ought* to be laughed at, *never* understood or pitied. They're such outlandish things, the front of a store built up to look like a second storey. They *ought always* to be seen that way, pretentious, ridiculous, *never* as Philip sees them, stricken with a look of self-awareness and futility. (7, my emphasis)

He sympathizes, she scorns. Even in the excruciating uncertainty which infects Mrs. B's life, perhaps because of that very doubt, her discourse bristles with modalities: all those oughts and nevers, the severe and judgemental adjectives appended to her namings. "It's all there," she adds, in language stripped of equivocation (7). Apparently.

For Mrs. Bentley cannot so easily name herself.[2] In a culture in which as a rule naming is in others' hands, she is hardly allowed to do so. Even as she mocks whatever names present themselves to her, or are presented to her, she chafes under them, the gall of their inevitability, their excruciating unfairness. Mrs. Lawson, who manages her own husband like a terrier round a Clyde, scolds him for asking Mrs. Bentley to play a hoe-down: "'The minister's wife, and Sunday afternoon,' Mrs. Lawson snapped at him" (28). What do we make of those two noun phrases brought into familiarity, set in some equivalence across the coordinate construction, without even the felt need for a verb? Mrs. Lawson speaks in such surety of definition, she can only imagine that whatever cultural codes impinge upon the noun "Sunday afternoon" hold equally for whatever it is she understands "the minister's wife" to mean as falling within its ambit. Evidently the mere naming is enough, each phrase reciprocal to the other. More accurately, we might suppose that the lexical domain "Sunday afternoon" in her economy subsumes the smaller domain "the minister's wife," swallows it within its hierarchy. There is no need to predicate so obvious a conjunction. Within the cultural names available Mrs. Lawson feels no need for elaboration. Her terms, she knows, will be taken for simple and known truth.

In these definitions Mrs. Bentley is further bent from personal presence into a role defined by Puritan limits. She is all the more removed from self-definition in becoming the object of someone else's possession—"the minister's wife." She is doubly positioned in a naming which makes her known in a marital relationship and in a religious-moral domain. In either case her name is beholden to someone else: her husband's profession, her husband's ownership. At the same time she is herself possessive, possessed with ownership. The name of the book itself, with its pronouns, is in the first-person as far as Mrs. Bentley is concerned.[3] Needless to say, when others do the naming it does not always sit well with her.

Something happens, then, when Mrs. Bird, neighbour, announcer of kinship, arrives to declare that she herself is an appendage to her husband, he who figures in her account as "the doctor" and "Dr. Bird." Mrs. Bentley, only too aware of such naming, writes that evening in her diary: "'It will be made up to him [Dr. Bird] though,' the parson's wife remembered to say" (29), then silently adds, a few minutes later, "said the parson's wife appropriately" (30). The irony in Mrs. Bentley's parodies does not altogether protect her. Nor does the facetious inversion in syntax, "said the parson's wife," even as it ridicules the prissy roles she is asked to assume, the pinching names she is asked to wear. Not even that inversion enables her to ward off unwanted namings.

A measure of how much she loses herself, loses control over the names by which she is known, and under whose edicts she exists, is her propensity here to designate herself in the third person. Even as she mocks that grammar—"I met the preacher's wife" (31)—she accedes to it, falls prey to what substitutions complete the syntax.

And yet, she thinks, she must "keep myself intact" (13), must guard against "yielding my identity" (22). She needs to bring those predicates back under her own jurisdiction, regain the nouns that trail frighteningly off the ends of her verbs. Needs, too, to shake off other names, metonymies—all the "Horizons" she forever moves into and out of—which threaten to engulf her.

*   *   *   *

Ventriloquism of speaker (Mrs. B.)
Speaks for Ross_ But this is voice -judgmental

She is not without her resources, this Mrs. Bentley. For all her subjection to others' namings, and for all her restlessness under them, she is herself more than willing to glue her own names onto the world. To apply herself. "The real trouble is Philip himself" (13), she announces at one point. The familiarity of her idiom should not allow us to overlook the radical nature of her equation. She puts "real trouble" and "Philip" into a mutual relationship by virtue of that copula. It's not that Philip causes trouble (and therefore can be presumed able to mend his ways); Philip *is* trouble. Mrs. Bentley, as we see in this instance, habitually writes her world as a field of fixed nouns. "Philip's a born dreamer" (70), she decides, "It's a man's way, I suppose, and a woman's," "I knew that with Philip it was the only way," "He was the kind to" (22). There is more of this construction, lots more: "it's a sullen, hopeless kind," "He's cold and skeptical," "He's not the kind to" (24). How often the nomination falls on the heels of that verb, a verb that supposes the name, the naming, exists beyond recall or revision. How little doubt the verb permits, what small oppositions it will tolerate.

The grammar predicates a world of known and inalterable identities, a completion that is so sufficient there is no room for additions or alternatives, virtually no chance to reconstitute yourself or to slough off namings. Nouns that are stable. Interesting, too, how (in these examples at least) the nominative—"it"—that begets the predicate permits virtually any completion, insists upon no constraints. "It" could be anything. "It," it turns out, across that small buzz we hear as "is" and "was," is something else. "It" is something more definite, more narrowly delimited. A structure of open possibilities gives way to a more constricted, more certainly constructed, denomination. Is, was: this, that; one name after the other.

A language of definition, then. Mrs. Bentley speaks of essence, immutability. "He was the kind" (22), "He's a failure," "I'm a failure" (23), "Horizon is his due" (24). And yet, as we know, these names will not hold, do not hold. What's needed, and what arrives, finally, is the active verb, the transitive verb, that dissolves that grammar of being into a new nomination. A verb that will lift Mrs. Bentley and her world from stasis of definition and empower a narrative in which she and others actually can *do* something.

*   *   *   *   *

Reminds me of Buss article.
Mrs. B naming her characters —
she then can manipulate them as she wants

It is not easy for her to escape her encumbrance of naming, however. Once she discovers, or thinks she discovers, Philip's affair with Judith, she is thrown into a consternation whose terms fall regressively into a Puritan rhetoric. As she struggles with the trauma, she lapses into a naming so predictable and so exclusive in its binaries that it blinds her to other namings and hence impedes her chances of understanding in other ways what has happened. Discovering what she takes to be "adultery," she immediately thinks she has "a right now to be free," a revealing evaluation, one that may say something about her interest in Paul. Her next thoughts turn towards "my house" and hopes to get Judith "out of the house." The semantic domains "my house" and "adultery" evidently cannot overlap for her, so set is she on her categories. The name "adultery" cannot at any edge or to any degree impinge upon the naming she proprietarily would observe in "my house." Hence the agency of semantic contamination, Judith, must be removed. In every extent the domains must be kept apart: if Judith means "anything" to him, he would "hate me" now. Mrs. Bentley would herself "hate" a first husband if Philip later happened along. "But Judith—another woman—do I mean then so little to him? Does she do just as well?" "Another woman," "so little," "just as well" (164)—lexia of hurt, yes, but terms of the strictest exclusion as well: love / hate, love me / hate her. Mrs. Bentley insists on a naming that allows no nuance and no other interpretations. She has already admitted, "I haven't much to tempt him [Philip] with" (19) and yet she does not understand, cannot bring herself to admit, to name, a condition within which her husband might want or even seek another woman. We see how this might happen: Mrs. Bentley's tight lips, her desire to manage and direct; we see also Judith's breasts, her voice, her strong response to Philip's art. He perhaps desires no more than his wife desires—something more, something more gratifying or exciting. Though she finally admits to her own attraction to Paul after the longest time of denying it exists, she still enforces her sharp Puritan dichotomies on Philip.

*   *   *   *   *

It may well be that Mrs. Bentley *does* do something significant when in the end *she* decides on the name for Judith's baby. Though she perennially has assented to Paul Kirby's namings, here in the end she shows no reticence whatsoever in deciding on a name: "My baby—his baby—all I have of him. It's going to be a boy, of course, and I'm going to call him Philip too" (207).[4] She does this, you will recall, in the face of Philip's doubts. Should there be two with the same name? "'Sometimes you won't know which of us is which'" (216). The moment stands out for us. Mrs. Bentley, who in some ways wants fixed names and fixing names for others, here seeks the ambiguity of a destabilized name: one signifier, two signifieds. She persists in her celebrated last words, unspoken words, which end the novel: "That's right, Philip. I want it so" (216). Philip, we remember, who by virtue of his clerical role perhaps, as one who baptizes, has up until now been entrusted with whatever naming has been needed. It is he who christens El Greco (107), and it is he, much to his wife's chagrin, who chooses not to rename Minnie (139–40).[5]

The change in jurisdiction is not a total surprise, however, for Mrs. Bentley has shown a propensity for names and passing out names all along. It is she, thinking of how oil paints ooze and glisten (how tactile she is, so devoid of touch she trembles in thought of it), who confesses to herself: "I used to like the names the colors had myself—*terre verte* and *sienna*, *gamboge*, *vermilion lake*, *ultramarine*—just as names they suggested so much that the colors themselves always fell a little flat" (107). This is quite a run of names —Italian, French, Latin, Cambodian—for someone so susceptible to the parsimonies of a Puritan economy that she measures out her emotion in the name of "thrift" and of what is "waste" or "frugal" or "spendthrift" (30, 31, 38, 134, 136 for examples). Extravagant, exotic, rare, romantic—these names speak of intensity (bright yellow, bright red, deep blue), of shaking off the smallnesses her life is burred with. They glow with something more than she commonly experiences. They permit, brief flares, an escape from the high-mindedness of meaning. They release Mrs. Bentley into the pleasures of a naming which exceeds "reality." In linguistic terms we would say this naming, these signifiers, shrug off the constraints of signifieds. The passage is so little beholden to the "world," it opens some space for Mrs. B. to operate briefly in what approaches—how "childish," how irresponsible— a free play of namings.

She can be, for a moment, even faintly risqué, this Mrs. B., in her naming. She approves of Steve's facetious name for their tilting outhouse, the Leaning Tower of Pisa: "A rather good name too, by virtue of a bad pronunciation," she adds wickedly (83). Names, she knows, can carry cachet. Proper names can. She invokes Thomas Carlyle's name—received name, renowned name (re-nouned name, a renaming in homage) with its power to endorse and legitimize—to bolster her romantic precepts (135). El Greco becomes so "handsome" and "almost graceful," so replete with "courtly, old-world elegance," Mrs. Bentley thinks, they perhaps should consider promoting him (from Philip's naming) by calling him "Romney" or "Gainsborough" (139).[6] She flirts here with the possibilities of becoming a bestower of names, fairly humming with romantic and aristocratic reverberations. She's nursed a hankering to be a conferer of names all along, then, and is more than ready to seize the prerogative when the chance comes.

*   *   *   *   *

She's more than willing, too, to name "the real Philip." There is, she claims, "The Philip before the Horizons" (29), there is "the old Philip" (165), "the real one" (166), "the old Philip, the one I've always known" (177). There is an objectionable Philip who upsets her with his laughter; this one "wasn't Philip" and she is able "to restore him to his actual self" (191). For her, there is a true self and a false self. She confidently names both, even if in reversal of her expectations: there is once in a while "the one I've always known" and "the real one" (177). The naming coincides with a Puritan narrative and its lost self or undiscovered self whose task it is one's to recover or to discern and so to bring to redemption.

Believing identity is preserved in a name, Mrs. Bentley perseveres in her reiterations. This, this one I object to, do not like this Philip, the one who acts beyond my ambit of safe naming—he is not Philip, Philip is the one *I* know, *I* name. There is a kind of egotism in this, it seems to me. She *knows* and will place Philip forever within the ambit of a name she fits him with and confines him to—*this* name, *these* properties. Once more her namings or her structure of naming may in its tendency towards exclusive binaries—false self, real self—get in the way of understanding.[7]

Ultimately, she makes even greater inroads on Philip Bentley's name. In taking charge of their future, she usurps the name, speaks on his behalf, *in his name*. "I write dunning letters every other week in Philip's name" (192). She so fully appropriates his name, she presumes to speak on his behalf —more, as if she *were* Philip. She shelters herself under that proper noun, improperly speaks as if it were hers to use. She so utterly takes over the name, she presumes to have its voice—together with its authority and intention, its guarantee that the signature whose emblem she makes would endorse what she has written. If within the statutes of matrimony Mrs. Bentley has surrendered with her maiden name a profound part of herself, here she acts with a vengeance to take over her adopted marital name—to so obliterate the distinctions between herself and her husband that she will occupy all space beneath his name, become signifier to a signified whose outward manifestation would be the very name she takes so totally unto herself.[8]

There is another side to her use of the Bentley name. Even as she lays claim so dubiously to Philip Bentley's name, she generously uses it to provide shelter and opportunity, legitimacy too. In a flurry of negations and commands, Mrs. Bentley instructs Philip on what he is to say to Judith: "I told him he must," "I want," "I won't let her," "Make it clear," "Tell her," "You tell her." "Tell her that we can give her child opportunity and a name" (156). Here the name is not so much lent as bestowed. Mrs. Bentley would do Judith and her baby a genuine favour by bringing the child within the Bentley household and housing it within the Bentley name. The gesture is not simply an act of presumption to bring someone in under her (second-hand) name, for to go with no name or the wrong name into the world, this world with its Puritan rules, would be ruinous, as she well knows. Fully aware of these political realities, Mrs. Bentley offers a family name, would share a good name, which would at once mask improper origins and promise a privileged upbringing.

* * * * *

There are moments when Mrs. Bentley's rigid grammar of definitions puts her on the edge of a truth she cannot know: "It's Judith tonight he's drawing" (33), she says, the odd syntax permitting, for just a moment, the expression "It's Judith." Yes. It *is* Judith.

* * * * *

Other namings. Intertextual namings? So we find in the pale, powerfully voiced Judith West a namesake to the tempestuous Judith Gare in Martha Ostenso's *Wild Geese*. Philip: yes, we know his name says he is a lover of horses, but is he? What about Miss Twill and Mrs. Wenderby in *As for Me and My House*? Miss Wiggins, drill-master music teacher in "Cornet at Night"? They could be names out of Dickens (a childhood author to Ross), characters in fealty to their names. The same could be said for Sonny and Mad, "crazy names" in *Whir of Gold*, "craziest names you ever heard of" (1). The names, L. K. MacKendrick notes, locate the two in an intriguing relationship. "Mad" spelled backwards is "dam" or "mother," and it is she who offers "Sonny" love and care.[9]

Then there is Mrs. Paynter in *The Well*. Mrs. Paynter, the self-righteous keeper of morality, is filled with complaints about her aches and pains: "Mrs. Paynter, ostentatiously sabbath-minded, however godless the others might be, funerary and severe in black silk and jet beads, sat down on the chesterfield between the two Chris's" (110).

* * * * *

There's Paul Kirby too (curber, restrainer?). If there is a character in Canadian fiction more obsessed with names I can't think of one. Here are the etymologies he comes up with:

- noticing Mrs. Bentley's book of organ music, he tells her that "*offertory* comes from a word meaning *sacrifice*." It is in this same scene that he announces he is a philologist: "Philologist, you know—lover of words" (11)
- later that day when the Bentleys and Paul get stuck, he remembers that the word "weary" comes from a word that means "to walk across wet ground" (12)[10]
- "the word *automobile* is a very corrupt one, a hack and unscholarly job of splicing a Greek prefix to a Latin root, the sort of thing that in the best philological circles simply isn't done. Himself he prefers

car, a good, straightforward Celtic word, that originally meant *war chariot*" (26). A few hours later, he lets Mrs. Bentley know that religion is based on a desire to control the weather: "pagans singing Christian hymns . . . *pagan*, you know, originally that's exactly what it meant, *country dweller*" (26–27)[11]

- "*nausea* is from a Greek word meaning *ship* and is, therefore, etymologically speaking, an impossibility on dry land" and it is more correct to say "company" instead of "guests" because "company" means "the ones you break bread with—the most appropriate word of all" (47)
- dressing and playing cowboy for Mrs. Bentley, Paul "went philological then—*mustang* meant *stray*, *pinto* meant *painted*, a skewbald was a pinto with markings any color but black" (54)
- the name *sponge* cake is a corrupted form of *Spanish* cake (63)
- fuchsia is named after somebody whose name this was (an eponym) (71)
- *belly*, he announces to a comically priggish Mrs. Bentley (though he refrains from laying out its origins) is a perfectly fine word (92).[12]

The pattern comes to a climax when Paul finds Mrs. Bentley in the garden and lets go in a veritable orgy of names:

> Did I know, he asked, that *garden* and *yard* and *court* were etymologically all related? That a king's pomp and retinue is descended from a peasant's chicken run? *Paling*, too, he said, with a nod toward the fence, there was another social climber: in actual possession of the palace now that once it guarded as a humble palisade. (101)

Paul goes on to comment on what radical alterations have occurred in the use of *retaliate*, a word that once meant "to reply in kind, kindly or vindictively," then turns (or at least Mrs. Bentley in her journal turns) to a more daring series of entries which have gained a bit of attention: "You learn a lot from a philologist. Cupid, he says, has given us *cupidity*, Eros, *erotic*, Venus, *venereal*, and Aphrodite, *aphrodisiac*" (101). And that, that outrageous entry, dated June 7, is for some time the last of Paul's entries, entreaties every one of them. Perhaps. Perhaps not. Paul does pop up at the end of June to report the latest in his struggles with Mrs. Wenderby. She warns him "that if he insists on saying *sweat* in the classroom instead of *perspiration* she'll use her influence to have the school board ask him to resign" (120). He returns from the hiatus of summer holidays, pages later, to gloss the Bentleys' lives in a series of pointed notes:

- a painter's easel is "a little ass," unkind shot at Philip (137)[13]
- "enthusiasm" means "the *god within*," he says "dryly" (138)
- a *fool* is a *windbag* (169)[14]
- a "fly-trap" is what you create when you strike one of your tor-

mentors: the rest, attracted, swarm quickly around, make your suffering worse (174–75)

– a "coyote" means "*half-breed*" and it should be pronounced in three syllables instead of two (179)

– a raven is like a writing-desk, he says "brusquely" and "cryptically" (208)[15]

– the name "Philip" means "'a lover of horses'" (213)[16]

– "Did I know, he asked gravely, that in the early ages of our race it was imitation of just such a little wail as this [the baby Philip's cry] that had given us some of our noblest words, like father, and patriarch, and paternity" (213).[17]

This is an intriguing list of announcements, tantalizing as much in its sequence as its contents. True, Paul is a structural convenience enabling Ross to play with meanings he could not so readily otherwise have introduced into his realist text. It is true, too, that his unrestrained penchant means Ross risks losing our sympathies for him, and patience with the book, as readers have done. Yet we make something of Paul himself, that inveterate and telling namer. As "philologist," his name perhaps puts him into further association with Philip, the suffixes of their names rhyming them into rivals or doubles—these two men of the word. For it is Paul who announces himself as a "lover of words." Not a lover of women evidently, but a lover of words. As a namer of names, is he beholden to their sources and histories? Is he neglectful finally of the very woman he woos, more committed to the origins of names than their effects and meanings? Although Mrs. Bentley, infatuated with Paul in ways she cannot admit, decides Paul is a poet, we wonder. Is he? Certainly not in any desire to use words in new ways. He does not push, as a poet might, into neologism, nor does he advance into a dominion where the word is made flesh. Paul's names are determined and confirming. His names, in other words, are for the most part confined to what once was.

Paul, full as is his Biblical namesake with missionary zeal, would fulfil the word.[18] Even as he sends his own word into the world, he would be guided by the already written. Textually bound, he would insert those traces, that residue, into the present moment, would have us read the present under governance of the past, precedents whose erosions have occurred in time. Even as Paul gives us the word, faithful to its source before dissemination and corruption have set in, he is monkish in his ministrations. He would appear to be so in his zeal to instruct. When we recognize that Paul does not confine himself to reporting etymologies, but extends into matters of usage and pronunciation, this becomes even clearer. In a number of his interventions, then, he actively proscribes: "automobiles" is an objectionable construction; "nausea" perhaps shouldn't happen or cannot happen in Saskatchewan, a place where you should have "company" instead of guests; "belly" will do as a word, and so on.

Is he monkish too in his evasions, his scholarly niceties? His oblique namings? Why that sudden lapse in fall, when his etymologies arguably turn cranky and mysterious? The nature of his change takes on even more radical significance when we remind ourselves it is Philip who, in the interim between Paul's two runs of etymologies, gives Mrs. Bentley another etymology. The word *umber*, he tells her, comes from a word that means shade, shadow, gives us the *umbrella* (107).

We detect, clearly, an escalation in Paul's reports. The first tend to be short, modest, inoffensive. At this stage lexia run towards dailiness or what for Mrs. Bentley in Horizon would be dailiness—church, travel, visiting, horses, food, flowers. As his ties with Mrs. Bentley tighten, his own offerings, his gallant sacrifices, take on more and more suggestion, become in a sense more and more provocative. They take a new turn in his talk of bellies, culminate—climax one might say—in that flurry of names which, even as they perhaps criticize Mrs. B. (Mrs. B. the chatelaine, hoity-toity), woo her too. Paul, the courtly lover, speaks of courts and gardens, hints of carnal pleasures before trailing off next fall into dry and brusque and grave offerings, statements that ring possibly with uncertainty and despair. No wonder. These are daring things he has said to her, transgressions of a shocking sort: drastic words to say to the Puritan wife of a Puritan minister in Puritan small-town Saskatchewan. What is this naming, oblique though it may be, of the erotic, venereal, the aphroditic? Who is this Paul, hopes up, brought into likeness with a Hereford bull beneath whose sire Mrs. Bentley—glad "to escape the Horizon matrons for awhile"—stretches in bed? The hints of reprieve from a narrow morality are distinct and become more sharply focused when we see how Mrs. Bentley speaks of the pictures that adorn her room. There is a curious naming here too. It is "Gallant Lad the Third" under whose picture she lies. We learn more. This bull's son is alive and kicking, "carrying on" is what Mrs. Bentley is led to believe. This calf "belonged to Paul, and instead of Gallant Lad the Fourth he's Priapus the First" (130). The unexpected name, "Priapus," represents an important adjustment in the pattern of naming and solidifies the connections between Paul and the Priapic bull, "studs" both of them. The interruption in names brings a redirection in ethos—from gallantry to sexuality. It is one which the "gallant" Paul (and how often do we hear of Paul's gallantry?) re-enacts, I'm suggesting, in his own sequence of derivations.

This is perhaps Mrs. Bentley's escalation too, for these are *her* words, not Paul's, that we immediately read here. It is she who draws out the sexual namings and who reports, in apparent innocence, the satisfaction she takes, beyond reach of the matrons' disapproval, beyond reach of the "matron" she herself was back home (128), lying in bed beneath the bull. Here, as elsewhere, she flirts with the possibility of radical redefinition by placing herself in another role. It is when she is at the ranch too—scene of permission and release, for both Bentleys—that she flirts with "my stripling cowboy"

(129), a verbal construction that may reveal more than she supposes. She does, after all, wander off alone with the cowboy "Sam" (128) and she does slap his (male) horse on the hips and belly (129), an adventure that meets with some dismay in Paul's reproval. And it is here, at the ranch, that Mrs. Bentley allows herself to tell a tantalizing story:

> For there's a story that a goddess once, enamored of a mortal, sought for him from the other gods the gift of immortality. But not of youth. The years went on, and her handsome lover grew bald and bleary-eyed. Young and beautiful herself she begged the gods again either to grant him youth or let him die like other men, but this time they were obdurate. And she hardened at last, and found another lover, and to escape the first one changed him into a grasshopper. (127)

Parallels to Mrs. Bentley's own situation are inescapable, perhaps all the more because she never actually names the figures. There is "a goddess once" (soon to become "Young and beautiful") and "her handsome lover" and "another lover." We know part of the story in Tennyson, say. Yet we are struck by the multiple anonymities. They allow Mrs. Bentley to dream her way in under the characters, there is so much room under the names. The absent (proper) names permit her to enter the story without owning up to it, to say things without saying them, vicariously to be somebody without having to admit what she would be. The device allows her freedom into the role and absolution from its consequences or from even having to admit to the projections in the first place.[19]

And yet Paul's words, for all their transgression, are opaque too. Even as they would seem to open areas of lexical risk, they sidestep them in a dance that is at once approach and evasion. Despite Paul's declared preferences for direct language, not once does he actually declare his passion, nor do his words register on Mrs. Bentley, at least not as clear overtures. And why should they? Paul's naming is so equivocal, so beholden to source, so committed to lexical system and enfolded upon itself, that he falls back into it, spider in a toilet bowl. The strategy permits him to use words within that system, safely, without having to deposit them within a realm of public meaning or private message. Any representational acts would expose his desires and jeopardize him in such a way that he would have to answer for them or stand by them. Perhaps Paul is so doubtful Mrs. Bentley will "retaliate" by responding favourably to his approaches, is so unclear even in his own mind about what he wants, that he decides it is better to seek metalingual than other acts of the tongue. Better to bypass contact, to annul personal contract, by migrating to the archaic and the derivative.

*　*　*　*　*

Better maybe to bypass a direct naming when the consequences it would beget are unthinkable.

Chris Rowe, protagonist in *The Well*, flees into rural Saskatchewan, fearing he has killed someone in Montreal and that he will face trial for murder. He is taken in by a half-demented 66-year-old man named Larson and his 39-year-old wife, Sylvia. The first thing he does is to announce that his name is "Chris McKenzie." He christens himself on the spot, brings himself into being. He becomes what one of the townspeople calls old Larson's "new man" (61). A new man, then. In part unnamed, in part newly named and self-named, he sheds his old name and attempts to bail out of the personal history his name drags with it. Chris's actions are entirely motivated within the conventions of realist fiction, but they enter too an intricate and dizzying chain of crossed identities, shared namings, sought innocence.

No sooner has Chris announced his partial pseudonym (he is *not* who he says he is, or not quite what he says he is, for he is "Chris" but he is not "McKenzie") than Larson announces "'We've got a Chris in the family too.'" "Real name's Christian," he adds in his laconic way (4). And right from the start the name ties "Chris McKenzie" to his past, for the name comes from an old *teacher* of Chris's and so provides that continuity with his past. In a different direction his name becomes entangled with another doubling, a seven-year-old boy who is dying from a bad heart. The novel will take us through Chris Rowe's education as he learns how to be good-hearted —"Christian," we might say—to acquire his "real" name Chris.

Ross yo-yos those homonyms up and down the novel, plays Chris Rowe off against his "real" name, his true self—the small boy who is the same age (seven) as was the young Chris when his own world came tumbling apart in uncertainty. The loss of self, loss of innocence, comes for Chris Rowe when an unnamed stranger emerges in his life and his mother's. Obviously her lover, the man never rises out of the anonymity of pronoun. Here is what the mother tells her son to do: "'Be nice to him now, and tell him how much you miss him. It's all up to you—tell him you're frightened when I go to work and leave you alone, and this time he'll maybe stay'" (83). The next afternoon they go for a sundae, the two males. "'Just the two of us this time,' he [the mother's lover] said. 'It's about time we got acquainted.'" But then, "pushing his own sundae away, he said there was a little business he had to attend to, but he would be gone only a few minutes" (84). He disappears for good, not once having taken on the presence a proper noun would accord him and as a result never having grown into Chris's knowing. That's all he ever becomes, this man: "he," "him." He hides his activities behind euphemism ("a little business"), is himself hidden in pronoun. He withholds himself, never makes himself known to the young Chris Rowe, and from here on Chris is thrown into a search for some noun, some proper noun, that will accommodate him.

Before he finds himself in a special relationship with young Chris and comes to identify with the boy as a namesake, keeper of the very name he himself needs to claim, he lapses, fearfully, into a desire for anonymity.

To remove a name so that one exists without name and is therefore unidentified can provide protection for a fugitive: "he had to get lost again, trim himself down to anonymity" (87). Chris Rowe seeks in a sense to unname himself and to return to a realm beyond reach of names. He wants to re-enter a state from which no one can call him by name. At least for much of the novel that is what he believes: if they don't have your name, they can't get you.

The temptation to lose his name may spill over into the first meeting with his young counterpart when he teases "'So you're the young fellow who's been stealing my name.'" Sensing that the boy wishes "to escape identification" with his fussy mother, Chris Rowe then supposes they will have a talk "Chris to Chris," just the two of them (109). And so they do. They head off to the barn to inspect the animals, the older Chris instructed to keep knowledge from the boy, to preserve him in some innocence. Innocence in *The Well* seems to be a state of unknowing characterized by a lack of names. Chris protects his young namesake with euphemisms or polite renamings, lies actually: the pregnant Minnie has a "stomach ache" (114) and so the boy cannot sit on her. False naming.

Then when an anxious voice calls them back to the house, their identities merge in homonym: "Mrs. Paynter's voice broke in on them, shrill and anxious. 'Chris,' she called, 'what are you doing there? Chris, do you hear me? Where are you?' And they answered in unison, 'Here—in here with Minnie'" (116). In one voice they answer to their name. One voice, one name—they in that instant coincide. We get, as Ken McLean has pointed out, a Chris-crossing of names.[20] Another doubling then: there are to be two Philips; here we have two Chris's. In either case we have two signifieds wobbling under one signifier and all the ambiguity that that creates.

The doubling finds its most dramatic point later when Chris Rowe, "like a child" (210), ends up in difficulty delivering Minnie's colt. As Larson and Chris stand admiring the colt and the wonder of its birth, Sylvia yells from the house "to tell them that young Chris had just died" (211). Died for his namesake maybe? There is a birth—a colt. A death too—young Chris. There also is another birth—Chris Rowe is confirmed in his new role, new man at the Larson place, his old self sloughing off with the afterbirth. He alters, as if the young Chris has died so that the older Chris might be restored, be young again. Christened. Christ-like. This chapter has begun with Chris thinking of "wonder" and "a miracle" and what is "offered" (205), and in the end he is delivered into a childlikeness so apparent that cynics begin to suppose, Chris confesses, "'I'm trying to get away with something, pass myself off as the boy'" (228). What a terrible irony: this is the man who, when he *was* passing himself off as someone else, faced little suspicion; now that he has become someone genuine, become in a sense himself, he is viewed as a fraud.

Further irony: old man Larson has appropriated Chris Rowe as his own lost son. Again and again he refers to Chris as "son" (23, 39, 41, 74, 83, 178, 139), perhaps becoming the father Chris never found in his mother's anonymous lover. Old man Larson in Chris's dream announces to him "you're the one" (84) and so totally confuses wish with fact that he at moments slips into addressing Chris as if he were actually his own begotten son (105). The namings begin to take on bizarre configurations when Larson insists "'We're going to be a happy family yet.'" The happy family will consist of himself, Chris, and Sylvia, with whom (unknown to Larson) Chris is having an affair. "'Treat him right,'" he admonishes Sylvia, and there will be "'Just the three of us'" (123). Yes, but not as he supposes, since in the sexual relationship between Chris and Sylvia, the big-breasted, milk-giving Sylvia mothers Chris. Incest? Ménage à trois? Something more? When a bit later Larson repeats his wishes, "Just the three of us—just like a family," (140) we might wonder too at Chris's expression—"'Jesus!'" (98)—when Larson produces a watermelon out of nowhere. We might become suspicious when Larson takes Chris to the old well he dug on his first farm: "Half-way between house and stable the grey cribbing of a well projected two or three feet above the ground, with uprights and a cross-piece like a make-shift gallows" (99). And suddenly "the three of us" takes on all the weight of an old story, one that incorporates these names and these details with surprising ease. A Chris-crossing, yes, and a crossing over, the entangled lives of these many-crossed people.

*   *   *   *   *

A story. A lot of stories: "'so that's your story'" Sylvia says when Chris tries to put off her prying (50). "'You hear a lot of stories,'" a curious man tells Chris (59), and Elsie, a young town girl whom Chris seduces, says "'there's a different story every week'" (147). Lots of stories. And lots of names.

There is no ease, though, in another story this novel gives us. Sylvia (sweet Sylvia of Renaissance love, we remember) conspires to kill her husband and solicits Chris's help. The words by which they name the act come with great reluctance to Chris. Ross first introduces the possibility when Sylvia, driven to a desperation made bold by frankness, says "'I'll do something . . . . I'll kill him'" (165). For a long, long stretch she and Chris circle around the idea, never again naming the act for the next 26 pages, though all that while they talk about it. The frightening prospect is something that Chris, increasingly compassionate, ever more true to himself, wants never to face. And so he puts it off, this possibility, names it by not naming it. It floats, dangerously, in a lexical gap between what they realize and what they dare say. For the time being they can speak of murder only in euphemism. It is a "job" (165, 183, etc.), sometimes a "little job" (187). It also is a getting

(165). More commonly the prospect occurs as pronoun: "it," "what," "whatever." How they welcome the pro-noun, word whose suffix ensures mystery and imprecision, sink into the sanctuary of that. Chris's main strategy is to pretend he is involved in a game and is playing a role. It is a stance he's well prepared to assume, having spent much of his life in roles and games, at every turn assuming a self he manufactures in front of the mirror.[21] But those devices no longer sustain him, so changed has he become: "'Stop it,'" he tells Sylvia. "'Talk like that and first thing you will try something. It'll grow on you'" (166). Saying will bring a thing into being, he now realizes, naming will make it real.

The name of his game, therefore is putting off disturbing realities by holding them in abeyance, inside some jar of unknowing whose contents are precisely those names he refuses to pluck into being. Above all else he fears Sylvia will spill them out. Once the names are on the table, he then will be redefined. The naming is more than acknowledgement; it will be a kind of commitment too, he knows. Like saying "I love you," it can beget its own occasion, take on the status of the irrevocable.

*　　*　　*　　*　　*

Many other names or references to names pop up in *The Well*. Chris in his dreams, or coming out of his dreams, sees someone who is "Sylvia and not quite Sylvia" (126). He mentions a "woman called Flanders. He had forgotten her first name" (134). Sylvia, tormented by her dependence upon Larson and Larson's clinging to the name of his first wife, says, "'I'm not his wife. He's still got Cora'" (181), only to insist a few minutes later, laying claim to obligations she supposes are owed to her position, "'I said I was his wife'" and "'I'm his wife'" (182). She oscillates between claim and disclaimer, torn between what economic benefits the name "wife" might provide her and what lack it registers when in a romantic sense it is so nominal.

Other names show a similar instability in what they mean or what they effect. Larson had "four or five Minnies" (115). Chris's aunt accuses his mother of being "the first ever to disgrace their name" (114). Sylvia tells a poignant story about her days as a waitress: she would "'sit looking at the men in the catalogue in their suits and ties, and I'd pick one I liked and maybe give him a name'" (162). How telling it is that she would promote him from anonymity in the catalogue to a name in her story, bring him into her ambit, *her* telling, by virtue of naming him. More, as narrator she can then control the tenses, write off her past and her present, project a future in which names fall into place, in which figures carry *proper* nouns. There is power in that. Rickie, a thug and old chum of Chris's, was "a name and a power" on Boyle Street (153), a name to be reckoned with in a world where tough characters travel under nicknames meant to capture their essential quirks or selves. Chris, whenever it is convenient, announces "'I'm just

Larson's hired man'" (145) and names himself, he hopes, into safety. In a sense he promotes himself (demotes, perhaps) from the precariousness of proper name—your name is known, they have your name, know who you are—to immunity in a common name. It is there, under the generic label, he believes he can hide, beyond identification, sharing with impunity *this* name, "hired man," with others. The name, being transferable, cannot be stuck to one person and so cannot put him in jeopardy. In effect its refuge is as sure as what any anonym could provide.

Part of Sylvia Larson's power over Chris is the fact that she has names—secret names, powerful names, names from his criminal past. She might at any moment recall names that would incriminate him. "'Then tell me,' [she says] 'do you know a girl called Helen?'" (192). "'What about a man you used to know called Baxter?'" (193). She is relentless in naming names: "'Yes, Chris—Baxter'" (193). Chris, whose project it is to manage names, is held by them. He is so daunted by the prospect that she will come forward with the names, is so susceptible to certain proper names whose mere naming would jeopardize his life, that he asks himself, as if in resignation, in recognition that he cannot escape the names, "'Who's Baxter?'" (225). It's at this point he is brought most fully into the pull of old names he orbits and fears he may crash on.

There is yet another wrinkle on names and naming in this novel. At the climax of the story, when Sylvia has shot Larson and Chris refuses to join her, Chris clings to the hope that Larson will sign a statement on his behalf: the signature that endorses, the written name that guarantees truth—that here, juridical, would ensure protection, absolve him of guilt.

Chris, who characteristically has measured himself by the mirror, who has traded in presented selves, tries for much of the novel to cling to his old but no less manufactured self and to define himself by that old name and the bravado he has come to associate with it. Pleased with the thought that Sylvia has gone to great trouble and danger to join him in bed, he feels reassured and restored to his name: "The same old Chris Rowe . . . He wasn't slipping after all" (92). Later, faced with the realization that he has apologized to Larson, Chris thinks, "It didn't make sense—not Chris Rowe" (177), not with a name like that, surely. Still later he wonders, "should he, Chris Rowe, have to admit his stupidity or ineptness" (188). That proper noun to which he clings in times of crisis or self-doubt, even as it reassures Chris in continuity and definitions of himself—"Chris Rowe scared!" (43)— impede him in his journey towards himself.

*   *   *   *   *

Then there are horses' names in Ross: Old Ned (37), Minnie (39), Fanny (40)—these in *The Well*. There's Jake, Sarah's horse, in *Sawbones Memorial*. (There's also "Rip," Doc's horse.) And there is a host of horses in the stories collected in *The Lamp at Noon and Other Stories*: Bess and Prince (19), Isabel "the outlaw" (25), "old Pete" (26), "Old Rock" (35), the black mare Bess (again?) (54), "my pony Gopher" (84), the horse called "Tim" (119). And so on. There are many more of these names in Ross. Friendly names, pet names, human names. A common thing in Ross, those affectionate names and the continuity they suggest between a human and animal order:

> Ellen and the wheat seemed remote, unimportant. At a whinny from the bay mare, Bess, he went forward and into her stall. She seemed grateful for his presence, and thrust her nose deep between his arm and body. They stood a long time motionless, comforting and assuring each other. (*Lamp* 19)

Does the area of shared naming come in recognition of the horses or in acceptance of their fellow creatureliness? Perhaps it speaks an extension of human order into animal life. It certainly conforms to the prominent patterns of personification by which horses are known in Ross. At every turn they are vain or playful or knowing or sympathetic or tormenting. The human qualities are seemingly endless. Whatever happens to occasion the naming, a crossing-over is evident, especially in the frequency with which boys identify with horses, exulting; men lean on them, shaking.

A consonance that is broken, perhaps, in the horse "Smoke" ridden by "Sam" in *As for Me and My House* (129) and in the stallion's name—North—in *The Well*. Does the name acknowledge that this horse, stud horse, exists beyond the pale of human limits and hence naming, and therefore exacts some other principle of naming? Then there are "the Diamonds" in the story called "The Runaway." No personal names for them; they exist in some realm where they can be known and named only as extraordinarily endowed creatures. Theirs is a special category (certainly it is that in the mind of the kid's proud father) that resists the pull of the domestic and puts them beyond reach of a familial calling. The pattern of opposition finds its most overt expression in "A Day with Pegasus," where there is "Biddy" (*The Race and Other Stories* 37), "Lulu" and "Marie" and "Peter" (38) and "Tony" (41), when what's needed for the romantic young boy is "a name to match the miracle" (41). The young boy needs for his pony "Peter" "another name—a real name" (41), one that is commensurate with his dreams, something special and regal like "King" or "Prince," only they are taken (39). In the face of the boy's romanticism, Mrs. Parker persists: "'Bill's a good name . . . . Short and sensible. Or Mike, or Joe. We had a Buster once'" (39).

*   *   *   *   *

More names. Many more names. A stranger in "Cornet at Night" introduces himself as "'Philip Coleman—usually just Phil'" and the young protagonist, feeling his way into town, eager to be worthy, responds: "'Mine's Tommy Dickson. For the last year, though, my father says I'm getting big and should be called just Tom'" (44). How grateful he is for that altered naming, the removal of the sissy suffix, which rescues him from childhood and transforms him into an adult.

Ross's naming is never Adamic or epic, as it is so often in Canadian writing, scene of what Dick Harrison has called "unnamed country."[22] Nor does it often point to places, there curiously being few toponyms in Ross and none that name actual places on the prairies. But the naming goes on, generally in social and familial ways. It goes on and on. There is no end to this naming, this Canadian fascination with names, this interminable naming. This awful stumbling towards names.

[handwritten: Semiotic arbitrariness]

NOTES

1.   Sandra Djwa draws out the religious elements and adds this stimulating footnote on Biblical names in *As for Me and My House*: Stephen, a devout Christian, was the first martyr; Paul (formerly Saul) witnessed the stoning of Stephen by the mob and was converted to Christianity; Judith, in the *Apocrypha*, gave her body to save her townspeople and was honoured by them. Mrs. Bentley, unnamed in the novel, would appear to have many of the characteristics of the Rachel of Genesis. She has no children, receives a son through a maidservant and finally does have a son of her own. This Rachel is also associated with the successful theft of her father's household "images" (gods) which she brings to her husband. Added to these references is the suggestion of the "bent twig" implicit in the name "Bentley" (205).
2.   We find quite a different claim advanced in Jeanette Seim's article "Horses & Houses: Further Readings in Kroetsch's *Badlands* and Sinclair Ross's *As for Me and My House*." Seim writes of Mrs. Bentley, "What she fears most is the power of language, of naming" since "to legitimize something is to acknowledge its status, name it into existence, validate it and make it part of a larger system of relationships" (104). What this means specifically for Seim is that Mrs. Bentley fails to name her own activities as writer, as one might name or rename and so reconstitute her life. Mrs. Bentley gets entangled in periphrasis on the one hand and excessive naming on the other, both signs she misses the mark. As will be evident, I do not agree with the point about excessive or "over" naming.
3.   Diana Brydon put the matter this way: "The novel's title suggests . . . anxiety, its emphasis on 'me' and 'my' indicating a concern with possession" (99).
4.   In Robert Kroetsch's words, Mrs. Bentley, god-like, here "creates the son in her husband's image—and in her own" (221).
5.   Mrs. Bentley complains, silently to herself, in a strain that is typically romantic and emergingly feminist: "Philip hasn't even given her another name. In an hour or two the sorrel would have been Sleipner or Pegasus anyway, but for a mere mare plain Minnie has to do" (139–40).
6.   The name El Greco may not participate so simply in the circuit of romanticism. It is tempting at first blush to add it to a long list of high European artists and perhaps we should. It is possible, however, to exclude his name on the grounds that his work hardly entered the realm of elegant or aristocratic beauty.

His darkly gruesome paintings brooded over monstrous sufferings of simple people and were anything but "pretty" or ornamental. See Barbara Godard, "El Greco in Canada: Sinclair Ross's *As for Me and My House*." Her argument supposes, convincingly I think, that Philip is in fact a talented artist and that Mrs. Bentley has misnamed him. Godard traces a series of connections between Philip Bentley and the Spanish artist, El Greco. The essay would, silently, seem to concur with what I am saying. As would Wilfred Cude's remarks on El Greco in his "'Turn It Upside Down': The Right Perspective on *As for Me and My House*" (470).

7.   Mrs. Bentley does show some tolerance for growth or change in the self. "We all change and grow," she admits, however briefly (177).

8.   Perhaps this is too hard on Mrs. Bentley: her epistolary zeal would seem at the very least to have her husband's tacit support; in a sense she is acting as secretary or amanuensis to his name and well within the ethos of those to whom she writes—namely, their multiple obligations to the Bentleys. And yet, if in the lakes of names Ross's characters swim in we seek to know fish from fowl, how then are we to account for this sailing under false colours?

9.   Information supplied in conversation in Ottawa during the Sinclair Ross conference in April, 1990.

10.   I am unable to corroborate this claim. Neither *Webster's New World Dictionary*, nor *The Oxford Dictionary of English Etymology*, nor the *Oxford English Dictionary* (*OED*) confirms Paul's derivation. What does emerge is this: to be weary is to have gone astray or wandered off during a journey and as a result to have become exhausted, giddy, or faint, or irritable. The word also carries overtones of drunkenness, presumably what contributes to or what results from the getting lost or exhausted on some actual or figurative journey. A further elaboration: the word in earlier manifestations referred to fits of madness or insanity. It may ultimately be derived, the *OED* speculates, from a sense of being bewildered or stupefied. But there are no muddy tracks, not a one. It's tempting to find Paul in error and to assign some significance to the slip-up.

11.   David Williams writes that Paul Kirby errs modestly in his etymology here. Williams traces the word to other roots in *A Sanskrit-English Dictionary* (166). According to *Webster's*, however, "pagan" does indeed mean what Paul says it does—"country dweller."

12.   The word "belly," Paul does not tell us, is related to "bellows," something that forces a stream of air through a narrow tube, much like the human system.

13.   *Webster's New World Dictionary* takes the edge off the derivation by adding a related lineage that means "little horse," a linkage which, even as it tells us something about Paul, at this point opens intriguing readings of Philip's career, he who in name is a lover of horses, as we discover elsewhere.

14.   The word "fool" also means a "bellows," as does the "belly" he earlier brought up. It is not my purpose here to trace out Paul's derivations in every detail, neither their lapses nor their thickenings, but one glimpses possibilities. The word "fool," by the way, and variations upon it, appears all over the novel, ironic index to the characters' mistakes.

15.   Williams's gloss on this passage is intriguing (161), as he links it with Lewis Carroll and Edgar Allan Poe.

16. To my reading Philip is clearly a lover of horses. He is in his drawings, certainly, where horses figure prominently and sympathetically. (It would be rewarding to trace out the whole set of Philip Bentley drawings.) He further proves himself a lover of horses when he determines to get young Steve a horse. The point is worth emphasizing in the face of some readings that see him as weak and ineffectual, false to himself ultimately. We appreciate the fact that his rival, Paul, wants Mrs. Bentley to see him as "spavined" in his role as minister (93).

17. In his tantalizing (though dubious) argument, Williams claims that Paul Kirby has been drawn not to Mrs. Bentley but to Judith West and that it is not Philip Bentley but Paul who is the father of Judith's child. Williams also stresses the inaccuracy of Paul's derivation for "paternity" (166) and assumes that the mistake is expressive of Paul's grief over Judith's death (161).

18. Evelyn J. Hinz and John J. Teunissen link Paul to his New Testament namesake, who was "noted for his aestheticism and misogyny" (109). Hinz and Tennissen overreach themselves, however, by imposing inappropriate "generic" claims upon Ross's novel. Here, for instance, in skittered logic, is part of what they say about names: "Paul Kirby is another 'St. Paul' in the sense that like the Apostle who was knocked off his horse and subsequently changed his name, so the schoolteacher loses his initial belief in the value of a horse . . . just as his interest in word changes is a central aspect of his character" (110).

19. Seim draws out later configurations of Mrs. Bentley's own later "hardening" and so strengthens the connections between goddess and Ross's narrator (111).

20. In discussion at the Sinclair Ross conference at the University of Ottawa in April 1990.

21. Gail Bowen has noted this same dependence upon mirrors. She writes that "Chris finds his only assurance of existence in the reflected image of himself . . . . His treatment of people is marked by his need to find reflected in them an image of his own worth" (45).

22. Dick Harrison, *Unnamed Country: The Struggle for a Canadian Prairie Fiction.*

WORKS CITED

Bowen, Gail. "The Fiction of Sinclair Ross." *Canadian Literature* 80 (Spring 1979), 37–48.

Brydon, Diana. "Sinclair Ross." *Profiles in Canadian Literature*, Vol. 3. Ed. Jeffrey M. Heath. Toronto and Charlottetown: Dundurn Press, 1982, 97–103.

Cude, Wilfred. "'Turn It Upside Down': The Right Perspective on *As for Me and My House.*" *English Studies in Canada* 5 (Winter 1979), 469–88.

Djwa, Sandra. "No Other Way: Sinclair Ross's Stories and Novels." In *Writers of the Prairies.* Ed. Donald G. Stephens. Vancouver: University of British Columbia Press, 1973, 189–205.

Godard, Barbara. "El Greco in Canada: Sinclair Ross's *As for Me and My House.*" *Mosaic* 14 (Spring 1981), 54–75.

Harrison, Dick. *Unnamed Country: The Struggle for a Canadian Prairie Fiction.* Edmonton: University of Alberta Press, 1977.

Hinz, Evelyn J., and John J. Tennissen. "Who's the Father of Mrs. Bentley's Child?: *As for Me and My House* and the Conventions of Dramatic Monologue." *Canadian Literature* 111 (Winter 1986), 101–13.

Kroetsch, Robert. "Afterword" to Sinclair Ross, *As for Me and My House*. Toronto: McClelland and Stewart, 1989, 217–21.

Ross, Sinclair. *As for Me and My House*. Toronto, McClelland and Stewart, 1989.

———— . *The Well*. Toronto: Macmillan, 1958.

———— . *The Lamp at Noon and Other Stories*. Toronto: McClelland and Stewart, 1968.

———— . *Whir of Gold*. Toronto: McClelland and Stewart, 1970.

———— . *Sawbones Memorial*. Toronto: McClelland and Stewart, 1974.

———— . *The Race and Other Stories*. Ottawa: University of Ottawa Press, 1982.

Seim, Jeanette. "Horses & Houses: Further Readings in Kroetsch's *Badlands* and Sinclair Ross's *As for Me and My House*." *Open Letter* 5, 8–9 (Summer–Fall 1984), 99–115.

Williams, David. "The 'Scarlet' Rompers: Toward a New Perspective in *As for Me and My House*." *Canadian Literature* 103 (Winter 1984), 156–66.

Cooley – Post-struct fascination with language
– grounded in difference.

Gilhow – Linguistic approach
Examination of language on level of syntax
a discourse – connection (cohesive) beyond the sentence.

Makes us more aware of how we experience what we read –– how we are and/manipulated.
how we are affected by what we read.
Almost like critics of music analysis mathematics of music

A Reference Guide
to Sinclair Ross

DAVID LATHAM

The first half of this checklist of writings by and about Sinclair Ross begins with the editions of his four novels and two collections of short stories. It continues with the original publication in periodicals or anthologies of his short stories, articles, and memoir. The inclusion of a story in *The Lamp at Noon and Other Stories* or in *The Race and Other Stories* is noted at the end of the entry by the abbreviation *LNOS* or *ROS*. The selection of reprinted anthology contributions includes translations of his stories into Chinese and German.

The second half of the checklist is devoted to Ross's critical reception. It begins with four books on Ross, continues with articles and sections of books, with theses and dissertations, with interviews, and with adaptations of his fiction for radio and television. Those critical works that focus on a specific novel or story, and whose titles are not self-explanatory, have their subjects identified within brackets at the end of the entry. (Detailed annotations of the books, articles, and reviews published before 1981 are available in my bibliography of Ross published in the *Annotated Bibliography of Canada's Major Authors*, Vol. 3 [ECW Press, 1981].) In addition to the abbreviations for the two collections of short stories, *LNOS* and *ROS*, I have abbreviated *As for Me and My House* and *Sawbones Memorial* as *AMMH* and *SM*. The selection of book reviews concludes with reviews of the *Macmillan Anthology I*, since reviewers invariably singled out for praise its publication of Ross's most recent work, his 1988 memoir "Just Wind and Horses."

PART I

Works by Sinclair Ross

Books

As for Me and My House. New York: Reynal and Hitchcock, 1941. 296 pp.

――――― . Introd. Roy Daniells. New Canadian Library, No. 4. Toronto: McClelland and Stewart, 1957. x, 165 pp.

――――― . Introd. David Stouck. Bison Book. Lincoln: University of Nebraska Press, 1978. xiii, 165 pp.

――――― . *Au service du Seigneur?* Trans. Louis-Bertrand Raymond. Montreal: Éditions Fides, 1981. 238 pp.

――――― . Introd. Lorraine McMullen. New Canadian Library, Canadian Classic Series. Toronto: McClelland and Stewart, 1983. 165 pp.

――――― . Afterword Robert Kroetsch. New Canadian Library. Toronto: McClelland and Stewart, 1989. 221 pp.

The Well. Toronto: Macmillan, 1958. 256 pp.

The Lamp at Noon and Other Stories. Introd. Margaret Laurence. New Canadian Library, No. 62. Toronto: McClelland and Stewart, 1968. 134 pp.

Whir of Gold. Toronto: McClelland and Stewart, 1970. 195 pp.

Sawbones Memorial. Toronto: McClelland and Stewart, 1974. 140 pp.

――――― . Introd. Lorraine McMullen. New Canadian Library, No. 145. Toronto: McClelland and Stewart, 1978. 144 pp.

The Race and Other Stories. Introd. Lorraine McMullen. Ottawa: Univ. of Ottawa Press, 1982. 137 pp.

Contributions to Periodicals and Books: Short Stories, Articles, and Memoir

Short Stories

"No Other Way." *Nash's Magazine* 95 (October 1934), 16–17, 80–84. *ROS.*

"A Field of Wheat." *Queen's Quarterly* 42 (Spring 1935), 31–42. *LNOS.*

"September Snow." *Queen's Quarterly* 42 (Winter 1935), 451–60. *LNOS* ("Not by Rain Alone. Part II: September Snow").

"Circus in Town." *Queen's Quarterly* 43 (Winter 1936), 368–72. Rpt. in *Country Guide and Nor'west Farmer* 61 (June 1942), 12, 57. *LNOS.*

"The Lamp at Noon." *Queen's Quarterly* 45 (Spring 1938), 30–42. *LNOS.*

"A Day with Pegasus." *Queen's Quarterly* 45 (Summer 1938), 141–56. Rpt. in *Country Guide an Nor'west Farmer* 61 (April 1942), 12, 36–38. *ROS.*

"The Painted Door." *Queen's Quarterly* 46 (Summer 1939), 145–68. *LNOS.*

"Cornet at Night." *Queen's Quarterly* 46 (Winter 1939), 431–52. Rpt. in *Country Guide and Nor'west Farmer* 61 (May 1942), 9, 23–27. *LNOS.*

"Not by Rain Alone." *Queen's Quarterly* 48 (Spring 1941), 7–16. *LNOS* ("Not by Rain Alone. Part I: Summer Thunder").

"Nell." *Manitoba Arts Review* 2 (Winter 1941), 32–40. *ROS.*

"One's a Heifer." In *Canadian Accent.* Ed. Ralph Gustafson. Harmondsworth: Penguin, 1944, 114–28. *LNOS.*

"Barrack Room Fiddle Tune." *Manitoba Arts Review* 5 (Spring 1947), 12–17. *ROS.*

"Jug and Bottle." *Queen's Quarterly* 56 (Winter 1949), 500–21. *ROS.*

"The Outlaw." *Queen's Quarterly* 57 (Summer 1950), 198–210. *LNOS.*
"Saturday Night." *Queen's Quarterly* 58 (Autumn 1951), 387–400. *ROS.*
"The Runaway." *Queen's Quarterly* 59 (Autumn 1952), 323–42. *LNOS.*
"Spike." Trans. Pierre Villon. *Liberté* 11 (mars-avril 1969), 181–97. Rpt. in English
 in *Sinclair Ross, A Reader's Guide.* Ken Mitchell. Moose Jaw: Coteau Books,
 1981, 95-107; *Erindale Review* 1 (1982), 49–59. *ROS.*
"The Flowers That Killed Him." *Journal of Canadian Fiction* I (Summer 1972), 5–10.
 ROS.

Articles and Memoir
"Why My 2nd Book Came 17 Years Later." *Toronto Daily Star*, 13 September 1958,
 32.
"Montreal and French-Canadian Culture: What They Mean to English-Canadian
 Novelists." *The Tamarack Review* 40 (Summer 1966), 46–47.
"On Looking Back." *Mosaic* 3 (Spring 1970), 93–94.
Letter to the Editor. *Financial Times*, 9 December 1974, 9.
"Just Wind and Horses: A Memoir." *The Macmillan Anthology I.* Ed. John Metcalf and
 Leon Rooke. Toronto: Macmillan, 1988, 83–97.
Reprinted Anthology Contributions: A Selection
"A Field of Wheat." In *A Miscellany of Tales and Essays.* Ed. N.R. Fallis. Toronto:
 Clarke, Irwin, 1935, 154–69.
"The Lamp at Noon." In *A Book of Canadian Stories.* Ed. Desmond Pacey. Toronto:
 Ryerson, 1947, 262–73.
"The Outlaw." In *Canadian Short Stories.* Ed. Robert Weaver and Helen James.
 Toronto: Oxford University Press, 1952, 237–48.
"Cornet at Night." In *Saskatchewan Harvest.* Ed. Carlyle King. Toronto: McClellend
 and Stewart, 1955, 189–212.
"One's a Heifer." In *Canadian Anthology.* Ed. Carl F. Klinck and Reginald Watters.
 Toronto: Gage, 1955, 364–76.
"The Lamp at Noon." In *Canadian Short Stories.* Ed. Robert Weaver. London: Oxford
 University Press, 1960, 189–215.
"Parson's Wife." In *A Book of Canada.* Ed. William Toye. Toronto: Collins, 1962,
 399–404. *AMMH* (excerpt—"Saturday Evening, April 8").
"A Field of Wheat." In *Prose Pageant.* Ed. C.J. Porter. Toronto: Ryerson, 1963,
 145–55.
"One's a Heifer." In *Canadian Reflections.* Ed. P. Penner and J. McGechaen. Toronto:
 Macmillan, 1964, 10–26.
"The Lamp at Noon" and "The Painted Door." In *Modern Canadian Stories.* Ed. Giose
 Rimanelli and Roberto Ruberto. Toronto: Ryerson, 1966, 106–16.
"Die Lampe am Mittag." Trans. Walter Riedel. In *Kandische Erzähler.* Ed. Armin
 Arnold und Walter Riedel. Zurich: Manesse, 1967, 339–58.
"The Painted Door." In *Great Canadian Short Stories.* Ed. Alec Lucas. New York: Dell,
 1971, 96–115.
"A Day with Pegasus." In *Stories from Western Canada.* Ed. Rudy Wiebe. Toronto:
 Macmillan, 1972, 106–18.
"One's a Heifer." In *Kaleidoscope.* Ed. John Metcalf. Toronto: Van Nostrand Reinhold,
 1972, 42–58.

"The Lamp at Noon." In *The Oxford Anthology of Canadian Literature*. Ed. Robert Weaver and William Toye. Toronto: Oxford Univ. Press, 1973, 440–48.

"The Outlaw." In *The Evolution of Canadian Literature in English, 1914–45*. Ed. George Parker. Toronto: Holt, Rinehart and Winston, 1973, 235–42.

"The Painted Door." In *The Canadian Century*. Ed. A.J.M. Smith. Toronto: Gage, 1973, 330–49.

"There's an Old Man Dying." In *Canadian Literature: Two Centuries in Prose*. Ed. Brita Mickleburgh. Toronto: McClelland and Stewart, 1973, 191–93. *AMMH* (excerpt—"Wednesday Evening, October 18").

"The Lamp at Noon." In *Selections from Major Canadian Writers*. Ed. Desmond Pacey. Toronto: McGraw-Hill Ryerson, 1974, 199–204.

"One's a Heifer." In *Singing under Ice*. Ed. Grace Mersereau. Toronto: Macmillan, 1974, 74–79.

"The Lamp at Noon." In *Isolation in Canadian Literature*. Ed. David Arnason. Themes in Canadian Literature. Toronto: Macmillan, 1975, 31–43.

"Cornet at Night." In *The Artist in Canadian Literature*. Ed. Lionel Wilson. Toronto: Macmillan, 1976, 16–35.

"Die Frisch Gestrichene Tür." Trans. Walter Riedel. In *Kanada. Moderne Erzhäler der Welt*. Ed. Walter Riedel. Tubingen und Basil: Horst Erdmann, 1976, 167–89.

"A Field of Wheat." In *Horizon*. Ed. Ken Mitchell. Toronto: Oxford University Press, 1977, 151–58.

"The Lamp at Noon." In *Literature in Canada*. Vol. II. Ed. Douglas Daymond and Leslie Monkman. Toronto: Gage, 1978, 177–86.

"One's a Heifer." In *The Best Modern Canadian Short Stories*. Ed. Ivon Owen and Morris Wolfe. Edmonton: Hurtig, 1978, 78–89.

"Circus in Town." In *Voices of Discord: Canadian Short Stories from the 1930s*. Ed. Donna Phillips. Toronto: New Hogtown, 1979, 108–12.

"The Outlaw." In *Great Canadian Adventure Stories*. Ed. Muriel Whitaker. Edmonton: Hurtig, 1979, 16–27.

"The Flowers That Killed Him." In *More Stories From Western Canada*. Ed. Rudy Wiebe and Aritha van Herk. Toronto: Macmillan, 1980, 248–66.

"One's a Heifer." In *New Worlds*. Ed. John Metcalf. Toronto: McGraw-Hill Ryerson, 1980, 54–66. [Commentary 153–56].

["The Painted Door."] Trans. Zhang Yun and Liu Xun. *Foreign Literatures* [Beijing Foreign Languages Institute], No. 10 (1981), 30–38.

"Circus in Town." In *Visions of Canada*. Ed. Clifford B. Theberge. Toronto: Passageways, 1982, 109–15.

"A Field of Wheat" and "One's a Heifer." In *An Anthology of Canadian Literature in English Vol. I*. Ed. Russell Brown and Donna Bennett. Toronto: Oxford University Press, 1982, 448–66.

"One's a Heifer." In *Heartland: An Anthology of Canadian Stories*. Ed. Katheryn Maclean Broughton. Toronto: Nelson, 1983, 176–91. [Teacher's edition includes commentary, T55–57].

"The Lamp at Noon." In *The Oxford Book of Canadian Short Stories in English*. Ed. Margaret Atwood and Robert Weaver. Toronto: Oxford University Press, 1986, 73–81.

"The Painted Door." In *The New Canadian Anthology: Poetry and Short Fiction in English*. Ed. Robert Lecker and Jack David. Scarborough: Nelson, 1988, 306–20.

"The Painted Door." In *The Last Map Is the Heart: Western Canadian Fiction*. Ed. Allan Forrie, Patrick O'Rourke, and Glen Sorestad. Saskatoon: Thistledown, 1989, 226–44.

"The Painted Door." In *From Ink Lake. Canadian Stories*. Ed. Michael Ondaatje. Toronto: Lester & Orphen Dennys, 1990, 81–100.

"The Lamp at Noon" and "The Painted Door." In *The Short Story in English*. Ed. Neil Besner and David Staines. Toronto: Oxford University Press, 1991, 426–49.

PART II

Works on Sinclair Ross

Books, Articles and Sections of Books, Theses and Dissertations, Interviews, Audio-Visual Material, and Book Reviews

Books

Chambers, Robert D. *Sinclair Ross and Ernest Buckler*. Toronto: Copp Clark, 1975, 1–52, 99–105.

McMullen, Lorraine. *Sinclair Ross*. Twayne's World Authors Series, No. 504. Boston: Twayne, 1979. 159 pp.

Mitchell, Ken. *Sinclair Ross, A Reader's Guide*. Moose Jaw: Coteau Books, 1981. 115 pp.

Woodcock, George. *Introducing Sinclair Ross's As for Me and My House*. Toronto: ECW Press, 1990. 67 pp.

Stouck, David. *Sinclair Ross's* As for Me and My House. Toronto: University of Toronto Press, 1991. 238 pp.

Articles and Sections of Books

Stubbs, Roy St. George. "Presenting Sinclair Ross." *Saturday Night*, 9 August 1941, 17.

The Editors [R. D. Colquette and H. S. Fry]. "A Canadian Writer." *Country Guide and Nor'west Farmer* 61 (April 1942), 38.

McCourt, Edward. "Sinclair Ross." In *The Canadian West in Fiction*. Toronto: Ryerson, 1949, 94–99.

Pacey, Desmond. *Creative Writing in Canada. A Short History of English-Canadian Literature*. Toronto: Ryerson, 1952, 173–75.

Daniells, Roy. Introduction. In *As for Me and My House*. By Sinclair Ross. New Canadian Library, No. 4. Toronto: McClelland and Stewart, 1957, v–x.

Tallman, Warren. "Wolf in the Snow. Part One: Four Windows onto Landscapes." *Canadian Literature* 5 (Summer 1960), 7–20. "Wolf in the Snow. Part Two: The House Repossessed." *Canadian Literature* 6 (Autumn 1960), 41–48. Rpt. in *A Choice of Critics: Selections from* Canadian Literature *1964–74*. Ed. George Woodcock. Toronto: Oxford University Press, 1966, 53–76. Rpt. in *Contexts of Canadian Criticism: A Collection of Critical Essays*. Ed. Eli Mandel. Chicago: University of Chicago Press, 1977, 232–53. Rpt. in *Open Letter*, 3rd Ser., No. 6 (Fall 1977), 131–49. [*AMMH*].

Sylvestre, Guy, Brandon Conron, and Carl F. Klinck, eds. "Sinclair Ross." In *Canadian Writers/Écrivains canadiens*. Toronto: Ryerson, 1964, 119.

McPherson, Hugo. "Fiction 1940–1960." In *Literary History of Canada: Canadian Literature in English*. Gen. ed. and introd. Carl F. Klinck. Toronto: University of Toronto Press, 1965, 704–06. Rpt. 2nd ed. Toronto: University of Toronto Press, 1976. Vol. 2, 217–18.

Stephens, Donald. "Wind, Sun and Dust." *Canadian Literature* 23 (Winter 1965), 17–24. Rpt. in *Writers of the Prairies*. Ed. Donald Stephens. Vancouver: University of British Columbia Press, 1973, 175–82. [*AMMH*].

King, Carlyle. "Sinclair Ross: A Neglected Saskatchewan Novelist." *Skylark* 3 (November 1966), 4–7.

Story, Norah. "Ross, Sinclair (1908–)." In *The Oxford Companion to Canadian History and Literature*. Toronto: Oxford University Press, 1967, 727.

Laurence, Margaret. Introduction. In *The Lamp at Noon and Other Stories*. By Sinclair Ross. New Canadian Library, No. 62. Toronto: McClelland and Stewart, 1968, 7–12.

Pearson, Alan. "James Sinclair Ross: Major Novelist with a Banking Past." *The Montrealer* 42 (March 1968), 18–19.

New, W. H. "Sinclair Ross's Ambivalent World." *Canadian Literature* 40 (Spring 1969), 26–32. Rpt. in *Articulating West: Essays on Purpose and Form in Modern Canadian Literature*. By W. H. New. Toronto: new press, 1972, 60–67. [*AMMH*].

Jackel, Susan. "The House on the Prairies." *Canadian Literature* 42 (Autumn 1969), 46-55. Rpt. in *Writers of the Prairies*. Ed. Donald Stephens. Vancouver: University of British Columbia Press, 1973, 165–74. [*AMMH*].

Fraser, Keath. "Futility at the Pump: The Short Stories of Sinclair Ross." *Queen's Quarterly* 77 (Spring 1970), 72–80.

Jones, D. G. *Butterfly on Rock: A Study of Themes and Images in Canadian Literature*. Toronto: University of Toronto Press, 1970, 38–42. [*AMMH*].

Djwa, Sandra. "No Other Way: Sinclair Ross's Stories and Novels." *Canadian Literature* 47 (Winter 1971), 49–66. Rpt. in *The Canadian Novel in the Twentieth Century: Essays from Canadian Literature*. Ed. George Woodcock. Toronto: McClelland and Stewart, 1975, 127–44.

Atwood, Margaret. *Survival: A Thematic Guide to Canadian Literature*. Toronto: House of Anansi, 1972, 185–86, 189, 191–92, 207–08, 210. [*AMMH*].

Reference Division, McPherson Library, University of Victoria, B.C., comp. "Ross, Sinclair 1908– ." In *Creative Canada: A Biographical Dictionary of Twentieth-Century Creative and Performing Artists*. Vol. 2. Toronto: University of Toronto Press, 1972, 238–39.

Kostash, Myrna. "Discovering Sinclair Ross: It's Rather Late." *Saturday Night* 87 (July 1972), 33–37.

Djwa, Sandra. "False Gods and the True Covenant: Thematic Continuity between Margaret Laurence and Sinclair Ross." *Journal of Canadian Fiction* 1, 4 (Fall 1972), 43–50. [*AMMH*].

Thomas, Clara. "Sinclair Ross." In *Our Nature—Our Voices: A Guidebook to English Canadian Literature*. Vol. 1. Toronto: new press, 1972, 128–32.

Benson, Eugene, ed. *Encounter: Canadian Drama in Four Media*. Methuen Canadian Literature Series. Toronto: Methuen, 1973, 139. ["One's a Heifer"].

Cude, Wilfred. "Beyond Mrs. Bentley: A Study of *As for Me and My House*." *Journal of Canadian Studies* 8 (Feb. 1973), 3–18. Rpt. in *A Due Sense of Differences: An Evaluative Approach to Canadian Literature*. Washington, D.C.: University Press of America, 1980, 31–49.

Ricou, Laurence. "The Prairie Internalized: The Fiction of Sinclair Ross." In *Vertical Man/Horizontal World: Man and Landscape in Canadian Prairie Fiction*. Vancouver: University of British Columbia Press, 1973, 81–94.

S[tory]., N[orah]. "Ross, Sinclair (1908–)." In *Supplement to the Oxford Companion to Canadian History and Literature*. Ed. William Toye. Toronto: Oxford University Press, 1973, 281.

Moss, John. "As for Me and My House." *Patterns of Isolation in English-Canadian Fiction*. Toronto: McClelland and Stewart, 1974, 149–65.

French, William. "Too Good Too Soon, Ross Remains the Elusive Canadian." *The Globe and Mail*, 27 July 1974, 25.

Stouck, David. "The Mirror and the Lamp in Sinclair Ross's *As for Me and My House*." *Mosaic* 7 (Winter 1974), 141–50.

Djwa, Sandra. "Biblical Archetypes in Western Canadian Fiction." In *Western Canada Past and Present*. Ed. A. W. Rasporich. Calgary: University of Calgary and McClelland and Stewart West, 1975, 193–203. [*AMMH*].

Colombo, John Robert. "Ross, Sinclair." In *Colombo's Canadian References*. Toronto: Oxford University Press, 1976, 453.

Pacey, Desmond. "Ross, Sinclair." In *Contemporary Novelists*. Ed. James Vison. London: St. James, 1976, 1171–73.

Sutherland, Ronald. "Canadian Fiction—Comparatively Speaking." *Review of National Literature* 7 (1976), 24–29. Rpt. in *The New Hero: Essays in Comparative Quebec/Canadian Literature*. Toronto: Macmillan, 1977, 8–13. [*AMMH, SM*].

Gaskin, Geraldine, and the Atlantic Work Group. *Women in Canadian Literature*. Toronto: Writers' Development Trust, [1977], 49–50. [*AMMH, LNOS*].

Harrison, Dick. *Unnamed Country: The Struggle for a Canadian Prairie Fiction*. Edmonton: University of Alberta Press, 1977, 126–30, 134–36, 148–55, 188–90, 197.

Dawson, Anthony B. "Coming of Age in Canada." *Mosaic* 11 (Spring 1978), 47–62. ["One's a Heifer"].

Endres, Robin. "Marxist Literary Criticism and English Canadian Literature." In *In Our Own House: Social Perspectives on Canadian Literature*. Ed. Paul Cappon. Toronto: McClelland and Stewart, 1978, 123–26. [*AMMH*].

Gutteridge, Don. *Mountain and Plain*. Toronto: McClelland and Stewart, 1978, 71–72, 79–83. [*AMMH*, "A Field of Wheat"].

MacDonald, Bruce. "*As for Me and My House* and the Aesthetics of Illegitimacy in the Canadian Novel." *The Literary Criterion* 13, No. 1 (1978), 34–52.

McMullen, Lorraine. Introduction. In *Sawbones Memorial*. By Sinclair Ross. New Canadian Library, No. 145. Toronto: McClelland and Stewart, 1978, 5–11.

Ross, Morton. "The Canonization of *As for Me and My House*: A Case Study." In *Figures in a Ground: Canadian Essays on Modern Literature Collected in Honor of Sheila Watson*. Ed. Diane Bessai and David Jackel. Saskatoon: Western Producer Prairie, 1978, 189–205. Rpt. in *The Bumper Book*. Ed. John Metcalf. Toronto: ECW Press, 1986, 170–85.

Stouck, David. "Introduction to the Bison Book Edition." In *As for Me and My House.* By Sinclair Ross. Bison Book. Lincoln: University of Nebraska Press, 1978, v–xiii.

Kroetsch, Robert. "Fear of Women in Canadian Fiction: Erotics of Space." *The Canadian Forum* 58 (Oct.–Nov. 1978), 22–27. Rpt. in *Crossing Frontiers: Papers in American and Canadian Western Literature.* Ed. Dick Harrison. Edmonton: University of Alberta Press, 1979, 73–83. Rpt. in *The Lovely Treachery of Words: Essays Selected and New.* Toronto: Oxford University Press, 1989, 73–83. [*AMMH*].

Bowen, Gail. "The Fiction of Sinclair Ross." *Canadian Literature* 80 (Spring 1979), 37–48.

Dooley, D.J. "*As for Me and My House*: The Hypocrite and the Parasite." In *Moral Vision in the Canadian Novel.* Toronto: Clarke Irwin, 1979, 38–47.

Dubanski, Ryszard. "A Look at Philip's 'Journal' in *As for Me and My House.*" *Journal of Canadian Fiction* 24 (1979), 89–95.

Cude, Wilfred. "'Turn It Upside Down': The Right Perspective on *As for Me and My House.*" *English Studies in Canada* 5 (Winter 1979), 469–88. Rpt. in *A Due Sense of Differences: An Evaluative Approach to Canadian Literature.* Washington, D.C.: University Press of America, 1980, 50–68.

Birney, Earle. *Spreading Time: Remarks on Canadian Writing.* Book I: 1904–1949. Montreal: Véhicule, 1980, 66. [Ross as a soldier].

Cavell, Richard. "The Unspoken in Sinclair Ross's *As for Me and My House.*" *Letteratura Lingue Idee* 14 (1980), 23–30.

Denham, Paul. "Narrative Technique in Sinclair Ross's *As for Me and My House.*" *Studies in Canadian Literature* 5 (Spring 1980), 116–26.

Hicks, Anne. "Mrs. Bentley: The Good Housewife." *Room of One's Own* 5, No. 4 (1980), 60–67.

O'Connor, John J. "Saskatchewan Sirens: The Prairie as Sea in Western Canadian Literature." *Journal of Canadian Fiction* 28–29 (1980), 157–71.

O'Neil, Mary Sheila. "Point of View in *As for Me and My House.*" In *Human Fulfillment in Literature.* Scarborough, Ont.: Medallion Books, 1980, 23–31.

Woodcock, George. "Rural Roots." *Books in Canada* 9 (October 1980), 7–9.

Godard, Barbara. "El Greco in Canada: Sinclair Ross's *As for Me and My House.*" *Mosaic* 14 (Spring 1981), 54–75.

Jones, Joseph, and Johanna Jones. *Canadian Fiction.* Boston: G.K. Hall, 1981, 72–74.

Kroetsch, Robert. "Contemporary Standards in the Canadian Novel." *Essays on Canadian Writing* 20 (Winter 1980–81), 7–18. Rpt. in *Taking Stock: The Calgary Conference on the Canadian Novel.* Ed. Charles Steele. Toronto: ECW Press, 1982, 9–20. [*AMMH*].

Latham, David. "Literature." *The American Review of Canadian Studies* 11 (Spring 1981), 127–28.

Latham, David. "Sinclair Ross: An Annotated Bibliography." In *Annotated Bibliography of Canada's Major Authors Vol. 3.* Ed. Robert Lecker and Jack David. Toronto: ECW Press, 1981, 365–95.

Wee, Morris Owen. "Specks on the Horizon: Individuals and the Land in Canadian Prairie Fiction." *South Dakota Review* 19 (Winter 1981), 18–31.

Brydon, Diana. "Sinclair Ross." *Profiles in Canadian Literature Vol. 3*. Ed. Jeffrey M. Heath. Toronto: Dundurn Press, 1982, 97–103.

Hagiwara, Takao. "The Role of Nature in *An'ya Koro* and *As for Me and My House*." *Selecta* [Journal of the Pacific North West Council on Foreign Languages] 3 (1982), 1–8. Revised as "Man and Nature in Sinclair Ross' *As for Me and My House* and Naoya Shiga's *A Dark Night's Passing*." In *Nature and Identity in Canadian and Japanese Literature*. Ed. Kinya Tsuruta and Theodore Goossen. Toronto: University of Toronto—York University Joint Centre for Asia Pacific Studies, 1988, 19–33.

Moss, John. "Mrs. Bentley and the Bicameral Mind: A Hermeneutical Encounter with *As for Me and My House*." *Modern Times. A Critical Anthology: The Canadian Novel* Volume III. Ed. John Moss. Toronto: NC Press, 1982, 81–92.

Osachoff, Gail. "Sinclair Ross: A Reader's Guide." *NeWest Review* 8 (October 1982), 14.

Whitman, F. H. "The Case of Ross's Mysterious Barn." *Canadian Literature* 94 (Autumn 1982), 168–69. ["One's a Heifer"].

Davey, Frank. "Sexual Imagery in Sinclair Ross." *Surviving the Paraphrase: Eleven Essays on Canadian Literature*. Winnipeg: Turnstone Press, 1983, 167–81.

Ferres, John H. "An Introduction to the Novels of Sinclair Ross." *Commonwealth Novel in English* 2 (July 1983), 1–21.

McMullen, Lorraine. Introduction. In *As for Me and My House*. New Canadian Library, Canadian Classic Series. Toronto: McClelland and Stewart, 1983.

Rose, Marilyn. "As for Me and My House"; "Sinclair Ross." In *The Oxford Companion to Canadian Literature*. Ed. William Toye. Toronto: Oxford University Press, 1983, 29–30; 715–16.

Chapman, Marilyn. "Another Case of Ross's Mysterious Barn." *Canadian Literature* 103 (Winter 1984), 184–86. ["One's a Heifer"].

Colombo, John Robert. "Prince Albert." *Canadian Literary Landmarks*. Toronto: Hounslow Press, 1984, 238. [Includes drawing of Ross by Isaac Bickerstaff].

Comeau, Paul. "Sinclair Ross's Pioneer Fiction." *Canadian Literature* 103 (Winter 1984), 174–84.

Shirwadker, Meena. "Conscience and Conflict in Sinclair Ross' *As for Me and My House*." *I[ndian]PEN* 46 (May–June 1984), 12–16. Rpt. in *Indian Readings in Commonwealth Literature*. Ed. G. S. Amur, V. R. N. Prasad, *et al*. New Delhi and New York: Apt, 1985, 151–56.

Stouck, David. "Sinclair Ross." In *Major Canadian Authors: A Critical Introduction*. Lincoln: University of Nebraska Press, 1984, 111–26.

Thacker, Robert. "'Twisting toward Insanity': Landscape and Female Entrapment in Plains Fiction." *North Dakota Quarterly* 52 (Summer 1984), 181–94.

Williams, David. "The 'Scarlet' Rompers: Toward a New Perspective in *As for Me and My House*." *Canadian Literature* 103 (Winter 1984), 156–66.

York, Lorraine M. "'It's Better Nature Lost': The Importance of the Word in Sinclair Ross's *As for Me and My House*." *Canadian Literature* 103 (Winter 1984), 166–74.

Bishop, Karen. "The Pegasus Symbol in the Childhood Stories of Sinclair Ross." *Ariel: A Review of International English Literature* 16 (July 1985), 67–87.

Bonheim, Helmuth. "F. P. Grove's 'Snow' and Sinclair Ross's 'The Painted Door'—

The Rhetoric of the Prairie." In *Encounters and Explorations: Canadian Writers and European Critics*. Ed. Franz K. Stanzel and Waldemar Zacharasiewicz. Würzburg: Königshausen and Neumann, 1986, 58–72.

Keith, W. J. *Canadian Literature in English*. London: Longman, 1985, 139–41.

Adachi, Ken. "Ex–banker's Literary Talent an Investment." *Toronto Star*, 10 March 1986, C2. [Ross compared to other literary bankers].

Banting, Pamela. "Miss A. and Mrs. B.: The Letter of Pleasure in the *Scarlet Letter* and *As for Me and My House*." *North Dakota Quarterly* 54 (Spring 1986), 30–40.

Daymond, Douglas. "Ross Re–examined." *Journal of Canadian Fiction* 35–36 (1986), 142–46.

Dyck, E. F. "Introduction." *Essays on Saskatchewan Writing*. Ed. E. F. Dyck. Regina: Saskatchewan Writers Guild, 1986, xi–xii. [Ross is the originator of Saskatchewan writing.]

Hinz, Evelyn J., and John J. Tennissen. "Who's the Father of Mrs. Bentley's Child?: *As for Me and My House* and the Conventions of Dramatic Monologue." *Canadian Literature* 111 (Winter 1986), 101–13.

Hughes, Kenneth James. "Sinclair Ross's 'The Lamp at Noon.'" In *Signs of Literature: Language, Ideology and the Literary Text*. Vancouver: Talon, 1986, 170–74.

Mitchell, Ken. "The Ross File." *Ambience*, CBC Radio, 6 July 1986. [Interviews with Ross's contemporaries of the 1930s].

Denham, Paul. "A Halo of His Anonymity." *NeWest Review* 12 (December 1986), 14. [Review of Ken Mitchell's "Ross File"].

Stratford, Philip. "The Two Sides of Main Street: Sinclair Ross and André Langevin." *All the Polarities: Comparative Studies in Contemporary Canadian Novels in French and English*. Toronto: ECW Press, 1986, 30–44. [*AMMH*].

Thieme, John. "Robert Kroetsch and the Erotics of Prairie Fiction." *Kunapipi* 8, No. 1 (1986), 90–102.

Matheson, T. J. "'But do your thing': Conformity, Self-Reliance and Sinclair Ross's *As for Me and My House*." *Dalhousie Review* 66 (Winter 1986–87), 497–512.

Bogden, Deanne. "Feminist Criticism and Total Form in Literary Experience." *Resources for Feminist Research* 16 (September 1987), 20–23. ["The Painted Door"].

Cooley, Dennis. "The Eye in Sinclair Ross's Short Stories." *The Vernacular Muse: The Eye and the Ear in Contemporary Literature*. Winnipeg: Turnstone Press, 1987, 139–65.

Craig, Terrence. "The Synthesis of Multiculturalism 1939–1980." In *Racial Attitudes in English-Canadian Fiction 1905–1980*. Waterloo: Wilfrid Laurier Press, 1987, 118. [*SM*].

Moritz, Albert and Theresa. *The Oxford Illustrated Literary Guide to Canada*. Toronto: Oxford U. P., 1987, 71, 184, 196–200, 207, 228.

New, W. H. "The Tensions between Story and Word, 1930–1980." *Dreams of Speech and Violence: The Art of the Short Story in Canada and New Zealand*. Toronto: University of Toronto Press, 1987, 82–3. [*LNOS*].

Deacon, William Arthur. *Dear Bill: The Correspondence of William Arthur Deacon*. Ed. John Lennox and Michèle Lacombe. Toronto: University of Toronto Press, 1988, 216–21. [Correspondence with Ross].

Gadpaille, Michelle. *The Canadian Short Story*. Toronto: Oxford University Press, 1988, 32–34.

Kaye, Frances W. "Sinclair Ross's Use of George Sand and Frederic Chopin as Models for the Bentleys." *Essays on Canadian Writing* 33 (Fall 1988), 100–11.

Latham, David. "Sinclair Ross." In *The New Canadian Anthology: Poetry and Short Fiction in English*. Ed. Robert Lecker and Jack David. Toronto: Nelson, 1988, 304–05.

Mitchell, Barbara. "Paul: The Answer to the Riddle of *As for Me and My House*." *Studies in Canadian Literature* 13, 1 (1988), 47–63.

Gerry, Thomas M. F. "Dante, C. D. Burns and Sinclair Ross: Philosophical Issues in *As for Me and My House*." *Mosaic* 22 (Winter 1989), 113–22.

Kroetsch, Robert. Afterword. In *As for Me and My House*. New Canadian Library. Toronto: McClelland and Stewart, 1989, 217–21.

Kroetsch, Robert. "The Moment of the Discovery of America Continues." In *The Lovely Treachery of Words: Essays Selected and New*. Toronto: Oxford University Press, 1989, 4–5. [Ross's influence on Kroetsch].

McMullen, Lorraine. "Sinclair Ross." *Dictionary of Literary Biography Volume 88: Canadian Writers, 1920–1959 Second Series*. Ed. W. H. New. Detroit: Gale Research, 1989, 268–73.

New, W. H. *A History of Canadian Literature*. London: Macmillan, 1989, 155, 175–77.

Thacker, Robert. "A Complex of Possibilities: Prairie as Home Place." In *The Great Prairie Fact and Literary Imagination*. Albuquerque: University of New Mexico Press, 1989, 197–207, 221. [*AMMH* and *LNOS*].

Denham, Paul. "Sinclair Ross in the Nineties." *NeWest Review* 15 (Aug.–Sept. 1990), 5–6. [Review of the 1990 Ross Symposium in Ottawa].

Lacey, Liam. "The 'Cosmopolitan' Prairie Boy." *The Globe and Mail*, 16 February 1991, C5. [Ross is writing a new novel].

Theses and Dissertations

Keller, Ella Lorraine. "The Development of the Canadian Short Story." M.A. Thesis Saskatchewan 1950.

A'Court, Mary. "The Faiths of Four Men: Emerson: The Peaceful One of Concord, Mitchell: The Boy of Crocus, Melville: The Wanderer if Nantucket, and Ross: The Bittern of the Dust Bowl." M.A. Thesis Toronto 1966. [*AMMH*].

Cameron, Doris Margaret. "Puritanism in Canadian Prairie Fiction." M.A. Thesis British Columbia 1966. [*AMMH*].

Lee, Annie Hope. "Some Themes of Community and Exile in Six Canadian Novels." M.A. Thesis Toronto 1966. [*AMMH*].

Spettigue, Douglas. "The English-Canadian Novel: Some Attitudes and Themes in Relation to Form." Diss. Toronto 1966. [*AMMH*].

Wing, Ted. "Puritan Ethic and Social Response in the Novels of Ross, Davies, and MacLennan." M.A. Thesis Alberta 1969.

Fowlie, Irene L. "The Significance of Landscape in the Works of Sinclair Ross." M.A. Thesis Calgary 1977.

Moores, Wallace Byron. "The Valiant Struggle: A Study of the Short Stories of Sinclair Ross." M.A. Thesis Memorial 1977.

Weis, Lyle P. "Dream and Fantasy in the Work of Sinclair Ross." M.A. Thesis British Columbia 1977.

Wainwright, John. "Motives for Metaphor: Art and the Artist in Seven Canadian Novels." Diss. Dalhousie 1978. [*AMMH*].

Sunega, Thomas George. "The Works of Sinclair Ross." M.A. Thesis Queen's 1979.

Stevens, Kathlene Mary. "The North American Prairie: American and Canadian Prairie Conflict in the Works of Willa Cather and Sinclair Ross." M.A. Thesis Eastern Washington 1981.

Beauchesne, Rosaire. "'Felicitations, docteur!,' traduction de *Sawbones Memorial* de Sinclair Ross." M.A. Thesis Sherbrooke 1982.

Burns, Karen. "Image, Symbol, and the Life of the Imagination in the Works of Sinclair Ross." M.A. Thesis Lakehead 1982.

Prytz, Ellen Jone. "A Look behind the False Fronts: A Study of the Main Characters in Sinclair Ross's *As for Me and My House*." M.A. Thesis Oslo 1983.

Wheatland, Heather D. "Narrative Technique in the Short Stories of Sinclair Ross." M.A. Thesis Queen's 1986.

Interviews

Sypnowich, Peter. "A Bachelor on the Run Comes Back to Canada." *Toronto Star*, 13 November 1970, 30.

Toppings, Earle. *Canadian Writers on Tape: Mordecai Richler/Sinclair Ross*. Ontario Institute for Studies in Education, 1971. (Cassette tape. 30 min.)

Audio-Visual Material

"The Outlaw." Read by John Drainie. *Canadian Short Stories*, CBC Radio, 21 April 1950. (30 min.)

Waldman, Marian. "As for Me and My House." Dir. Gus Kristjanson. *Summer Stage*. CBC Radio, 7 September 1958. (30 min.)

Cornet at Night. Dir. Gus Kristjanson. *Wednesday Night*. CBC Radio, 17 September 1958. (45 min.)

Cornet at Night. Dir. Stanley Jackson. National Film Board, 1963. (15 min.)

Waldman, Marian. "As for Me and My House." Dir. Esse Ljungh. *Stage*. CBC Radio, 10 April 1964. (30 min.)

Goldman, Alvin. "The Painted Door." Dir. Rudi Dorn. *Festival*. CBC Television, 17 January 1968. (30 min.)

Dorn, Rudi. "One's a Heifer." Dir. Laurel Crosby. *Programme X*. CBC Television, 25 March 1971. (30 min.)

Nichol, James. "Cornet at Night." Dir. Don Williams. *To See Ourselves*. CBC Television, 26 December 1973. (30 min.)

Blizzard. Dir. Rudi Wrench. Simon Fraser Univ. Workshop, 1975. (10 min.) ("The Painted Door.")

Cornet at Night. Dir. Bruce Pittman. Atlantis Films, 1983. (25 min.)

One's a Heifer. Dir. Anne Wheeler. Atlantis Films, 1984. (24 min.)

The Painted Door. Dir. Bruce Pittman. Atlantis Films, 1984. (24 min.)

Selected Book Reviews

As for Me and My House

Fadiman, Clifton. Rev. of *As for Me and My House*. *New Yorker*, 22 February 1941, 72.

Feld, Rose. Rev. of *As for Me and My House*. *New York Herald Tribune Book Review*, 23 February 1941, 14.

Hauser, Marianne. "A Man's Failure." *The New York Times Book Review*, 2 March 1941, 25, 27.

"Fiction." *Toronto Daily Star*, 22 March 1941, 28.

Easton, Stuart C. "Excellent Canadian Novel." *Saturday Night*, 29 March 1941, 18.

Davies, Robertson. "Caps and Bells." *Peterborough Examiner*, 26 April 1941, p. 4. Rpt. in his *The Well-Tempered Critic: One Man's View of Theatre and Letters in Canada*. Ed. Judith Skelton Grant. Toronto: McClelland and Stewart, 1981, 142–44.

Deacon, W. A. "The Story of Prairie Parson's Wife." *The Globe and Mail*, 26 April 1941, 9.

MacPhail, Alexander. Rev. of *As for Me and My House*. *Queen's Quarterly* 48 (Summer 1941), 198–99.

Brown, E. K. Rev. of *As for Me and My House*. *The Canadian Forum* 21 (July 1941), 124.

MacGillivray, J. R. "Letters in Canada: Fiction." *University of Toronto Quarterly* 11 (April 1942), 298, 300–02.

Stewart, H.L. Rev. of *As for Me and My House*. *Dalhousie Review* 22 (April 1942), 130.

Leberg, Ruth R. Rev. of *As for Me and My House*. *Canadian Welfare* 18 (January 1943), 39–40.

The Well

Honderich, Theodore. "Farmer, Wife and Hired Man." *Toronto Daily Star*, 30 August 1958, 28.

Hughes, Isabelle. "Long Awaited Second Novel." *The Globe and Mail*, 20 September 1958, 19.

Scott, James. "Sinclair Ross Has Forgotten Prairie Smells." *Toronto Telegram*, 20 September 1958, 37.

Mullins, S. G. Rev. of *The Well*. *Culture* 19 (December 1958), 458.

Weaver, Robert. Rev. of *The Well*. *The Tamarack Review* 10 (Winter 1959), 106.

Bissell, Claude. "Letters in Canada: Fiction." *University of Toronto Quarterly* 28 (Summer 1959), 369–70.

Weekes, H. V. Rev. of *The Well*. *Dalhousie Review* 38 (Winter 1959), 529–30.

The Lamp at Noon and Other Stories

Roper, Gordon. "Letters in Canada: Fiction." *University of Toronto Quarterly* 38 (Summer 1969), 363.

Spracklin, Floyd. Rev. of *The Lamp at Noon and Other Stories*. *CM: A Reviewing Journal of Canadian Materials for Young People* 17 (January 1989), 20.

Whir of Gold

Sypnowich, Peter. "This Author May Be the Man Who Could Rescue Literature." *Toronto Daily Star*, 21 Nov. 1970, 67.

Duncan, Chester. "Not All Is Gold." *Winnipeg Free Press*, 19 December 1970, 14NL.

Garner, Hugh. "Bamboozled by Time and Lumpen Losers." *Globe Magazine*, 2 January 1971, 17.

Dawe, Alan. "Moral for a Clarinet Player Down on His Luck." *The Vancouver Sun*, 22 January 1971, 35A, 39A.

Chelsey, Stephen. "*Whir of Gold* Builds on Past for Modern Tale." *The Varsity* [University of Toronto], 27 January 1971, 12.

Swan, Susan. Rev. of *Whir of Gold*. *Toronto Telegram*, 6 February 1971, 31.

Montagnes, Anne. Rev. of *Whir of Gold*. *The Canadian Forum* 50 (March 1971), 443–44.

Barbour, Doug. "Fine Novel from a Deceptive Author." *Edmonton Journal*, 5 March 1971, 60.

Stephens, Donald. "Fluid Time." *Canadian Literature* 48 (Spring 1971), 92–94.

Dafoe, John W. "Another Kind of Depression." *The Montreal Star*, 17 April 1971, 16.

Moss, John. Rev. of *Whir of Gold*. *The Fiddlehead* 90 (Summer 1971), 126–28.

Roper, Gordon. "Letters in Canada: Fiction." *University of Toronto Quarterly* 40 (Summer 1971), 384.

Sawbones Memorial

Woodcock, George. "Adele Wiseman and Sinclair Ross: Return Engagements." *Maclean's* 87 (October 1974), 110.

Stubbs, Roy St. George. "Ross Redivivus." *Winnipeg Free Press*, 12 October 1974, 20.

French, William. "This One Can Stand on Its Own." *The Globe and Mail*, 26 October 1974, 32.

Sandler, Linda. "Ross Turns Bigotry into Comedy." *Toronto Star*, 29 October 1974, F7.

McGillivray, Don. "Beyond the Oratory Canadian Tolerance Is Only Skin Deep." *Financial Times*, 4 November 1974, 8.

Laurence, Margaret. "Sinclair Ross Looks at the Prairies, His Time and Place." *The Gazette* [Montreal], 9 November 1974, 58.

James, Geoffrey. "Too Many Voices." *Time* [Canada], 11 November 1974, 16.

Hošek, Chaviva. Rev. of *Sawbones Memorial*. *Quill & Quire* 40 (December 1974), 22.

Mulhallen, Karen. "Onward and Upward with Sinclair Ross." *Books in Canada* 3 (December 1974), 9–11.

Atwood, Margaret. Rev. of *Sawbones Memorial*. *Sunday Supplement*. CBC Radio, 15 December 1974.

Scott, Kenneth. "Welcomed Guests." *Alive* 41 (1975), 35.

Davies, Barrie. Rev. of *Sawbones Memorial*. *The Fiddlehead* 105 (Spring 1975), 130–31.

Stouck, David. "Canadian Classics." *West Coast Review* 10 (June 1975), 47–48.

Sutton, Michael. "In Reality." *Canadian Review* 2 (July–Aug. 1975), 42–43.

Munton, Ann. Rev. of *Sawbones Memorial*. *The Dalhousie Review* 55 (Autumn 1975), 573–75.

Lauder, Scott. "Throbbing Life." *The Canadian Forum* 55 (November 1975), 37.

Shohet, Linda. Rev. of *Sawbones Memorial*. *Canadian Fiction Magazine* 19 (Winter 1975), 95–97.

Williams, David. Rev of *Sawbones Memorial*. *Queen's Quarterly* 82 (Winter 1975), 641–42.

Weis, Lyle. "Landscape Criticism Not Valid: Sinclair Ross's New Novel." *The Sphinx* 2 (Winter 1976), 45–47.

The Race and Other Stories

Mills, Sparling. Rev. of *The Race and Other Stories*. *Canadian Book Review Annual 1982*. Ed. Dean Tudor and Ann Tudor. Toronto: Simon & Pierre, 1983, 213.

Matyas, Cathy. Rev. of *The Race and Other Stories. Canadian Selection: Books and Periodicals for Libraries.* Ed. Mavis Carion, Sandra Cox, Alvan Bregman. 2nd ed. Toronto: University of Toronto Press, 1985, 264.

Just Wind and Horses: A Memoir

Adachi, Ken. "Anthology Produces Try, Try, Try Again." *Toronto Star*, 23 April 1988, M4. ["By far the most intriguing piece is" Ross's memoir.]

French, William. "The New Harvest." *The Globe and Mail*, 30 April 1988, C19. ["Among the highlights is (Ross's memoir), a real coup".]

Hamilton, Janet. "Inaugural Anthology a Positive Step for Contemporary Writing." *Quill & Quire* 54 (June 1988), 27. ["The memoir's special gift to us is in its struggle with the problem of description."]

Almon, Bert. Rev. of *The Macmillan Anthology 1. Canadian Book Review Annual 1988.* Ed. Dean Tudor. Toronto: Simon & Pierre, 1989, 250–51. [Ross's memoir is one of the two treasures.]

CONTRIBUTORS

Helen M. Buss, University of Calgary

David Carpenter, University of Saskatchewan

Dennis Cooley, University of Manitoba

Wilfred Cude, West Bay, N.S.

Frank Davey, University of Western Ontario

Charlene Diehl-Jones, University of Manitoba

Angela Esterhammer, University of Western Ontario

David Latham, University of Lethbridge

Marilyn Rose, Brock University

David Stouck, Simon Fraser University